FATE
of the
VULTURE

JESSACA WILLIS

Fate of the Vulture.

ISBN: 978-1-7339925-8-9

ASIN: B08B7LHFZ3

Front cover design by Luminescence Covers.
Editing by Sandra Ogle from Reedsy.
Proofreading by Kate Anderson.

Book published by Jessaca Willis 2020.

Jessaca Willis
PO Box 66574
Portland, OR 97266
https://www.jessacawillis.com

To my older cousin Kelsey,

I learned about strength by watching you.

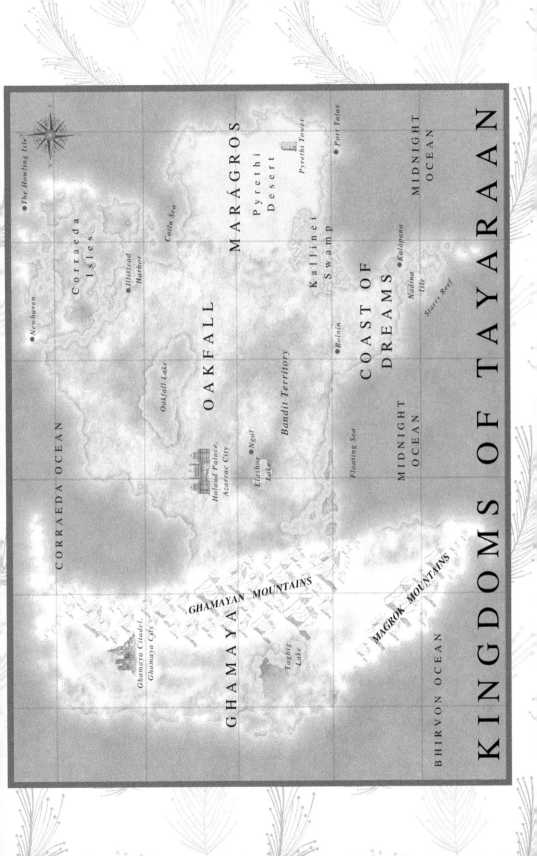

KINGDOMS OF TAYARAAN

The Howling Isle

CORRAEDA OCEAN

Corraeda Isles

• Newhaven

• Illstead Harbor

Cailu Sea

Oakfall Lake

OAKFALL

MARÁGROS

Pyrethi Desert

Pyrethi Tower

• Port Talas

MIDNIGHT OCEAN

Kallinei Swamp

• Kaldpana

Nádina Isle

Starry Reef

• Bolnin

COAST OF DREAMS

Bandit Territory

Haland Palace, Azarrac City

• Ngal

Elashor Lake

Floating Sea

MIDNIGHT OCEAN

GHAMAYAN MOUNTAINS

MAGROK MOUNTAINS

Ghamaya Citadel, Ghamaya City

Taghg Lake

GHAMAYA

BHIRVON OCEAN

BOOKS IN SERIES

REAPERS OF VELTUUR

Assassin Reaper, Prequel

Soul of the Crow, Book 1

Heart of the Sungem, Book 2

Fate of the Vulture, Book 3

1

PROLOGUE
ARIK

Beneath my hand, a small foot thrums against my palm.

I peel my eyes away from my wife's belly and beam into her honey brown eyes. "Some days it is impossible to believe that after all these years, we finally created life."

But the smile I expect to find in return isn't one of joy, but of sorrow and fear.

"What is it, Khastyl? What ails your mind?"

She lowers her head, dark hair shimmering like the waters of the Coast of Dreams, and hides her face.

I reach for her chin, cradle it between my calloused fingers, and meet her gaze. She always says that our child will be lucky to inherit my eyes, crystal blue like the clearest lake on a mountain. Of course, I hope for nothing but the opposite. For one thing, my eyes are gray, not the picturesque blue that Khastyl for some reason sees. For another, her eyes are like the maple syrup that pours from trees, warm and sweet, and so sticky that I get caught in their gaze every time I look into them.

"It's all right to be afraid," I reassure her. "Any new mother would be. Wings give me strength; I too am fearful of fatherhood and how we will raise this child—"

"It's not that, Arik." She bites the soft flesh of her lip, chewing it a moment. "There's something I should've told you a long time ago, the reason I always insisted we never bear children."

A chill trickles down my spine, but I ignore it. In the face of her vulnerability, of her distress, I must summon the strength she needs to feel brave.

"Then tell me now," I say gently, lowering myself to the chair beside her. I take her hands away from her stomach and into my own. "The child won't be born for another few moons. I dare say, we have time for any discussion we have yet to have."

Tears brim beneath Khastyl's brown eyes. This time, I'm unable to hide my unease. It is so very unlike her to break like this.

She draws a hand back from mine to wipe at her eyes before I can do it for her and musters the courage she needs to finally speak what's on her mind. "A long time ago, before we found each other, before I lived here, before...a lot of things, there was a woman. She foretold of a prophecy."

I scoff, unable to stifle my laugh. Prophecy is illusory. It's make-believe, no more than the falsehoods shared in fairy tales and childhood stories, meant to make little ones feel important while they're waiting to emerge into adulthood. It does not exist.

But the longer Khastyl holds my gaze, truth hardening every wrinkle in her brow, my smile starts to falter. "You talk of madness. There is no such thing as prophecy."

"I hope you are right." She looks to her belly, to the babe growing inside her, the one we've both already fallen in love with.

I scowl at my wife's worried state. It's unlike her to be so openly distraught. Khastyl is made of iron and droughted soil. She knows not how to shed tears, nor how to break or bend, even in a forge of blazing fire.

It's why it's always so troubling to see her like this, because these moments are incredibly rare and all the more worrying.

With a yielding sigh, I take her hand again. "Tell me of this prophecy you speak of."

She draws in a sharp breath. "I was told that I would have a daughter, that she was destined to destroy Veltuur."

Amusement furrows my brow. "Why does that cause you to anguish so? Prophecy or no, if the underrealm were gone, the Reapers would go with it. No one would live in fear any longer of the deaths they might bring us, nor of the consequences of killing game to provide for your family. It would be a blessing sent straight from the Divine Altúyur, wherever they may be."

She shakes her head. "You don't understand."

At her side, I fall silent and wait for her to elaborate. On this, and on most things, she is right. I don't understand. How could I? Such a prophecy, were it true—and I am not a superstitious man and so I am not inclined to believe it is—I would know as much about it as I do the intricacies of shoemaking. And yet, still, this supposed prophecy hardly seems the sort of thing to fret over. I would be proud to bear a daughter who would claim such greatness for our family, joyous to live in a world where Reapers did not exist.

I stare at Khastyl from the edge of my seat, patient and curious, but the silence only stretches. If my wife is iron that will not bend and drought to tears, she is also as stubborn as a magrok. Perhaps more so. If she does not want to speak, then she will not.

But as I have said, I do not enjoy seeing my love in pain, especially not when I am helpless to easing it.

"Tell me, my love," I say, inching closer and brushing the dark hair back behind her ears. "How would our daughter ever do such a thing? She will grow up with a doting mother and a loving father. She will want for nothing. She will know not loneliness, or anger, or fear. How would a girl like that ever encounter the underrealm?"

"The prophecy was unclear—"

I nod, like I've already proven my point.

"But there are ways, Arik. Plenty of ways. She could become a Reaper."

"Flightless bird, Khastyl! I've never heard such an outrageous suggestion. Did you not hear me? She will be loved. She will have us. She will never have any reason of *ever* becoming a Reaper."

"It could happen by accident—"

"No!" I shout, slamming my fists on my knees and springing from my chair. My boots thump on the wooden floor as I pace, the force of every enraged step shaking our glasses on the table. After I've taken a few paces around the small living space, I go to the hearth and gaze deep into the flames. My anger cools as my skin warms. "No. I promise you, Khastyl. Any daughter of ours will grow up understanding that life as a mortal far outweighs anything that life as a Reaper could give her."

After a long moment of silence, Khastyl moves, coming up behind me and tucking herself beneath my arm.

"I apologize," I say into her hair with a kiss. "Your speculations frighten me too. But I'll remind us both that our daughter will know no such fate. She will not become a Reaper—I vow it. And since she will not, we can both rest easy knowing she will stay in the mortal realm, far, *far* away from Veltuur."

Khastyl twists her head away from me.

"What? What is it? Is my word not reassuring enough?"

"It's nothing. You're right. I'm sure everything will be—"

Softening my voice, I spin her toward me. "What is it, Khastyl? You've all but said it now. If there's more, you might as well say it."

I search the golden brown of her irises.

She draws another deep breath, loosed through the smallest slit between her lips. "There's a gate, Arik. One that leads to the under-realm, and even if she doesn't become a Reaper, what if she finds the gate? What if she goes there of her own accord?"

I blink at my wife, growing increasingly curious about the woman standing beside me. "A gate to the underrealm? How do you know of such a thing?"

"I just do."

My eyes widen at her, insisting she give me more than that.

She sighs again. "The woman, the prophecy. It might've been mentioned there."

"And where, Altúyur tell, is this gate located?"

"It doesn't matter, Arik—"

"No, I think quite the opposite, my love. If I am to appease your mind and ensure that our child never sets foot near such a place, then I need to know the place she is forbidden to venture."

Khastyl purses her lips, wincing as she considers. She knows me long enough by now to know that she is not the only stubborn one. I will not let this conversation end without an answer.

"Kallinei Swamp," she says at last.

Nodding, I take her slowly back into my arms and breathe in the pine still lingering in her hair from our journey through the woods earlier.

"Then I swear on my life, Khastyl, that our daughter shall never set foot near the Kallinei Swamp."

She nestles her face deeper into my chest, and I squeeze her tightly. She sighs, a light and airy noise meant to tell me that her woes have finally been soothed. But if I know my wife, it is a trick. She does not want to worry me more than she already has, and likely doesn't want me to continue pestering her about a topic she's ready to stop discussing.

But it is late, and we had a long day. There is still time before the child is born for me to learn more about this supposed prophecy, about this gate hidden in the Kallinei Swamp.

For now, I simply hold her and comfort her as best I can. But there will come a day when I have more information, that I will do what Khastyl needs me to do to make her feel truly comforted. I will journey to the swamp, and I will destroy whatever gate I find there.

2

FORBIDDEN, FORGOTTEN, FREED
SINISA

"There," I stammer, pointing below through the trees and trying not to think about how far away the ground is. "I can see the palace."

"Indeed," the Divine Altúyur shouts over the wind and the flapping of his magnificent, black wings. "Then prepare for descent!"

Nothing could've prepared me for it, not even our rocky takeoff. Most birds are graceful creatures. They soar effortlessly through the blue sky, they're able to balance on the thinnest of branches without ever toppling over, and many are known for having the gift of lovely, chipper song.

For all the Altúyur's likeness to a bird, he shares none of its grace as we fall through the trees. Branch after branch pelt me in the leg, the arm, the face. He catches a bushel of leaves or two as well, sending us spinning for the woodland floor at a hastened, wobbling pace.

I squint my eyes closed and prepare for a painful landing. Fazing with my crow had never been like this. For all the grief I gave him about never being able to take us precisely where we needed to be, at least we always landed safely.

When my feet tap gently on the ground, I dare to open one eye to find that the realm hasn't toppled on its side.

"Scared you, did I?" As the Altúyur releases my stiff arms, I hear the smile in his voice. "Rest assured, I may not know who I am, but I *know* how to fly."

"Keep telling yourself that," I groan, rolling out my neck and shoulders.

He lands beside me, taking a moment to stretch and adjust to the solid ground as well. Apparently, spending a day in flight, dangling from the talons of an oversize bird-man is as foreign to my muscles as flying around with a mortal is for him.

The earth seems to ripple beneath me. It swirls and writhes like the dirt itself is made from thousands of bugs that are crawling beneath my feet. Green heat rises up my throat, and I have to pull my nauseous, disoriented gaze away from the ground to the smooth marble backside of Halaud Palace instead. It's just as radiant as I remember, and just as surprisingly unguarded.

I comb my fingers through the knots in my hair, trying to make myself appear at least a little presentable for what may come once we're inside. I know I'm no noblewoman, but perhaps with any luck, I won't stick out like a sore thumb. Although, when I glance down at the mud caked all the way up my trousers from where I waded through Kallinei Swamp, when I feel the salt from the Coast of Dreams and sand from the Pyrethi Desert still seasoning my hair, any notions I had of blending in are expunged.

The only solace I have is knowing that the entrance we're about to use will take us right to the Forbidden Garden, right to the place where the Divine Sungema is supposedly, possibly imprisoned.

"This way."

I motion for the Altúyur to follow me, along the backside of the palace, to the secret door buried in the forest floor. With him behind me, I descend into the dark tunnel, shove my way through the tiny enclosure, and push against the framed painting on the other side.

Despite my best attempts at being quiet, the large frame whines every time I shove it an inch. Anyone on the other side could've heard us from all the way down the hallways.

But fate is on our side tonight, because once I finally peek my head inside, the only guard around is one I already know.

"Borgravid," I say, equal parts surprised and relieved to see his extended hand. "I was hoping you'd be stationed here tonight."

"And what was your plan if I wasn't?"

Grimacing, I gesture to the tunnel's opening. "Probably just rely on scaring them to death?"

Borgravid's brow furrows as he watches the opening. "You brought the princess then?" he starts to ask, reminding me that the last time we'd spoken, I'd lied to him and told him that I'd bring Gem back to the palace to lay claim to the throne. Considering Acari has become king, and considering that Borgravid's eyes have gone wide, focusing exclusively on the tall, winged man exiting the tunnel behind me, thankfully I doubt I'll have to explain myself.

Borgravid surprises me when he drops down to his knees, head to the floor. "Divine Iracara, you grace us with your return."

I exchange a quick look with my travel companion to see if the name sounds familiar to him. Whether it does or doesn't, I can't tell, but he holds his head of spiky maroon hair high as he says, "Thank you, mortal human."

I glare at his theatrics and grab Borgravid by the arm to pull him back to his feet. He only budges because he wants to.

"I was hoping you could help us," I say, gritting through my teeth with effort.

"Anything for the Divine Iracara," he says, and starts to drop to his knees once more.

This time, I catch his arm again before he gets too far. "I need you to let us into the Forbidden Garden."

Borgravid scowl is dubious and skeptical. "Why?"

I heave a sigh. This would all be a lot simpler if I didn't have to tell him everything. For one thing, I don't even know it all myself. Leumas hadn't exactly been effusive with his instructions. All he told me was that I was supposedly prophesized to defeat Veltuur, but first he needs me to free the Divine Altúyur, starting with Sungema.

He'd been specific, sure. But I hadn't had time to ask questions. I'm not even sure I believe everything he said. Do I really think there was a prophecy, and that I'm a part of it? Do I really want to become enslaved to it, and let it guide my hand like Veltuur commanded me while I was a Reaper? When Leumas told me about fate and destiny, when Acari turned down my offer of help, I had been too surprised and confused to think for a second about whether I wanted to be involved in this or not. I've only just recently reclaimed my freedom. Am I so eager to release it?

But behind me, Iracara says chipperly, "We're here to release the Divine Sungema from where she is trapped in the memory tree. Sinisa is prophesized to do so."

Borgravid jerks his gaze away from Iracara back to me. "You what?"

Shaking my head, I say, speaking more to myself than Borgravid, "I don't know. But I was told she was trapped here, and I don't really like the idea of anyone being kept enslaved, so here I am. That's about as much as I know though."

Before he can formulate any of the questions buzzing in his mind like stigrees, I push past him and head down the corridor toward the Forbidden Garden. Iracara and Borgravid follow closely, but just as the captain's about to speak, I cut him off.

"Look, it's a long and complicated story that I don't have all the details of. What I do know is that we might not have much time to free her. Veltuur will figure out we've come here. He will try to stop us from releasing her. You can either help us or fight us."

He leans back and examines me with amusement.

"Oh, shut up," I snap. "I might not be able to best you hand-to-hand, but Iracara could contain you. His talons are quite strong, you know. And if he were to grab you and lift you into the air, he could fly out through the courtyard, and you'd be—"

"I have a duty to the Divine Altúyur. We all do. I took a vow to ensure that I would do everything in my power to help them return to Tayaraan," he says, uncrossing his arms. He leans across me, hands clasping the brass handles, and shoves the glass doors ajar. "If what you say is true, then I have no reason to fight you, but every reason to help."

I flash him a crooked smile, enter the garden, and make my way to the memory tree.

With Borgravid on my right and Iracara to my left, we stare up through the branches, speechless as we gaze upon what is said to be one of the other Divine Altúyur: Sungema, Preserver of Memory.

Borgravid flattens his hands over his chest and drags them down his front, as if he'll be able to smooth out the wrinkles in his leather armor any more than one can smooth out the ripples in the ocean. He fusses with his cape as well, then his beard.

I crook my eyebrow at him.

He grunts. "It's not every day you meet one of the Divine Altúyur, let alone two of them. Forgive me for wanting to appear presentable. One of us should, anyway."

Smirking, I roll my eyes. "I only look this way because I was sent on a wild goose chase through the swamp, which is where Iracara was finally freed, and where I learned that Sungema was trapped here. So, hopefully, she'll find it in her heart to forgive me."

"Do you think she has sentience?" Iracara asks beside me before Borgravid can respond. He inches forward to examine one of the hundreds, if not thousands of small leaves that brim Sungema's branches.

"How am I supposed to know?" I shrug, but then a thought hits me. "Did you?"

Iracara brings a thoughtful feather to his chin. "Hmm, I don't think I did."

Borgravid eyes him warily. "What were you before?"

"I believe I was a key. Certainly not the most glorious of lives, I imagine—but, no. I don't think I recall any of it."

"Hrmph," Borgravid grumbles, beard in hand. "It's just like the Reapers. They lose their memories too, according to the King."

"Interesting," Iracara sings. He flutters his feathered fingers together with glee.

As understandable as it is that either of them would find this all fascinating, none of what they're discussing matters and is only serving to distract me.

"Will the both of you be quiet?" I snap. "I'm trying to think."

Borgravid resumes his soldier's stance. Iracara on the other hand...

"Think about what?"

Snarling, I storm away from the both of them, grumbling more to myself than anyone, but I'm sure they hear me all the same. "Of how I'm supposed to set her free."

Leumas' words are twisting cyclones that tear through my thoughts. Talk of fate and destiny, of Veltuur and the Altúyur. The hints he gave me the other day about who Sungema was and the gifts she bestowed on the mortals, helped me decipher that she was here in Halaud Palace, caged inside the memory tree. But as I sift through the rest of Leumas' words, searching for meaning, for answers, I only discover that he never said anything about *how* to release her.

I approach the trunk of the memory tree and press my hand to the jagged bark.

I'm missing something. Something obvious, I can just feel it.

"I don't know how to release you," I whisper, resting my head against her. I blink down at the ground, to the thick roots rising through the soil. Dozens of green, coin-size leaves have fallen away from her to settle in the dirt, the very leaves that Acari gave me so that I could remember how I became a Reaper.

Then, like the slow rise of the sun, a realization dawns on the horizon of my thoughts. Iracara didn't change the moment he was rescued from the neko cave; he didn't even become himself again until long after we evaded the Deceptive Serpent. Something triggered his transformation.

"Borgravid," I call over my shoulder, taking a few steps back from the memory tree. "What gift does the Divine Iracara bestow?"

He frowns. "He's the Altúyur of Compassion. He provides us our humanity, our morality."

Nodding, I turn back to the tree, and to the puzzle solving itself before me. While we were in Kallinei Swamp, Iracara didn't change until after I showed the Deceptive Serpent the mirror, after Acari stormed toward the snake with his death-addled hand outstretched, after I stopped him from killing the creature. We showed the beast an act of compassion.

I examine the leaves on the ground and notice that none of them are yellowed. In a place like this, it's likely that the garden is cared for daily by a groundskeeper, to ensure a healthy and mani-cured sanctuary fit for royalty. Said person probably rakes every day before they water anything in here.

I scoop some of the leaves into my hand and race back toward my companions. "We use the memory leaves. We water the tree with the leaves still on the ground and it'll act like a tea, giving Sungema her memories back."

Iracara claps his black feathered hands together. "Brilliant!"

Borgravid is less convinced. "How do you know that will work?"

"I don't. But, when we were in the swamp, it wasn't until after I showed compassion for the serpent and spared it that Iracara was released from the key. And Leumas said that Veltuur is the Altúyur of balance, that he wanted to trap the others until he could return equilibrium to the realms. Maybe the only way they can be freed is if they witness the gift they bestowed upon the mortals. For Iracara it was compassion. For Sungema, it would be—"

"Memory," Borgravid finishes. He racks his fingers through his bushy beard. "If the Divine Iracara had to witness the act, then perhaps the Divine Sungema does too."

Chewing my lip, I turn back to face the tree. "You're right. Even if the groundskeepers are diligent about their work, the memory tree has been here a long time, and by now she would've likely been steeped in waters containing her own leaves at least once."

Borgravid nods, a single assured jerk of a motion. "We need to show her someone remembering something they have forgotten."

Slowly, both of us turn to Iracara. The bird-man is brushing the feathers along his arms, seemingly unaware of the conversation we've been having. It's hard to believe that he is one of the Divine Altúyur. I always imagined they'd be elegant, poised, perfect. But Iracara is far from any of those things. He carries himself with the wide-eyed wonderment of a child seeing a waterfall for the first time, not an immortal whose walked the realms since the dawn of time.

Sensing the heat of our gazes, Iracara shoves his arms behind his back and blinks up at us. "Did I miss something?"

I roll my eyes. "If we're to free Sungema, we need you to take the memory leaves."

He brings his wings before him again, crossing them shyly and hiding behind them like a shield. "I—I don't know. I'm afraid..."

We have no time for doubt and wavering. Leumas made it clear that Veltuur wasn't keen on us freeing Sungema. If Veltuur really wants her to remain trapped here for all eternity, there is an entire army of Reapers at his disposal to prevent us from releasing her.

Losing the last ounce of patience I have, I growl.

Borgravid plants a firm hand on my shoulder. "Compassion, Sinisa."

I'm about to growl at him next, but there's just enough reason behind his reminder that I'm able to soften my scowl. I know next to nothing about the Divine Altúyur, but what he's saying makes sense to me. If we want Iracara to do what we need him to do— what the *realms* need him to do—then we might need to take a gentler approach.

Unfortunately, I'm a little out of practice with pleasantness and kindness. It was one of the skills that Hayliel had brought to our little team. I can do courage, I can even do loyalty and determination, but compassion? That was more her style, and not for the first time today, I feel her absence like a chasm widening in the soil beneath my feet. Were she here, it would come all but naturally to her to ease Iracara. She'd soothe his fears, reassure him that the courage he needs is already inside himself, if only he'd just look there. But if I were to say the same, the words would come out all wrong. They'd be harsh and cold, likely sending him deeper into a retreat instead of building him up.

The courage he needs is already inside himself, the words repeat. Though they are my own, a mere replication of my impression of what Hayliel might say in times like these, I hear them in her voice and it's like she's talking to me now.

The courage you need is inside you. Just talk to him.

With a tilt of his head, Borgravid stares at me, waiting. It's possible I could insist I don't have a tender bone in my body, but between the two of us, both lacking what I think are proper social skills, I asses the man before me, the one built like a mountain magrok, hardened as stone, and then I look to myself. A former Reaper, sure, but Iracara never knew me as such. When he looks at me, he can't see any of my dark past, only a young woman who still hasn't even reached adulthood yet, a girl traveling all across Tayaraan in search of the Divine Altúyur to save them, a girl who's already saved him.

Perhaps I underestimate how intimidating I am to a stranger now that I'm not in Reaper's clothing.

I nod to Borgravid, swallow the lump in my throat, and step forward.

"I understand your fear," I say, the words heavy and dragging slowly across my tongue. "Not too long ago, I used some of the memory leaves to remember something from my past too."

Iracara perks up. "And?" he asks through his feathered fingers. "How was it? Were you happy with your decision or did you regret it?"

My laugh is dry and humorless. "Neither. Both. I'm not going to lie to you; it was a bad memory, one of the worst. The whole time I was reliving it, I just kept thinking about how much I wanted to forget it ever happened again. I had been content in my ignorance."

Watching him closely, I see the fear snaking its way through him again. It devours every hint of curiosity or courage he had until there is nothing but black in his eyes. Before my own doubt can creep in, I hear Hayliel's voice uttering my words again, encouraging me forward.

The courage you need is inside you. And then she adds, *You can do this.*

I know it's not really her, I know that she is forever gone, but I lean into her anyway and continue.

"But, you know what, Iracara? After the worst of it had passed, once I was able to sit with my long lost memories and figure out what they meant to me, what they made of who I was and who I had become, I was glad I took the memory leaves. They showed me a piece of myself I had forgotten, and as awful and horrible as that moment was, it was still a part of me, and it wasn't fair that someone else had taken that away from me."

Iracara smiles sadly, the red skin surrounding his surprisingly human mouth dimpling the deeper the smile grows, until he's gazing at me with pure gratitude.

"Thank you for that, Sinisa. I think you are right. I want to know who I was because that is a part of who I am."

"Does this mean you'll try the memory leaves then?" I ask, hopeful and trying not to sound too surprised.

"It does," he says boldly.

Glancing briefly to Borgravid, I hold out my hand and let Iracara take the memory leaves from me.

As his wary eyes rove over them, he winces. "I sure hope she's not sentient. I don't want to imagine what that feels like otherwise, having someone eat a part of you."

I shudder at the thought. "It's like you said earlier. You weren't conscious while you were the key. I doubt she is either."

Despite my reassurance, I'm not convinced. What if once Sungema becomes herself again, she's missing feathers from all the places where she has lost leaves? What if she's missing an arm or a leg or a wing from where one of her branches has fallen off?

I shove the thought aside and try focusing on Borgravid instead.

"Where are you going?" I call after him when he starts heading for the entrance.

He stops. "To retrieve a mug and water. To make the tea. It's how Acari did it last time…" His words trail off when he catches my raised eyebrow and he realizes his idiocy. "But he was a Reaper and so he couldn't touch the leaves without cooking them first."

"That, and the effects are probably the same, whether you drink the leaves, eat them, smoke them, or whatever."

"I'd rather not smoke anything," Iracara says, still eyeing the handful of foliage I handed to him dubiously."

"You don't have to. Just chew them. We'll know soon enough if it's working or not, and if it doesn't, *then* we can take the extra time to make you a nice, warm cup of tea. But for now, we should move quickly. It took us a day to get here. There's no telling how long it will take Veltuur to find us."

With a longing sigh, Iracara plucks a leaf from his hand and holds it out before him. "I don't suppose this will taste good."

Before I can growl at him to hurry, he sets the thing on his tongue and clamps his jaw shut.

"Remember to think about something from your past," I remind him, hopeful that he remembers the instructions I gave him while we were still in Kallinei Swamp, just before I'd gone through the gate to the underrealm.

Jaw working, Iracara gnaws on the leaf. A dent forms on his brow with each chew, but he doesn't stop until every last bit of it has become green paste in his mouth. When he finally swallows, his expression bitter, he smacks his tongue to get rid of the grainy flavor.

"I knew that was going to have a foul flavor to it."

Neither of us make a remark. We're too eager to see what will happen next. Though I've experienced the effects of the memory leaves firsthand, I've never seen them from the outside before. All I know is that when I drank the tea that Acari had made with them, the experience was so vivid and lifelike that I couldn't tell the past from the present. It felt like I had fazed from the inn in Ngal to the orphanage where I grew up three years prior, like no time had passed at all. My clothes had changed from my Reaper tunic to my nightgown, my body was three years younger, even the air had the distinct chill of winter, though we were in the middle of spring.

"How long does it take?" Iracara asks.

"Not long. For me it was almost instant—"

Before I can finish speaking, Iracara's face falls flat. His already bulbous pupils bleed black into his whites. His gaze grows distant as the memory leaves work their magic. I twist toward the tree, fully expecting to see it bursting with light, just as the key had done before Iracara's transformation, but nothing happens.

"Stop this madness, Veltuur!" yells Iracara.

His tone sends a chill through me. The rage and desperation in his voice is so unlike the cheerful wonder I'm used to hearing from him that it makes every one of my muscles stiffen. Even more alarming still is the name he yells, the title that I only just recently learned is the name of a cruel, forgotten Altúyur.

Slowly, I spin around to watch Iracara as the memory takes hold.

"You've proven your point. You brought war down on the Altúyur. You put malice in the people's hearts. You executed our Guardians and kidnapped our Prophets. How much further are you willing to go?"

There's a pause while Veltuur answers, though since Borgravid and I are on the outside of this memory, neither of us can hear what is said.

"You call this balance?" Iracara replies. "Look around us! There is no need for all this bloodshed. You've created a system where everyone is doomed."

Another pause, then Iracara throws out his wings. "I don't care about your reasons. Just put an end to this. Release our Prophets, release Dovenia, and let her bring peace back to the realm. *That* is your balance, Veltuur. Not this...this chaos."

The next interlude of silence is long and filled with various scoffs and half-spoken sentences from Iracara, but it seems like Veltuur has a lot to say. Eventually, Iracara stops trying to interject. He narrows his eyes at his invisible converser, squares his shoulders, and listens. But as the conversation continues, eventually Iracara loses hold of his resolve.

His pupils bloom wide. "You can't be serious. What will that prove? No matter my form, I am beloved to the mortals. They would hastily show me love once they discover what's become of us —" Iracara staggers back a step, fear twisting his already frightful expression. "I beg of you. It's not too late to change all of this. Permit compassion to enter your heart, Veltuur—No. No, no—"

Without further warning, Iracara's legs buckle beneath him. He crumples to the gravel, a limp mound of feathers and limbs. Borgravid and I race to his side, the captain reaching him first.

"Divine Iracara, are you all right?" he asks, lifting the Altúyur's head from the ground.

The small white rocks cling to his cheek, and Borgravid wipes them away as Iracara's eyes flutter.

"I...I..." Iracara mumbles weakly. "He turned me into a key. I—I had forgotten. All those years ago, that thick-headed, illogical, conniving birdbrain turned me into a key because he knew no one could feel compassion for a piece of iron! Why, when I get my hands on him, I'm gonna—"

All of us wince when a burst of light shines before us. I shield my face into the crook of my arm, but I can still see the roots retreating through the ground. The brightness grows and grows, consuming everything in the room in piercing white. But just as it did with Iracara, after a final shudder, the light blinks away. Once it's gone, once I'm finally able to see again without burning my eyes, I lower my arm and search the garden ahead.

I almost don't see her curled over her knees in the grass. The green, iridescent wings that lay flat over her back almost blend in completely with the now open pasture. But when she rises, blue hair dipped in ink falling to her shoulders, it's like nothing else in the room exists but her. Power emits from her very core. It's in the way she straightens, one vertebra at a time, in the way she keeps her eyes closed, her face poised, as if nothing around her could cause her any harm.

When she finally opens her eyes, I stagger in their shine. They are as golden and as striking as the sun itself, perhaps more.

Beside me, Iracara places his hands to his chest before striking them down and out to his sides. "Blessed Sister," he breathes.

Sungema inclines her head. For someone so small, her presence is giant, domineering. It fills the expansive, domed room like she is more important than the air.

She tucks one charcoal hand to her chest, and I realize her wings are not attached to her arms like Iracara's are. Her feet, too, are not wrinkly with talons, but rather humanlike.

She traces a finger lightly along the juniper wrappings around her chest as she speaks directly to me. "Thank you, young Sinisa Strigidae. I have been waiting for you, Prophesized One."

3

DISTRUST

ACARI

Pacing the bottom of the chasm, I stop abruptly to look up to Nymane lounging in her throne.

"I don't mean to rush you—or *him*, or whatever—I mean, if you don't mind Nerul taking forever then neither do I, but...shouldn't he be here by now?"

"He's busy," Nymane says through gritted teeth, barely glancing away from her long, pointed nails.

"Right, but...isn't doing Veltuur's bidding kind of more important than whatever Nerul's been tasked with? Isn't this a time sensitive matter?"

Nymane's white hair is so thin that when she snaps around to face me, the tendrils sticking out from under her bloodred hood don't even have enough weight behind them to whip as she spins. They simply float in the wake of her movement before settling back into place to dangle in patches around her face. "Do not belittle the work of your seniors. Nerul is tailing a Reaper who has developed a troubling pattern of killing of her own accord instead of claiming the single soul she was sent to retrieve. It is not a job I can simply pull him from without consequences."

"Right. No, I'm not saying what he's doing isn't important... I'm just saying...why am I still here? I could be back at the palace by now. Sinisa's probably already been there; she could already have freed Sungema and then—"

Nymane hisses. "And I suppose you're the Reaper to trust to do the job of killing her?" I fall silent and Nymane barks a laugh. "You may have Veltuur convinced, but I am no fool. You have no intention of killing the girl. You didn't in Kallinei Swamp, and you won't do it now."

"Then why send me at all?"

"Because unlike you, I understand the meaning of duty and loyalty. Veltuur has selected you for such a task, and I will not disobey him. However, I will not send you up to the mortal realm to ruin everything he has fought for without an escort to ensure you stay in your place. Nerul will be here shortly."

"Nerul is here now," sings a man from the disappearing smoke that had been his entrance. "Forgive me for making you wait. That Reaper sure does like to make a game out of her kills. Smart, that one. She saved her contracted kill for last so I had to wait until she'd butchered every last one of them, otherwise we would've had another Prophet running free—"

"Now isn't the time," Nymane snaps. She stands from her throne before disappearing behind a cloud of black and reappearing in the Pit of Judgment beside us. "You have another mission now. The Reaper King, here, has been tasked with returning to Oakfall to kill Sinisa Strigidae."

Nerul's eyebrows hike up his forehead. "What imbecile Councilspirit gave that contract to him?"

"Watch your tongue," Nymane says coolly. "No Councilspirit, but Veltuur himself. The boy is meant to put an end to an ancient prophecy. I'd like you to join him and ensure that he does."

"Is that all? Kill Sinisa? I've looked forward to watching her die for years."

"There is more, but the two are intricately intwined. Do not let her release Sungema. If she succeeds in doing so, Veltuur's demise will be well on its way."

Nerul eyes me then, a wicked grin playing at the edge of his lips, and just before we both disappear behind a veil of smoke, he says with sinister quiet, "Consider it done."

4

WAR OF DIVINITY

SINISA

Despite the imposing nature of Sungema's presence, the one that has Iracara and Borgravid both addressing her with nothing short of reverence and awe, I fight the instinct to do the same. So what if the Divine Altúyur are supposedly all powerful? So what if they are as ancient as time itself and utterly impervious to death? Other than bestowing mankind with a set of characteristics eons ago and then getting themselves imprisoned by one of their own, I've witnessed no real magnitude of power, no miracle to suggest that I should treat Sungema or any of them any differently than I would anyone else.

And right now, all this talk of prophecy and fate has me wanting answers.

"Why me?" I demand. "Why have you been waiting for me? Leumas could've sent anyone here to save you if he knew where you'd been all along. Why am I the one being roped into this?"

Iracara gasps. "Leumas lives?"

Confusion wrinkles my brow. "You know him?"

But he doesn't have a chance to answer before Sungema says plainly, "You were prophesized. It is as simple as that. He could send no other because only you could do what has been done."

If she continues to withhold from me any real answers, my teeth will be ground to dust by the time we're done here.

"That's not an answer," I snarl. "You just expect me to go along with this like my life isn't even my own, but I have news for you—it is. I am here by choice, and I will leave by choice if you don't tell me what I need to know—"

But as I'm stomping toward her, smoke fills the Forbidden Garden. Not the heavy black kind that I'm familiar with in the underrealm, but a lighter, whiter fog that seems to make all of the flora around us—the large-leafed plants, the colorful flowers, even the pebble walkway we're standing on—disappear behind a haze.

"Iracara?" I yell. "Borgravid!"

Neither of them answers, and I don't expect them to. Whiteness spreads as far as the eye can see in all directions around me, and I do not see them anywhere.

Sungema's voice fills the nothingness. "Before the Veltuur Empire, was the Age of Divinity, a peaceful time when the Divine Altúyur roamed the Tayaraan realm alongside the mortals."

A stone walkway appears beneath my feet, archways of the same slate gray blinking into view farther and farther down the bridge until an entire city and the mountain peak it rests upon emerges through the fog. Rows of buildings and towers are stacked on the mountainside, a single road winding between them all to reach the topmost level: a fortress.

But not just any fortress. The pewter spires and tall, gothic windows that line the gray, stone wall are defining markers of the Ghamayan Citadel. The snowy alps help too, but most of all, the Bridge of Evermore is unmistakable.

I wrap my arms around my shoulders when a mountainous gust blows past, following the wide bridge to the city's gate. As a Reaper, I've been to the citadel surrounding the castle many times before, and so I know what to expect when I arrive: a formidable stone wall, the portcullis that is almost always open, and the eight blue-gray statues who guard over the entrance as tall as the wall itself.

Only, this time as I draw nearer, I count nine of them.

A macaw.

A lorikeet.

An aracari.

A quetzal.

A dove.

An owl.

A peacock.

A sungem.

And the ninth is a vulture.

Veltuur's statue is perhaps the most avian of all. His head is bald and small compared to the rest of his towering frame. His nose is crooked, stretched forward into a sharp, angled beak. Like any vulture, he lurks above the bridge like he's waiting for a feast, for any of the mortals below him to drop dead so that he might swoop down and devour them.

"The Altúyur were once beloved by all," Sungema continues from somewhere in the ether. "Each and every one of us was worshipped for the gifts we bestowed upon the people: Macawna for her intellect, Lorik for his bravery, Iracara for compassion, Quetzi for integrity, Dovenia for peace, Owlena for fate, Pecolock for inspiration, myself for the gift of memory, and Veltuur for the balance he brought to the realm.

"Veltuur tempered Tayaraan's winters so that no longer would the people freeze during the unrelenting storms. He cooled the desert sands so that they would no longer melt all who dared to cross them. He brought the moon to counter the sun's light, and the oceans to cradle the land's masses.

"But Veltuur oversaw balance in *all* things, not just in the way in which the mortals preferred. Where there was life, he brought death; where there was wealth, he brought poverty. When the other Altúyur bestowed their gifts, he ensured that the people would know as many moments of our blessings as they would his. If they were to experience intellect, they'd also know stupidity; where there was inspiration, he gave them boredom; where there was memory there would also be forgetting; and where there was fate, there would also be choice. To bravery he brought fear; compassion was met with malice; integrity with deceit; and peace with war.

"Where the people once loved us all and rejoiced at our presence, they soon began to have their doubts about the Divine Veltuur, and they succumbed to the very malice and fear he bestowed upon them. The people quickly turned on him. They stopped their worship of him. And though he had no one to blame but himself, he held the other Altúyur culpable instead, felt as if we were claiming all the glory for ourselves and leaving him none.

"To his credit, he was not wrong about us. The balance Veltuur brought often felt like a betrayal to many of us. For centuries, we lived among the people and witnessed their prosperity, but the more he introduced his gifts, the darker Tayaraan became. People starved, and kingdoms went to war over misunderstandings and misaligned values. It broke our hearts, and so the Altúyur intervened.

"We created the Guardians. They could not do all, but we gave them the gift of healing and protection, to alleviate some of the deaths that Veltuur's *balance* had inflicted upon the realm."

Suddenly, the Ghamayan Mountains disappear, and I'm cast once more into the mist. As a new scene develops around me, a canopy of green overhead, a lush meadow at my feet, I'm overcome with a deep sense of familiarity toward the place, though I can't identify it. The sun here is gentler than the one I've bathed in, making every branch, leaf, and flower glow with a subtle, glorious hue.

Nine figures appear between the trees, circling a pool of the brightest blue at their feet. I recognize some of them, Iracara by his black and yellow feathers, and Sungema for her small stature, but even though the others are new to me, I know them for who they are: the Divine Altúyur, each and every one of them.

Including Veltuur.

He spreads his massive, black wings wide as he speaks, but once more it's not his words I hear, but Sungema's as she recounts what happened that day.

"But now it was Veltuur's turn to feel betrayed. He summoned the Divine Altúyur and accused us of abusing our powers and upsetting the balance of the realms. He demanded that we destroy the Guardians that we had created, but we could not. They were not created out of nothing, after all. They were exceptional mortals, hand-selected for their altruism and kind hearts. They were people, and we could not remove their powers without causing them harm, and so, we did not. But when none of us would abolish our Guardians, Veltuur saw imbalance once more.

"So he created the Reapers."

The meadow darkens, a shadow creeping overhead above the trees. People in red tunics step into view from all around the forest, closing in on the convening Altúyur. Their horrified faces say it all, say everything that the mortals once said to me: abomination, vile creature, wicked, deadly.

I can't shake the unsettled feeling of standing between the two sides, Reapers closing in at my back while the Altúyur stand gaping back at them in horror. I want to close my eyes. I want to run. I want to be no part of this.

Fortunately, the visions fades again, and for a while, nothing refills it. I stand on a white canvas of land, mirrored by a white sky, with not so much as a shadow to mark where one begins and the other ends.

"He claimed that the Reapers were the balance that the Guardians brought to the world. That they would be the vilest mortals in existence and that their servitude would be to repent for their sins.

"But what Veltuur did not know was that every person involved in murder would become a Reaper, not just the cruel and malicious. The babes who took their mothers' lives as they were born, the child who accidentally stepped on a beetle while crossing a path to embrace his mother, the young girl who fought off her attacker in self-defense. No fail-safe was set in place to determine who was worthy or not of repentance, and so they all were claimed as Reapers.

"And the Altúyur could not abide by such an atrocious act against humanity."

Sand starts to spill in beneath my feet, golden and warm. Heat presses down on me, as well as rises from below, as beige dunes pop into existence and scorch my toes even from the safe confines of my boots. A battle roars across the barren desert, robust with the clashing of metal on flesh, the agonizing cries of the dying, and the horrendous, gluttonous squawking of the crows as they feast on the fallen.

I find all but one of the Divine Altúyur overseeing the war, each of them standing side by side atop the tallest of the sandy peaks. But interspersed between them is someone neither feathered nor marked by the runes of a Guardian, but instead by prophecy. Cleft lips, clubbed feet, splotchy skin pigmentation. I scan their faces, searching through the slits of fabric that shield them from the winds for anything that I might recognize, and I'm surprised to find that one among them *is* familiar, even though I'm fairly certain that the war Sungema is showing me occurred many millennium ago.

Even though all I can see are his dark eyes between the scarf wrapped around his face and neck, and even though his pallor is far more vibrant than I've ever seen it, his skin less wrinkled than I'm used to, I'd recognize his stance anywhere, the way he keeps his hands clasped at his waist, slightly leaning to one side as he favors one of his legs.

Leumas is dressed head to toe in white, draping cloths. Although he won't see battle, he wears rose-gold plates over his shoulders and chest all the same, and as I scan the rest of his attire, I realize for the first time since I met him, that he has only one leg. I'd always just assumed he limped because he was ancient and decrepit. Never once had it ever occurred to me that he might've been a Prophet before his time in the underrealm.

The more I think on it though, the more it makes sense. How

else would he or the other Councilspirits be able to foresee deaths if they weren't Prophets themselves?

Leumas leans over to kiss the hand of the Altúyur beside him, the one who's wide, feathered face resembles that of an owl.

"To fight for humanity," Sungema continues at last. "To correct Veltuur's wrongdoings, we went to war. Of course, the bloodshed was unbearable and foolishly unanticipated. For every Reaper our soldiers slain, another was born. For every soldier Veltuur's Reapers took, one more innocent life was lost to his dark and twisted vision of a balanced realm.

"We were losing, and we all knew it. And so, we regrouped, the eight of us with our Prophets, and planned our final assault, one that we had sworn to never attempt."

The battle disappears and the quiet assaults my ringing ears. Nothing replaces the fog this time, but a single, shining blade floats down from the ether. It spins before me, the blade gleaming like the sun itself shone down just for it.

"Long before the war, Veltuur realized there was an imbalance among the realms. The Altúyur could not remain immortal forever without any threat of death existing. In order to keep the balance that Veltuur so cherished, he created such a threat, a possibility for any of us to meet our demise. The Blade of Immortality, carved from the forest of death, forged in the Pools of Prophecy, is said to destroy any Altúyur it should strike through the heart.

"We intended to use it to end Veltuur's tyranny. However, during our next convening, Owlena foretold of a prophecy. To strike him with the Blade of Immortality then would bring about the demise of us all. She saw the blade falling into Veltuur's hands and him, in time, using it against each of us until only he remained. Humanity would never know freedom from his reign. The Tayaraan realm would've been plunged into darkness.

"But should we hide the blade, there would come a time when another Guardian would be born, one who would be victorious in ending Veltuur and restoring balance to the realms. But it would require a great sacrifice from us all, accepting the imprisonment that Veltuur had planned for us, and leaving the mortals alone with only Veltuur to guide them for eons.

"Though we knew we were condemning many, we chose to save the ones we could and to fight another day. So Owlena cast the Blade of Immortality far away where no one would find it, and one by one Veltuur captured each of us. Though our gifts did not leave the mortals with our entrapment, every time he sealed one of us away, he lost that part of us inside himself. No longer could he feel compassion, or peace, or integrity. And once he captured me, he soon also forgot what had come to pass."

This time, when the fog finally clears, I find myself standing in the Forbidden Garden again, wedged between an equally bewildered Borgravid and Iracara. I glance to both of them, eye them as if to ask if they've just been shown the same thing I have. Borgravid gives a subtle, disoriented nod. Iracara blows between his lips.

Sungema approaches us, her wings hanging off her back but not quite reaching the ground. "You asked why we waited for you, Sinisa Strigidae, and the answer is simple. We waited because humanity needed us to. We waited because we had no other choice. We waited because we knew you were our only hope in defeating Veltuur, and considering you are standing here before me now, having already released Iracara from his binds, having already been set upon the path to free the rest of us, there is not a doubt in my mind that we waited for good reason."

I shift uncomfortably on my feet. Although I'd felt so confident in my questioning her, now I just feel foolish. Childish. This chain of events has been in the making for centuries. Maybe my life isn't as much my own as I had hoped, as I'd been promised upon leaving the underrealm.

Something carnal and innate inside me tears at that thought. As long as my lungs still fill with air, only *I* can decide how I live. I will not let anyone take my life away from me again.

But also...what else would I be doing if not setting out to free the Altúyur? Could I live with myself, knowing that I left them all to their binds while I enjoyed my freedom?

"Now what, then?" I ask her. "Leumas said once I freed you, you would know where to find the rest of the Altúyur."

Sungema inclines her head. "The Prophet speaks the truth. I am the keeper of memory. I know what became of each of the Altúyur and where they were discarded. Veltuur wanted each of us to learn to appreciate the counterbalance of our gifts, and he ensured we would spend our time in our confines learning that lesson. He turned me into a tree that could grant mortals their memories but forbade me from having any of my own. Iracara he turned into a key and hid away in a cave so that he could never know the compassion of another living being again.

"The others suffer similar fates. He turned Quetzi into a giant serpent that forces lies upon any who cross it—"

"The Deceptive Serpent is one of the Divine Altúyur..." I say breathlessly, recalling how it had made Hayliel believe Acari was there with her, how it had made my mother forget her entire life.

Sungema nods. "Dovenia, the Altúyur of Peace, he forced her to live out her days as an aacsi, a creature whose only purpose is to kill and feast on flesh to produce its offspring from decay."

Borgravid and I exchange a look.

"Didn't the king—the *other* king, before Acari—didn't he gather all of the aacsi?" I ask him.

Borgravid looks to the greenhouse. "All that could be found, he commanded be caged in there."

"Let us see if Dovenia is among them," Sungema says, strolling toward the humid building.

We all follow.

For each of Borgravid's strides, Sungema takes three just to keep up. Even still, never once does she lose her lead. She enters the greenhouse first, Borgravid shortly behind her. The place is so small and stuffy that Iracara and I opt to wait outside, but we don't have to wait long. They return shortly with Sungema holding one of the glass boxes, a wild aacsi lunging at the sides where her hands are.

Whereas most aacsi are dark in color, allowing them to blend in with tree bark and dirt, this aacsi is different than any other I've ever seen. Its shell is white, just like that of a dove for which Dovenia is named.

"That's her?" I ask, skeptically lowering my face to the glass. "The Altúyur of Peace... So, we just need to show her something peaceful. What about this garden? It seems peaceful enough."

But before Sungema can answer, the calm tranquility of the Forbidden Garden shifts. A shadow bleeds across the floor, tenebrous and slithering. The four of us huddle closer, Borgravid holding tightly to his spear as a cloud of smoke forms ahead on the path.

"Is it Veltuur? Has he found us?" Iracara asks, voice shaking.

But even before the smoke can fully dissipate, I recognize the two figures blocking our exit.

"No," I say in barely more than a growl. "He's returned the king to his throne and sent one of his lapdogs with him."

Nerul's grin is repulsive, but it's the sight of Acari beside him, a man I thought I could call a friend, that truly churns my stomach.

"Hello, Sinisa," Nerul snarls. "Going somewhere?"

5

OBEY

ACARI

Please *don't be here. Please don't be here. Please don't be here.*
My eyes are squeezed shut as we faze out of Veltuur, but I open one warily to take a peek at the garden as we arrive, and to my deepest regret, I spy Sinisa among the four before us. Of course she's here. Why would I have expected anything different? It seems fate is insistent on forcing our paths to cross, even when doing so will only hinder both of us.

Sinisa's eyes burn into mine, accusations unspoken, but felt all the same. I want to tell her I'm not here to fight her, I'm not here to stop her from doing what she believes she needs to do, just like she didn't try to stop me. But with Nerul beside me, if I so much as suggest I'm on her side, he'll send me back to Veltuur and I'll be locked away with the Wraiths for good. Nymane will have the proof she needs to show Veltuur that I can't be trusted, and they'll give Sinisa's contract to Nerul, who will take the utmost pleasure in siphoning her soul.

I can't let that happen. Not only can I not let her die, I'd never be able to set things right in Tayaraan for people like Gem, never be able to prove to my father that his way of ruling and abiding by the archaic Law of Mother's Love was wrong.

For now, I have to play my part in this, even though it wrenches me to see her looking at me with so much scorn.

"I'm afraid you're too late," Sinisa spits, sparing me and directing the taunt at Nerul. "We've already released the Divine Sungema. We know about the War of Divinity, what Veltuur did to the other Altúyur, where they are, and how to free them. We're going to stop him, Nerul. You failed."

The strike hits its mark. Beside me, Nerul's lip curls. "I never fail." He snaps to me next. "Do it. Kill her like you were told."

I gape at him, unable to breathe. This is happening too fast. I haven't had a chance to think of a way out of this yet.

Just before Nerul can lash out at me for my slow response, I sneak a cautious glance across the path to Sinisa. I try meeting her glare with a softness that says I don't want to harm her, a silent plea for her to find some way to evade me that doesn't show the terrifying Veltuur that I am not loyal to him, but I don't think she reads it on me.

Overhead, my father-crow squawks, pulling a glare from me and drawing it skyward. As soon as I can have a quiet moment in the throne room, review the ancient laws that king after king have ruled over, I can finally let him go, finally be free of his watchful eyes. After all, Sinisa only had to make peace with her past to be rid of her crow, and the only way I'll make peace with mine is by proving to my father that there was another way, that people like Gem don't have to die just because of the way they are born.

But until then...

I look back to Sinisa, then to Nerul, as I comb a hand through my dark hair. "This...wasn't supposed to happen. Veltuur wants the Altúyur to remain trapped, but she's already freed one—*two* of them. Forget about Sinisa. We should take Sungema back to the underrealm so Veltuur can—"

Nerul growls, striking at me like a viper. "Foolish boy! You do not decide what Veltuur wants. He tasked you with Sinisa's death, so that is what you'll do. Now kill her!"

I flinch at the spittle flying from his lips, but I hold my ground.

"Don't you think having the Altúyur of Memory would be far more valuable to him than killing a mere Guardian?"

Nerul doesn't answer me, but I see the anger boiling inside him like volcano about to blow.

Before he can say a thing though, Sinisa suddenly lights up. I can see her discovering a solution as clearly as I can see the fire stoking in Nerul's eyes, but I don't know what exactly she's planning.

But then, I think I figure it out. Sinisa is no longer a Reaper, but she isn't a mere mortal either. She has a different arsenal of talents at her disposal now.

"Good luck in pleasing Veltuur," she calls across the garden. "But it might be difficult to do since my death won't be among your victories."

And with that, she, the two Altúyur beside her, the random aacsi I'm just now noticing is in one of their hands, and Captain Borgravid blink out of sight.

Although it pains me to hear the hatred in her voice, to think that she actually believes that I would try to kill her, after everything, I'm too relieved that she's made her escape to worry too much about it. She is alive—for now—and that's all that matters.

Now that she's gone, I can resume my place at the palace. I can shift my focus to changing the Law of Mother's Love, and I can show my father before I set him free what a *real* king is like. I can leave the underrealm politics and drama to the rest of the Reapers, Shades, Councilspirits, and Veltuur.

"No!" Nerul shouts, fists clenched at his sides. If I didn't know any better, I'd think the shadows of the room quaked with fear in the presence of his fury. He spins on me. "You faltered, you spineless slug. We could've had her, we could've had them all, and instead you started yammering about alternatives to your orders instead of just carrying them out. Do you have any idea what you've done?"

It takes tremendous effort to hide the prideful grin that's fighting to get through my expression.

"Now she's as good as lost to us, thanks to you!"

I comb through my hair again, settling back into my act. "I-I'm sorry. I just thought Veltuur would've been happier if we'd returned with Sinisa—I mean Sungema. I didn't mean—"

"Save it, boy. Your intentions are of no concern to me. You'll have to plead for your stupidity before Veltuur."

My stomach sinks. "What do you mean? I thought I was staying here?"

Nerul scoffs. "If you had killed the Guardian like you were supposed to, then yes, Veltuur was going to station you on the throne of Oakfall for the time being. But you didn't complete your task, and therefore the prophecy remains in motion. If we are to stop it, we have to go back and ask him what he wants us to do next."

I feel like I'm sinking. To go back means to delay any progress I might make toward changing the laws, a task that I imagine will already take quite some time. To go back means delaying my grand, final farewell with my father-crow until I'm allowed to return to the mortal realm once more.

"Now that Sinisa knows she can protect herself and her friends from us, it's likely she won't leave us much of an opening to claim her life again. Come, Veltuur might have another plan to stop this forsaken prophecy from coming to fruition."

Without further warning, darkness seeps up from the pebbles, clouding at our feet like ominous fog. But just before we become engulfed, I see Sinisa and the others reappear, her barrier dropped, and though I'm not sure she sees me in time, I flash her an impressed smile before the underrealm swallows me.

6

FLIGHT OF ALTÚYUR
SINISA

s Acari and Nerul faze back to the underrealm, I drop the barrier I've been straining to hold. My powers as a Guardian still don't come as naturally to me as my powers did when I was a Reaper. If it weren't for Acari mentioning the Guardians, I wouldn't have even remembered I had such a trick up my sleeve. I'm still not used to doing the things I'm able to do as a Guardian, and maybe I'm wrong, but I think he knew it too. The smile he flashed me makes me wonder if he wasn't trying to remind me himself.

Long after they've gone, Borgravid continues to stare at the place where Acari was standing. He must feel my gaze on him because he straightens, blinking to tear his eyes away.

"How long have you known him?" I ask. "The prince—I mean king."

Borgravid's brow creases, but instead of ignoring me, which is what I think he's going to do at first, he purses his lips together and says, "Since he was a boy."

I'm quiet for a moment, considering what it must be like to watch someone you've known for that long become a Reaper, to see the way the underrealm changes them. When I became initiated, the Councilspirits ensured that my orders never put me on the path of what limited family I had left. No one recognized me when I surfaced for a kill. No one had to see who I'd become.

"He's...I think he's almost ready to return," I say softly, trying to offer what little reassurance I can. "He just wants to change the law that started all of this before he lets go of his father."

Borgravid raises an eyebrow at me.

"Oh," I say sheepishly. "I forgot not everyone knows about the crows."

The man's scowl deepens as he mulls over my words, but it doesn't take long for understanding to strike. "His father—the king is his crow?"

While I incline my head, snorting my disdain, Sungema chimes in.

"It was all part of the balance Veltuur had to maintain. For him to create Reapers out of those who had taken a life, too many would succumb to such a fate. They needed a possibility at freedom, as well as a link to the underrealm. The crows were the solution to both. He bound the souls of the fallen so that they could be released, should the Reaper so choose."

"But none of the Reapers know about their pasts," I snap, the topic a sore spot of conversation for me. "None of them know anything about who they killed or anything about their lives before becoming a Reaper. It's a cheated system."

In the first act of any sort of emotion I've seen from her, Sungema bows her head. Her green wings seem to curl over the curves of her shoulders, as if they were offering her a hug.

"That is a blame that I bear, not Veltuur."

I cock my head at her. "Why? What did you do?"

"Before my capture, the Reapers still remembered their pasts. Most were so tortured about them that, though forgiveness and peace were desirable to them, it was still difficult to muster. However, when Veltuur captured me, I took away from him memories. Not just his own, but, in some ways, the very idea. For each Reaper he claimed, he rebirthed them from the underrealm and bound them to their crow. They would have no memory of anything but what came afterward, and perhaps the smallest fraction of a memory of the crow that they were now bound to."

My fingers dig into my palms as she speaks. Every time I think I have someone to blame for the injustice of being fastened to my abuser for years after finally having murdered him to escape him, I discover there's someone new to be angry with.

But when Sungema lifts her chin, her golden eyes blinking at me, though she shows no inkling of emotion, I hear the sorrow in her voice all the same.

"None of this should've ever been permitted to pass. As the Altúyur, we should've protected humanity from the start; we should've stopped Veltuur from creating the Reapers before the thought had even crossed him. But I regret to say that the time for changing those outcomes is in the past. Rest assured, once we free the remaining Altúyur, once you reclaim the Blade of Immortality, I will restore the Reapers their memories. Each and every one of them."

Though the sentiment is heartfelt and reassuring, I'm too busy choking to catch most of what she said. "Wait, *I'm* to reclaim the Blade of Immortality?"

"You are the Prophesized—"

I groan, cutting her off. "Yeah, so I'm told. But no one ever said anything about a sword."

"Not a sword. Not exactly—"

"Okay, blade. Whatever. Where do we find it?"

Again, I'm not sure why I even ask. This quest doesn't feel like it should be mine. It feels like my path has been hijacked by someone far greater and far more important than I am. Only just recently being freshly remade a mortal, I should be out looking to start a profession, perhaps finding a home and thinking about making a family...but even as that thought crosses my mind it, too, feels wrong. The more I think about it, the less I'm sure what I'm meant to be doing. If I were to tell Sungema and Iracara that they are on their own in fulfilling this prophecy, if I were to leave here right now, what else would I do? I guess maybe that's why I'm indulging all of this. I don't know what my path is supposed to be, and though I want autonomy in choosing it, until I can decide, having something else to guide me helps make being in Tayaraan a little less... lonesome; it makes me feel less lost.

"What does it do?" I ask.

"If you are to defeat Veltuur, you will need to wield the blade," Sungema says. Then she holds out the box with the aacsi inside. It's stopped thrashing, so I'd almost completely forgotten it was even there. "But first, we free Dovenia."

"And how do we do that? This garden isn't working apparently."

Iracara holds up one of his bluish-black feathered fingers. "We show her a true place of peace, where the hunted are safe and protected, where even death cannot reach."

I scowl, shaking my head. "Where is a place like that?"

This time, it's Borgravid to answer. "He's suggesting the Guardian encampment, a place where the Prophets are brought to escape their deaths, where Reapers cannot cross."

"Precisely!" Iracara chirps.

"Okay," I say, going over what I know so far. "First, we free Dovenia. Then we find Lorik, Pecolock, Macawna, Owlena, and the Blade of Immortality?"

Sungema looks to Iracara first, wide-eyed and unblinking. For the first time I realize I don't yet know how much the memory tree leaves brought back for him, not to mention whether or not Sungema's awakening alone could've filled in any of his gaps. Judging from the way he twitches under her gaze and starts bouncing on one of his legs, I think even he knows more than what he's letting on.

Sungema returns her gaze to me. "First, we free Dovenia."

My scowl deepens. I *really* don't like being kept in the dark, especially when there's a prophecy that involves me and they're keeping details from me.

I open my mouth to bark an order for them to tell me what

they're not saying, but Iracara stretches his wing out and taps my shoulder with his hand.

"Veltuur will keep coming for us. There is more for you to know, but little time to tell it, and it is not safe here. If he sends more Reapers for us, how long can you hold up your shield?"

I close my mouth and start biting the inside of my lip.

"The encampment will have many Guardians to keep us shielded. We will tell you more then."

With a long sigh, I finally acquiesce. "Fine. But then there's no more room for secrets. If I'm going to be able to do this and fulfill this prophecy, I need to know everything."

"Of course," Iracara says with a bright smile.

"You should go," Borgravid says, drawing all of our gazes to him. "It's as the Divine Sungema says, Veltuur will send more for you. He'll be back."

"You're not coming with us?" I ask.

He plants his feet, crossing his arms over his bulging chest. "My duty is to my king, and according to you, my king has one task to complete before he can return to his true self."

"You want to help him change the laws."

"I want to help him leave the underrealm. I'm not so sure changing the laws will be as easy as either of you seem to think it will be, but I'll talk to him. I'll help him find his way back."

Hope soars inside me, a bubbling, airy feeling that makes me feel as if I'm weightless. Perhaps Borgravid will be able to do what I couldn't: convince Acari that what truly matters is not the dead, but the living.

"Then I wish you the best of luck," I say to him with a nod as Iracara, Sungema, and I make our way toward the entrance. "Will you..."

I can't seem to figure out what I want to ask him. When and if he saves Acari, I want to know, but once I leave the palace, I'm not so sure I'll ever be returning. I have five Altúyur to free and an enchanted sword—no, I'm sorry, an enchanted *blade* to locate—not to mention the Altúyur of Balance I'm meant to face at the end of all this.

"Just keep him safe," I say at last. "And let him know I'm sorry for getting him caught up in all of this. If I could go back and change all of it—"

A sharp nod. "Understood. The king will know of your loyalty."

The three of us exit the Forbidden Garden, leaving Borgravid where he stands, and make our way back to the hidden entrance. Behind me, though Sungema fits easily into the thin chamber, Iracara has to hunch over to be able to make it through. At the end of the tunnel, I push the door ajar, climb out into the fresh forest air, and turn around to aid the two of them out as well.

"Are you ready to fly again?" Iracara asks me.

I look out toward the trees, recognizing the woods and the path Hayliel and I had taken to get to the encampment.

"We can fly to Ngal," I say, thinking that the town should be easy to view from the clouds. "But once we're there, we'll have to walk. I won't be able to find our way to the Guardians' camp otherwise."

"A splendid plan!" Iracara gives three powerful blasts of his wings, hoisting himself off the ground with ease. "Shall we then?"

I glance over at Sungema to find that she's already in flight too, having lifted herself into the sky as silent as the hummingbird for which she's named.

Nodding, I hold out my arms for Iracara and he grasps me in his talons. "Ready."

7

SEER OF DEATH

ACARI

The underrealm appears around us one shade of gray at a time. There is the murky white cloud of fog that settles over the dark soil, the ashen hue that belongs to the trees in the surrounding forest, and the blackest black of the crows that perch overhead atop their branches.

"Wait here," Nerul growls.

"Where are you going?"

He exhales emphatically. "To seek the Councilspirits and request an audience with Veltuur to explain your insolence. Or have you forgotten why we've come here?"

Sheepishly, I bow my head, not raising it again until I feel Shade Nerul faze deeper into the underrealm.

I kick a rock at my feet while I wait, meander between the gnarled trunks, and duck beneath the twisting branches that seem to reach for me like black claws. The longer he takes, the more impatient and worried I become. There's no telling how Veltuur will take the news, what the Councilspirits will say to Nerul when he requests an audience. Up until today, I'm fairly certain they've mostly operated on their own accord. What's to stop them from punishing one of their Reapers for his failure today?

Caw!

Scowling, I turn my back to my father-crow. "Spare me the lecture. There's nothing you have to squawk about that I want to hear."

He flies around me, lands on the ground, and hops with another ear-twisting screech.

"I already told you. I don't want to hear anything from you—"

My words are cut short once he's hopped a few paces away, for it's only then that I realize he's not squawking at me, but at a small, green, glowing speck that's floating aimlessly at the foot of the trees.

I walk toward it, ducking beneath a low-hanging branch to get a better look. Considering the color, and the fact that I know of no other insects that dwell in the underrealm, I think it might be an abyss fly, though I've only ever seen them in the Pit of Judgment.

As I approach, my boot catches on a particularly protruding root, sending me tumbling forward. The abyss fly startles, rattling as it floats away. Instead of staying put like Nerul told me to, I find myself scrambling to my feet instead and racing through the ominous woods, my father-crow flying close behind me.

The deeper we go, the darker it gets. Even though the forest seems to stretch on and on, I somehow know that we're reaching the outskirts, a place I've never dared wander, never wanted to. But as I chase the bounding abyss fly—faintly aware that I've gone after a glowing critter in a dark wood before—there's not a bone in my body that wants to stop. I have to see where it's heading, even if it's only leading me back to its home in the Pit of Judgment; I can't stop myself.

The trees start to thin, the fog growing thicker until I feel like I'm walking through smoke. I can't even see the abyss fly anymore, can't even keep my bearings to tell which way is right or left or forward or backward; it's all just endless, dense haze.

My palms slam into an obsidian wall, cold and damp to the touch. I use it to guide myself down a chamber made from the same slick slab of stone, and I'm relieved to find that the farther I go, the more the fog weakens. I spy the glowing abyss fly up ahead once more, gently bouncing in the air as it, too, glides down the corridor.

It takes a sharp turn, disappearing from view. Worried I might lose it, I pick up the pace and jog to the exit.

But my jaw grows slack when I step into the room on the other side. The space is small, dark, and intimate. Only a modest bed made from branches and twigs sits in the corner, and a large black pool is in the center of the room. Black, thick walls enclose the entire space, leaving nowhere for the abyss fly to go, unless it ascended up the walls that also look as if they stretch forever. I might spend more time searching for the fly if I thought that was why I was here, but standing in this obsidian room, the space feels far too secluded and private to be ignored.

I walk on the outer rim of the black pool, gazing into the dark waters and realizing I find no reflection in them. Not of the walls, not of the nothingness overhead, and not of myself. But as I make my way around the pool, as I draw nearer to the mess of branches I mistook for a bed at first glance, my curiosity is struck once more by the feathers resting on the sheet.

My footsteps echo up the towering walls as I make my way to the bed—or rather, the nest—and I bend down to retrieve one of the inky black feathers. I hold it out before me. It's longer than my forearm, but when I twist it, there's no iridescent shimmer. It is the darkest of blacks, impenetrable and unsettling.

Adrenaline tingles in my chest. I know I shouldn't have such a feather, I'm almost certain it belongs to Veltuur himself, but I ignore the warning bells sounding inside me and instead shove it inside my tunic to be examined later. Thankfully, the belt cinched at my waist prevents it from falling through the bottom. It's as good as a satchel, for now.

As I turn around, my father-crow squawks loudly in my ear, swooping past me and causing me to slip. The ground is uneven with stones, slick from the fog and perhaps the pool in the room, and so instead of a simple, single blunder, the blunder escalates. I stumble backward, trip on an uneven stone, and fall backward, splashing in the inky black waters.

They're not like normal waters though. Instead of floating back up to the top, they pull me down deeper. I'm sinking, rapidly, like the pool itself has wrapped its claws around me and is dragging me under.

I flail my arms, kick my legs to try to swim, but it's like the more I struggle, the deeper I plunge.

And though that should be the worst of it, I'm startled to discover it's not.

When I can see the surface no longer, once everything has burned black, visions of death flood through me. Painful deaths and peaceful ones. Quick ones and slow. Brutal ones. Silent ones. Deaths performed by Reapers. Deaths performed by mortals. Dozens and hundreds and thousands of people and creatures die before my eyes, and I feel them all. I see the moments leading to their demise. I feel their agony as they pass away. For an eternity of seconds, I am suspended in the deaths of all who are living.

Suddenly, a brittle hand grasps my shoulder. The water whooshes past me, and I feel myself becoming lighter, becoming buoyant once more.

I reach the surface with a gasp, black slime oozing down my face, my neck, all of me.

"Insolent boy!" Nymane snarls. "You have defiled the order of the underrealm too many times. Wraiths! I summon thee!"

My eyes are still caked with ink, so I can't see them come, but I hear them. They scurry down the tall walls, creep up from the lagoon beside me. Their tenebrous claws scrape along the stone, and I feel the gust of their movements as they whir about the room.

"Take this pathetic excuse for a Reaper and remind him what's at stake for failing to fulfill an order. Veltuur will come for him when he's ready."

And then, I'm sinking again, but not into the pool of death.

Oh no, I'm sinking somewhere far, far worse.

8

THE POWER OF COMPASSION
SINISA

A s we fly over Owlena Forest, it dawns on me that this will be the third time I've been in Ngal since I received my five-thousandth kill order. Not much time has passed since that day, and yet it feels like a distant memory, another life.

I still can't believe how long I was deceived by my crow, how much longer I would've been a puppet of the underrealm if Acari had not fled the palace with his sister on a whim that he might be able to save her.

When the city of Ngal comes into view, Iracara and Sungema angle for their descents. Sungema lands first, with the Dovenia aacsi still clutched tightly to her chest. It takes a little more coordination for me and Iracara to land, but he manages to settle me on my feet without either of us toppling over.

My arms are stiff from where I was suspended for the flight, and I find that even as I roll them, I have to do it slowly so as not to hurt myself. Still, I wince with each rotation despite my best efforts.

And while I'm too busy catering to my sore limbs, I fail to notice the crowd drawing ever closer around us until we are surrounded by the astonished faces of the people of Ngal who have waited since the dawn of time for the return of the Altúyur.

"Th-they're back."

"Struck by the fate of Owlena...the Divine Altúyur have returned!"

The crowd erupts, rejoicing and applauding as if we were a spectacle to be viewed. The people squeeze in tighter. They reach and paw for the Altúyur beside me, begging for their gifts once more. Every one of them seems to believe they are deserving. They plead with stories of pity and worth, they tell us how dutifully they've maintained their altars and their weekly vows, never once faltering from their belief.

Iracara beams at them like a proud child who's just impressed his mother. To her credit, Sungema too musters an attempt at a smile for the people, her earnest devotees. But as the people close in, I grow uneasy. They claim their benevolence and worth, but I see the desperation in their eyes, and I have witnessed far too many times just what people will do when they believe they have no other option.

I lean forward to speak into Iracara's ear and to ensure he hears me over the crowd that grows even more unruly by the second. "We should go. Before they ask for something neither of you can provide."

Grabbing his arm, I shove my way through the mob, ignoring their withering demands.

"Fear not, dear mortals, we shall return soon," Iracara shouts as we leave. "But first, we must find the other Altúyur. Pray for their safe and speedy return, and you shall earn all our favors."

Fists pump into the air all around us, the massive crowd whooping and hollering as one.

By sheer force of will and a sturdy shoulder, I manage to barrel through the rest of the throng until we are back in an open street. But even here, we catch bystanders' eyes. For every corner we take, we encounter a new group of citizens who haven't yet heard the news that their beloved Divine Altúyur have returned to the mortal realm.

"This was a bad idea," I growl, pushing between two broad-shouldered men.

Iracara waves to everyone he passes, blowing kisses to nearly just as many. "I thought you wanted to go through the city."

"That was before I remembered who I'd be walking down the streets with. How can you stand this? They don't even give you any room to breathe."

Sungema shrugs. "It is the price one pays for the powers we have."

Once we're through the next crowd, I stop abruptly. "What powers are those anyway? I know I'm the last person who would claim to know much of anything about you two and the other Altúyur, but I've never heard anyone really talk about *what* it is you can do."

Grinning, Iracara glances to Sungema, a mischievous glint behind his eyes. But before he can answer me, a shrill voice claws its way across the street.

"Where is she?"

I spin to face the woman charging toward me, a stout thing with dark brown hair and eyes that are somehow familiar. It takes a second for recognition to kick in, but once it does, there's no denying the familiar warmth of her eyes, the dark pink of her runes. The sight of Hayliel's sister caves in my chest.

"Where is she? Where is my sister? She left with you on some reckless, impulsive quest, and here you are, having returned, but I don't see her with you. So, where is she? Where is Hayliel?"

"I...I..."

I can't speak. Never did it occur to me that I might face Hayliel's family again, nor that I'd be the one to relay the news of her death to them. Last I saw Hayliel's sister was when she and her husband slammed their door in my face and made me sleep outside by their forge.

"You, you, spit it out already, Reaper. Did you do it? Did you kill my baby sister?"

"What? No! I didn't—"

"Don't lie to me, foul thing. I warned her about you. I told her that Reapers cannot change and that you would kill her the moment you had the chance, but she wouldn't listen."

"I didn't kill her," I insist, looking to Iracara and Sungema as if they can prove my innocence.

Unfortunately, neither of them can though. Iracara only returned to himself after Acari's touch killed Hayliel. Even if he had been present, I'm not sure the woman before me would believe that the king had killed her sister.

"She is no Reaper," Sungema says plainly. "See her runes. They mark her mortal once more."

Hayliel's sister spits at my feet. "Lies. Filthy lies from a filthy creature."

Iracara steps beside me next. He takes my bare hand into his own. "There. See? I am not dead. She no longer has a Reaper's touch."

Fury flashes behind Hayliel's sister's eyes, but it fades when she notices Iracara's feathered fingers. Her gaze travels up him, along the green feathers covering his lanky legs, up the black tunic embroidered with the same shade of maroon as the disheveled hair atop his head. Then, her gaze flickers to Sungema, and though concern etches into her expression, she shoves it aside just as quickly as it appears and refocuses on what's most important to her.

She spins back to me, as angry and heartbroken as ever. "Where is she?"

"I—she...she's gone."

"Gone?" the woman breathes. It's only when she looks back over her shoulder that I see her husband stepping out from the shadows.

He taps a hammer against his palm as he approaches me, a forge of malice blazing in his dark eyes.

"Do it," the wife grits out, concealing a whimper behind the steel of her voice. "Make her pay."

As the large man advances, eyes trained on me, nothing but

instincts flood through me. I don't know whether he means to kill me or just beat me until I'm a hair's length away from death, but I shuffle backward regardless. With each step he takes, I mirror him, desperate to put some distance between us. But within a few strides, my back slams into a wall. I am trapped. I have nowhere else to go.

Panic ravages my throbbing heart. Desperation quickens my breaths. Without my Reaper touch, I don't know how to defend myself. I'm not strong, I never have been, and I don't know how to fight.

With a flash of hope, I remember that I'm a Guardian now. I should have some kind of powers of shielding and defense. But the hope dissipates when I remember my defenses are limited to concealing me from Reapers and granting my Prophet limitless protection.

Rage twists the husband's expression as he raises the hammer overhead. "This is for my wife's sister."

"That's enough of that," Iracara says with a snap of his fingers. "It seems to me that you're short on your compassion today, sir."

The husband stops midstep, hammer cocked back in his calloused fist.

Iracara strides toward him. He circles the man, frozen in place, looking him up and down with narrowed eyes. Then, he steps back, and fans a wing out over him. A gentle gust ruffles the husband's dark hair. To the naked eye, it looks like any normal wind or wake, but the moment the air brushes over him, the husband loosens his tight hold on the hammer, and his scowl softens, melting right off his face, leaving the most serene, weightless grin in its place as he lowers his arm and slumps to the cobblestone road.

"Cedric!" Hayliel's sister shrieks. She rushes to his side. "What have you done to him?"

With her back to Iracara, she can't see him prepping his wing for another gentle waft of power, and when it blows over her back and through her hair, she too succumbs to whatever ancient magic flows from him.

"Now, where were we?" Iracara spins on his heels, a pleasant smile creasing his eyes. "Ah yes, before you were so rudely attacked for something you did not do, I believe you had a tale to share about this poor woman's late, beloved sister."

Slowly, I peel myself away from the wall, never once letting my eyes drift from Iracara. I've never seen the likes of his power before. I know rationally, I have nothing to fear from an Altúyur of Compassion, but I still feel the tendrils of unease wriggling in my gut. On the face of it, what he's given these people is benevolent. He's soothed their rage with a gentle caress of air, turning them docile. But he's also violated them. The woman has every reason to grieve over the loss of her sister, to hate me for dragging her into matters that I knew from the start were too dangerous for someone as sweet and good-natured as Hayliel. And her husband has every right to defend the woman he loves.

But Iracara has taken that right away from the both of them, like he's ripped a part of them away, and it's all too much like what the underrealm did to me for me to be okay with it.

"If you'd like," Sungema calls, taking slow, steady strides toward the couple who have slumped together like docile nekos on the ground. "I can show them if you'd rather not speak of it."

My amazement only continues to grow, equally matched by the slick, oily feeling in my belly. I had no idea that Sungema could give people other people's memories. I know that she showed me the War of Divinity after I freed her in the Forbidden Garden, but I just assumed that was...different. That memory belonged to her, and being the Divine Altúyur of Memory, it made sense that she could do with her memories what she wanted. But this? Letting Hayliel's sister and husband actually *see* what happened to Hayliel? That, too, feels wrong to me.

I watch Hayliel's sister's eyes widen as she snaps her attention to the Altúyur of Memory. I think about what it was like being there when Hayliel died. I didn't see it, not exactly, but I remember what it was like knowing she died so close by, knowing that I might've been able to do something but couldn't. Seeing her body resting in the moss, she looked so peaceful and yet so wrong. I still can't get the image of her sinking into the swamp out of my head, and I'm sure if it was in Hayliel's sister's mind, she wouldn't either.

"Don't," I say. "Unless, that is, they want the memory of it. But I can just tell them."

Sungema inclines her head at me before looking back down on the mortals.

The woman's lip quivers. She tears her gaze away from Sungema's just long enough to flit her eyes at me. "Tell me what happened."

It takes me a long time to find the right words. Every time I think I've found them, I wonder if it's how Hayliel would've liked the story to have been told. I remember us telling Gem about Acari becoming a Reaper, and how delicately she tried conveying the news, and my approach to such matters is always vastly different. For her, though, I try to say it as gently as I can.

"It was an accident. She died at—"

"No," she says, soft yet stern, the voice of a mother, of an older sister, of a confident wife, as she rises to her feet and walks toward me.

I stand my ground. I might've been frightened by a thick man with a sledgehammer, but I do not fear this woman. For the first time since meeting her, I'm actually able to see the kindness in her eyes. Maybe it's all Iracara's doing in this moment, but I can tell that it was there all along.

She stops just out of arm's reach. Her gentle eyes hold mine. "Tell me everything. Tell me of my sister's journey and her final days in Tayaraan. I want to understand why she went with you, what she endured, and what she might've been thinking in her final moments."

And so, I do. I tell her how Hayliel braved the neko cave, and was only one of two to survive it. I tell her how she crossed the Midnight Ocean and traversed the Pyrethi Desert on the back of a magrok. I tell her how Hayliel braved the Tower of the Lost, only narrowly escaping the dark magic entrapped there, but escaping nonetheless. And then I tell her of Kallinei Swamp.

I spare no details of Hayliel's fierce determination, the impressive courage she showed at every challenge, and the devoted friendship she gave to both me and the prince-turned-Reaper-turned-king we were trying to save.

"Your sister was one of the best people I ever met. She helped me in more ways than she will ever know. And I wish I could've saved her. Tayaraan needs more people like her."

When I'm finally done retelling our tale, her eyes are wet as she peers up at me. "She died knowing she was loved, then. She died in the arms of a friend, thinking she had succeeded in her quest. It's more than most are given."

The husband helps his wife up and they embrace. He holds onto her as her sobs come heavy, unburdened, and once it becomes obvious that they will be like that for a while, the rest of us say our farewells and leave the two of them so that we can continue on to the Guardian camp.

If one thing's for certain, talking about Hayliel has reminded me what I'm fighting for. She only died because Veltuur turned Quetzi into a serpent and unleashed him to prey on any of those who dared to venture too close to the underrealm. She died because Veltuur made the Reapers and fashioned the rules that turned me into one and forced Acari's hand to do the same.

Hayliel's death will not be in vain. Now, more than ever, I want to see Veltuur brought to his knees, and I want to be the one to do it.

9

WHAT LURKS IN THE SHADOWS
ACARI

Suspended in the void, I hear the Wraiths skittering around me, feel the breaths of their hisses as they close in, and I am not embarrassed to admit that I am shaking violently with fear. It would be one thing to be able to see them as they came for me, no matter how horrendous they may be. It would be better than not knowing where they are, than not knowing how close they crawl, and I wouldn't be left on the edge of terror.

"It has returned," the Wraiths hiss as one, a thousand wretched voices twisted into a single howling wind. "It comes to us for punishment. A contract failed."

I twist and turn, following the voices as best as I can, but they assault me from every direction. There is no way to tell which of them will strike first. Even if there was, I have no defense against shadows.

Behind me, a creature unhinges its maw with a breathy exhale. I feel it lunging for me, but it's too close. I don't have the time to move. The Wraiths will devour me. Over and over again, they will sink their teeth in my flesh, they will drink my blood—I've heard the stories; I've heard the cries of the Reapers they torture.

Flinching, I cover my head in my arms and pray that this will be quick and painless.

But just as the creature's tongue reaches the back of my neck, it shrieks and writhes away.

"It possesses a feather of Veltuur."

I peek through my shielding arms, and all I see is thick, impenetrable darkness, but I'm aware of the Wraiths as they retreat farther back. Mindlessly, I press a hand to my chest, to the long feather resting inside my tunic. What did I stumble onto in that strange, eerie room?

"It comes to save us. To release us."

"It—what? Are you talking about me?"

"Yessss. It possesses a feather," the Wraiths say, their voices now a safe enough distance away that I'm actually able to breathe again. "It is the only way to trap Veltuur, the only way to release the spirits held captive in this realm."

"Spirits? Who are you?"

"We are the collected."

It—or they—say no more. It takes me a moment to decipher their meaning. The collected what? The collection of Wraiths? Of terrifying, tenebrous creatures that dwell in the darkest reaches of the underrealm? What even are they? Shadows that dwell in a place of utter darkness, where no light touches and therefore shouldn't even be able to create shadows.

But then it hits me like I've run face-first into a thick oak tree. The collected. The souls that the Reapers are sent to retrieve, the ones our crows consume...

"You're the dead," I say breathless.

"Not the dead." Their voices circle around me like a coiling serpent twisting in the sky. "The suspended. The captive."

Blinking through the thoughts that whir in my mind, at the magnitude of what they're saying, I can barely speak. "But...that would mean...there would have to be thousands of you. Millions."

The sizzle that pulses through the air might actually be a cackle. "We are more, still."

I blink again, my eyes straining in the dark. For eons, since the dawn of time I'd imagine, Reapers have existed and claimed the souls of the dead and told that they would be reborn in the mortal realm once they were returned to the underrealm. All this time, they were just brought here and left to rot.

"I'm so sorry." My hand, still pressing firmly over my chest, reminds me of what the Wraiths had said about the feather, about releasing them, and I'm not yet sure how those two things are connected. "Why can't you leave? How does this feather help free you?"

"Only a feather of Veltuur can contain such a being, just as the feathers of the others contained them."

I look down at my chest, even though I can't see a thing, and even if I could, I wouldn't be able to see the feather concealed beneath my red tunic. So that's how he did it, that's how he trapped the others.

"I don't understand. How can this feather contain him? He's covered in them already."

"A breath blown over the feather, an utterance of the words *conundrum become*. The gust that reaches Veltuur will do the rest."

"Conundrum become," I mutter to myself. Then, squinting my eyes, I cock my head at the ominous abyss around me. "So I just blow on it, and he...what? Disappears?"

"Becomes contained."

"What does that mean though?"

There's a breathy silence. The Wraiths shift and maneuver around in the void like aimless winds. When they finally speak, I feel their very words blow through me like the chill of the night. "We know not how its containment will look, for it has not ever been done before."

"Great. No pressure then. You just want me to contain one of the most powerful, terrifying creatures ever to exist, using a feather that I stole from I think his nest, by performing some mediocre ritual that no one has ever actually performed before and therefore we have no idea if it would actually work."

"We know it works. It has been done before—"

"But you just said—"

"It has been done to the other Altúyur. Each took a form unique to their gifts, but we do not know what would become of Veltuur for it was the only Altúyur to remain free."

The combination of my inability to see anything and the disturbing, confusing information I'm learning makes my head spin, and I succumb further to my disoriented state. The one thing I do know, though, is that I'm not sure I would mind Veltuur being captured. With him out of the way, perhaps I can avoid punishment for failing to kill Sinisa, maybe even return to the mortal realm finally.

And for some reason, it's that thought that draws my suspicions out. "What happens once I've trapped him? Not to him, but to everything else. Does the underrealm disappear?"

"In ways. Once Veltuur is gone, the realm will return to the way it was. No longer will it be clogged by death. The balance will return, and we will finally be able to find peace."

"*The realm will return to the way it was. No longer will it be clogged by death.* What does that mean, clogged by death? The Reapers? Are you talking about the Reapers?"

The Wraiths hiss, rearing on me with fangs and talons readied. "It asks many questions for one with few options."

A claw traces down my spine. I jump, spinning around to face the darkness. Another shadow caresses my cheek. One pulls on my arm. They pluck and poke and toy with me until I become a dizzied top spinning and spinning around.

"Will it contain Veltuur for us? Or will it choose to suffer beneath our claws?"

The Wraiths sift back into the void only long enough for me to answer. "I—I will do what I can. I will, but...what happens to the Reapers once Veltuur is captured? To the crows?"

"Ah, it fears for itself."

I shake my head firmly. "No. Not exactly. But there's something

I'm trying to do. I want to make sure I don't die before I can finish it."

Silence fills the void, punctured only by the low groaning of what I think are the breathes of the Wraiths.

"We are intrigued. Tell us. What would it like to accomplish?"

"I...want to abolish the Law of Mother's Love."

"Hmmm, ambitious, altruistic, perhaps overconfident as well. What makes it think it can change such an ancient law?"

Bowing my head, I ball my hands into fists. "I don't *think* I can. I *must*. The Law of Mother's Love is why I'm here, why I'm a Reaper. If it didn't exist, my father wouldn't have been able to send a Reaper after Gem, I wouldn't have had to flee the palace with her to try to keep her safe, and I wouldn't have had to kill him just to ensure the contract ended. I never wanted the responsibility of being king, but now that I have it, I intend to do what I can to make Oakfall a better place."

They don't speak for a long while. All I hear is the humming of silence as their shadows hover in the ether around me.

But just as I open my mouth—to say what, I don't know—their voices creep out as one. "Many of us perished because of the Law of Mother's Love. It would please us to see its abolition, and for that, we shall let it leave and return to the mortal realm."

I'm overcome with triumphant glee. I can't believe I actually convinced the Wraiths to spare me. But the moment fades quickly when I realize I don't think my father-crow is with me to help me faze to the mortal realm. Even if he were, once we arrived, I'm fairly certain he would just send me straight back to the Councilspirits, to Veltuur.

"I can't faze back to Tayaraan."

"Not faze. Leave."

My brow furrows. There's only one way that I know of to leave the underrealm, and it requires the cooperation of my father-crow, who I don't think is presently with me. Without him, I'm stuck here.

Unless...unless I took a more permanent action.

"I'm not *leaving*-leaving until I can show my father that he was wrong about me, that I make a great king, one better than him who doesn't summon Reapers to kill his own flesh and blood."

The Wraiths hiss, writhing in the shadows like tidal waves. "It is blinded by petulance and pride. It would make the others wait just so its maker could bear witness? Selfish. Arrogant."

I recoil as they press in on me. My feet become tangled, and I trip, crashing to the floor where more shadows await. They wrap and roll over me, talons sharp and slicing over the exposed skin of my hands and face and neck. They cut through the thigh of my trousers, sever an opening in the front of my tunic.

Instinctively, I reach up to protect the feather of Veltuur.

"Stop!" I yell, and I'm surprised that despite the shakiness of my voice, there is power behind it. I clutch onto it, throw it over my chest like armor. "I will do as you ask. I promise, I will. All I ask in return is that you let me end the law first, *with* my father-crow still intact to bear witness."

"*Father-crow?*" Curiosity calms the Wraiths and draws them nearer. "Its maker is no longer living?"

I give a quick, vigorous shake of my head.

"Ah," the Wraiths breathe. "So it knows of the suffering of the crows."

"You never answered me," I say, losing my resolve. "What happens to the crows once Veltuur is *contained*?"

"Nothing happens unless their Reapers will it."

Sighing, I feel myself relax a little, growing increasingly more open to fulfilling the task they're asking of me.

"So will you let me try to end the Law of Mother's Love *with* my father-crow at my side still?"

"We have waited ages. It asks us to wait longer?"

"I—I do. This is important to me."

Another wet hiss. Another shadow slithering in the air around me. But the temper in the room shifts. Like the passing of an ocean storm, the waves of the shadows settle, the winds they produce become calm. "It is bold to request anything from us, but it is also bold to attempt such an exploit. We will help it on its quest, and in return, it will contain Veltuur for us."

"Y-yes—of course."

"Very well. To change the Law of Mother's Love, it should seek the Divine Lorik of Bravery and the Divine Iracara of Compassion."

Startled, I nearly choke on my own saliva. "That's what Sinisa is doing. She's searching for them, to set them free. It's part of this prophecy or something. But what will they do for me?"

"To end such a law will require changing the people who were following it. The Divine Altúyur will aid in the process. They can restore humanity's compassion when facing difference and their bravery when embracing change."

"Do you know where I can find them, the Divine Iracara and the Divine Lorik?"

"One already walks the land of Tayaraan. It imparts compassion on humanity as we speak. The other is a malevolent satyr that resides on Howling Isle, the northernmost island of the Corraeda Isles."

"How will I find this creature, this satyr?"

The Wraiths chortle, a throaty, vile laugh that turns my spine to ice. "A beast that stands as tall as a boulder, that walks on two legs like a mortal, but has hooves for feet and horns on its head, a face that is bovine and gnarled. It will not be so easily ignored, we promise—" Suddenly, the Wraiths shriek. "They have returned."

All around me the sinister creatures scatter. Some dive deeper into the shadows, their absence known only by the wind of their wakes, while others dive for me. They swirl around my body, slide up and over me, leaving me chilled and uneasy. But once the shadows finally pull back, I realize my clothes are tighter. I press my hand to my chest, to the gaping hole their talons had created, and find it has been repaired. Some of the other tears, too, have been mended, though they left most of them, likely to convince the Councilspirits and Veltuur that I didn't go entirely untouched during my time here.

"It should not forget to use the feather once it has completed its undertaking."

"I won't. I promise. Once the law has been changed—"

"Not the law. The law will take time. Once the Altúyur are free, it will return to free us as well."

I work at my lip, chewing on their proposal. What difference does it make if Iracara and Lorik are free? The law will still be unchanged, and my father will still not know what I can accomplish.

Then again, freeing an Altúyur is quite the feat, and the Wraiths are right—this will take time. Can I honestly live with myself knowing that all that stands between the Wraiths' freedom is me and a single feather? Can I live with myself knowing my father-crow won't get to witness my most glorious moment? Or would I be just as bad as him for keeping the Wraiths imprisoned longer, just for my own gains?

"Okay. Once Lorik is free, I will come back to the underrealm, and I'll use the feather of Veltuur to trap him and free you."

Even in the darkness, I hear the Wraiths' lips pull back into wicked grins. "It would please us."

I nod, surprised to find that I don't feel at all frightened by having made a deal with the creatures of shadows. By all accounts, for all the vile rumors I've heard about them, they weren't half bad. Then again, they might've treated me differently if I didn't have one of Veltuur's feathers with me.

Which reminds me, someone else I know is down here too.

"Wait," I say, turning around in the black void to face the source of the voice. "Do you have Councilspirit Leumas? Is he here with the Wraiths—with you?"

They are silent for a moment, considering, before finally saying, "Yessss."

My throat is dry when I swallow, like it's clogged with the dust from my bones that are surely about to be pulverized for even asking for anything more from the Wraiths. "I—I know I have no room to ask you for any other fervors—*favors*, when you've already permitted me so much."

"Ask quickly, for it will not be long before the Councilspirits retrieve it."

I clear my throat. "Please, leave Leumas alone. He's close to a friend of mine, and honestly he's on your side anyway, so torturing him is only doing Veltuur's bidding and—"

"We do not torture Councilspirit Leumas."

"You don't?"

The wind swooshes in the ether like the mammoth Wraith is shaking its head. "It has tried aiding us. We do not punish friends."

I have nothing but their word to assuage my concern, but it's enough. For me anyway.

"Remember, to visit us means torment and torture. Do not allow the Councilspirits to see that we did not treat it poorly."

Without further warning, a slender hand grabs hold of the back of my tunic and yanks me to the surface. I emerge, eyes burning in the dimness of the Pit of Judgment that feels so much brighter than it ever has, like the candles are lit by suns, and the abyss flies are mirrors aiming all the light back down on me.

"I hope the Wraiths taught you what it means to fail me." The very ground beneath me rumbles with the force of Veltuur's voice, and I use it as a reminder to perform.

I stagger, clutching my thigh where I know one of their talons dug the deepest, surprised faintly that the wound persists. Perhaps any injury sustained here is one that will keep, as opposed to the many I've suffered in the mortal realm.

As I draw my head up to the Councilspirits above me in their thrones, I'm not sure what to expect here. The Pit of Judgment is the place Reapers go *before* they're sent to the Wraiths, not after.

As my eyes behold Veltuur's rigid shoulders, the twisted face that's mostly grotesque beak and black eyes, I clutch the feather inside my tunic protectively. Whatever is about to happen, I suppose at least I'm grateful to know that I now have a safeguard, a backup plan should I ever need to escape.

"Your Altúyur asked you a question," Nymane snarls, pushing off from her throne to lean over the edge. "You will speak when spoken to, Reaper Acari."

"I—what was the question?"

Seething, Nymane's pupils explode with rage. "Insolent fool—"

"That's enough," Veltuur says. "The Reaper is right. I posed no question. But I will now. Have you learned what it means to fail me?"

Fear comes naturally to me in his presence, so it's not part of my act when I start quivering. "Y-yes, Veltuur. Forgive you—I mean thank me—I mean—"

I hear his wings shift, but I keep my eyes trained on the cold, stone floor.

"You may go."

I snap my eyes up to his, a mixture of disbelief and shock rolling through me. It feels like a trick. It has to be. There's no way he'd let me leave.

"Almighty Veltuur," Nymane says with a bow of her own. "Forgive me, but his punishment has not been sufficient—"

"You question me, Councilspirit Nymane?"

"No. Of course not—" she utters, but Veltuur barrels over her.

"Am I not the Altúyur of Balance, Lord of the Reapers, Protector of the Realms? Do I not hold the interest of all and make my decisions based on what will maintain everything we have built?"

Nymane keeps her head low and stays mute.

"Oakfall has been without its king for days. Without a monarch, the people will be forced to create their own rules. There will be anarchy and chaos, and the balance we have created will be lost. As long as the Altúyur walk freely in Tayaraan, I do not need any more surprises to deal with. The best place for this Reaper is on his mortal throne." He twists back to face me, beady eyes scowling down at me. "Besides, he's proven inadequate to us anyway. For the time being, he will return to Halaud Palace until I can think of a better use of him."

Unsure of what to say or how to react, and afraid that my elation might be noticed, I lower my head once more.

"But you will remain at the palace. You are only permitted to fulfill your kingly duties. No more day-trips to the Coast of Dreams, no more private tea parties with your royal guard."

I stiffen. He knows. He knows about everything. It's...it's not possible.

Still, I keep my eyes cast downward until smoke starts blooming at my feet. And as my father-crow and I faze back to Tayaraan, I can't help thinking just how difficult it's going to be to find a way to sneak out of the palace and go to the Corraeda Isles without Veltuur finding out.

10

SORROWFUL PEACE

SINISA

Through the trees, I spy the tall cedar wall that wraps around the Guardian encampment up ahead.

"We're approaching the barrier," I say over my shoulder, nodding to the box in Sungema's hands that contains the aacsi. "Should we take her out before we cross it?"

"There is no need."

My brow crinkles. "But...when she changes, if she's anything like either of you, she'll be too big for that container. Couldn't the glass break and cut her or something?"

Iracara chuckles, the tuft of feathers on top of his head swaying. "She is the Altúyur of Peace. Even if she wasn't immortal and impervious, it is impossible for anything dangerous to happen because of her."

My scowl deepens, but I'm too exhausted to demand a more plentiful explanation. Instead, I sigh and quicken my pace. The sooner we cross the boundary, the sooner I'll have every answer I need, and if they believe she will be fine, then that's all that really matters anyway.

This time when I approach the gate, it's not Rhet who's standing guard. A woman with blonde braids bites her nails from where she leans against the wall. When she notices us, her reflexes do not fail her. She slings the bow from around her shoulder, an arrow notched not a moment later.

But as she takes aim, I step more plainly into view.

"Sinisa?" Miengha lowers her bow, a smile ticking up one side of her face. "Flightless bird, is Aulow gonna be happy to see you guys. She was starting worry that..."

But her smile disappears almost instantly when Iracara joins me, Sungema and the aacsi close behind him. I have been dreading this moment for days now.

"Wings give me strength... are those... are they..."

Iracara spreads his wings wide and folds over. "Iracara, my dear, the Divine Altúyur of Compassion. And allow me to introduce Sungema, the Divine Altúyur of Memory."

Sungema ignores him. She's too engulfed by what's happening —or rather, not happening—in the glass box. "Why hasn't she changed yet? We crossed the boundary. We have arrived, yes?"

"Where are the others?" Miengha asks, and like a ball tossed between children, I'm thrown back into conversation with her. "Dethoc and Rory, they stayed to help you and—where's Hayliel? What happened?"

Sungema steps beside me. "Perhaps it's not enough that we've arrived at the safe haven. Perhaps Dovenia needs to *see* that the Prophets are being protected here."

"Are they all right?" Miengha urges, not breaking away from me. "The others, are they all right?"

My head spins. I bounce back and forth between the two of them and their demands, and I don't know how to help either of them.

"I don't know," I say by way of answering them both.

"You don't know?" Miengha snarls. "Did they survive or not? Where is Dethoc? Where's Rory?"

"That is enough for now," rings a voice, stern but kind, from the entrance. I see her red curls from the corner of my eyes, recognize the woman with a birthmark on her face as she clings to Aulow's arm. Aulow presses a hand against the woman's and says to me, "Welcome back, Sinisa. It seems we have much to discuss."

They glance to my present company with a mixture of awe and grief.

Before I can attempt to explain and give them the closure they deserve, a bright light surges from between Sungema's hands. I expect her to shriek as shards of glass are surely about to burst next. But instead, I hear sand as it trickles between her fingers to the forest floor.

Once the light fades, I bring my gaze to meet the white-feathered woman before me. Much like Iracara, her wings are attached to her arms, long, white reams that almost drag on the ground while she stands. But unlike the disheveled patch of maroon feathers on top of Iracara's head, Dovenia's feathered hair is silken against her scalp, like it's been smoothed to flow down her back. Feathers protrude from her neck like one of the ruffled collars of the Ghamayan royals.

"Oh," Iracara chirps. "It would seem I'm behind an introduction. Greetings, Dovenia, Divine Altúyur of Peace." He leans over to me then and whispers in my ear, "I told you she'd be fine."

Dovenia inclines her head at all of us.

Aulow blinks. "Like I said, it seems we have *much* to discuss."

Every head turns in our direction as Aulow guides us through the camp, and I manage to dodge all of their gazes. With three Divine Altúyur to focus on, it's easy for me to hide, but I know the conversation that awaits me once we reach the main hut. Telling Hayliel's family about her death was different. She wasn't leaving behind a child, like Dethoc. She didn't die slipping from my grip, like Rory.

Aulow and Belsante enter the chieftain tent hand in hand. Rhet waits for us inside, twisted locks hanging over each of his shoulders, his arms crossed until he witnesses the three Divine Altúyur walk in behind me.

"Flightless bird…"

With a shake of his head, Iracara shrugs. "I never did understand that one. Only one of us can't fly, and he's not among those who stand before you, which means we are, in fact, entirely able of flight."

Wide-eyed and showing more emotion than I've ever seen from him, Rhet glances to Aulow.

"I'm afraid I know about as much as you at this point, Rhetriel, but I'm hopeful Sinisa can shed some light on the events that have transpired since we last saw her."

Swallowing the tumor of grief that's lodged itself in my throat, I take to the center of the half circle of people and Altúyur.

"There is no easy way to say this, so I'm going to be direct. Rory didn't make it out of the neko cave. The moment Hayliel, Dethoc, and I reached the cliffs, a Shade came to claim the soul that Rory had been protecting until her death. Dethoc died swiftly and painlessly, I'm not sure the same can be said for Rory because she...I didn't see...she just..."

Aulow pulls Belsante tighter under her arm as the woman's eyes begin to wet. Even Rhet's expression grows long and sorrowful, his usually rigid posture wilting from the weight of the news.

"Hayliel and I barely survived the Tower of the Lost, but we managed to escape with a shard of the Mirror of Truth"—I indicate to the jagged fragment wrapped in the fabric of Hayliel's old trousers at my waist—"but when we faced the Deceptive Serpent, we succumbed to its magic before we could act. It almost devoured her but Acari intervened. He shoved her out of the serpent's path and saved her life. He even managed to do it without letting his skin come into contact with hers. But she was still under the serpent's spell, and when she saw Acari, she forgot he was a Reaper and she touched him of her own accord before he could get away. She died in Kallinei Swamp."

I pause, haunted once more by the memory of the coldness of her skin as I dragged her through the clearing, the bubbles that emerged from between her lips as her body sunk to the bottom of the green waters. But at the gentle touch of Iracara's wing to my cheek, I shake myself out of the memory I'm spiraling into.

"Acari was going to kill the serpent, but I stopped him. I don't quite understand it, but that act of compassion, I guess, triggered another spell, one that was unknowingly cast over the key we had retrieved from the caves."

"A key?" Aulow asks. "I thought Gem's prophecy foretold of a neko trapped in the cave?"

"I misinterpreted her vision. I grew up along the Coast of Dreams believing a legend about a neko trapped in the cave. I'd even heard it mewling for help on more than one occasion. Everyone who lives there has. So when Gem shared the prophecy with me, I made my own conclusions, and assumed the vision was about the neko legend foretold. But once we reached the cave and followed the sound, all that was there was a key, the same key that turned into Iracara when we were in Kallinei Swamp."

"What?" Belsante gasps. She and Aulow exchange a look.

But it's Rhet who speaks. "What was the Divine Iracara doing cursed as a key and discarded to the bottom of a sea cave?"

It's at this point in the story that I step aside for the beholder of memory to take over. Sungema tells them everything. Just like she did with me a few hours ago, she walks them through the creation of the Guardians and the Reapers. She recounts how she and the other Altúyur begged Veltuur to stop the War of Divinity. She tells the three of them about the prophecy Owlena shared, and how each and every Altúyur thereafter let themselves be captured and imprisoned until one fated girl would come along.

"So that's why you're traveling with three of the Divine Altúyur," Aulow says, taking all of this a lot easier than anyone should. "You set out to free them, to stop Veltuur, to fulfill your destiny."

I shrug. "It's not like I really had a choice. I'm not going to be the reason they remain imprisoned. And all the deaths—Hayliel's, Rory's, Dethoc's—they're all Veltuur's fault. Then there's Leumas I have to worry about too. He said Veltuur was coming for him. I can't save Hayliel, or Dethoc, or Rory, but I might be able to save Leumas and the Altúyur. I think. Besides, I was apparently already doing it without even realizing."

"Who's Leumas?"

"He's..." The word *friend* comes to mind, but given everything I've learned about the underrealm and the forgotten histories of the Altúyur, I'm not entirely sure what he is.

"Leumas was Owlena's Prophet," Iracara says. The news is shocking at first, but it reminds me of his relief earlier when I told him Leumas had survived, makes me remember the memory Sungema showed me of Leumas kissing Owlena's hand before battle.

"That's how you knew him. But...why did the Altúyur of Fate need a Prophet? What is he doing in the underrealm?"

"She did not *need* one. You have to understand though, to be delegated as a Prophet to one of the Altúyur was a great honor. Prophets from all across Tayaraan sought such a position. And to serve under the Altúyur of Fate herself? It was the highest honor any Prophet could hope to achieve.

"Leumas began studying under Owlena so that he could learn from the best of the best, but he stayed for far more."

"They fell in love," I say to the room, remembering the sight of the two of them together during the War of Divinity.

Iracara nods. "They weren't the only ones."

A frown dims my face for so many reasons. I wonder who he fell in love with, what happened to them, and if Dovenia or Sungema have a similar tragic tale. I wonder, also, how it is that Leumas, Owlena's Prophet and lover, fell into the servitude of Veltuur.

When suddenly, it hits me.

"After you took the memory leaves," I say to Iracara. "You relived a conversation you had with Veltuur. You told him to release your Prophets. He abducted them?"

"He claimed that he needed them to guide his Reapers," Iracara sneers. "That only the best Prophets could help them find the souls that were on the brink of death. He said it would only be temporary, but it didn't matter. He had no right to take them against their wills, against ours."

"What were their names?" My voice quakes when I ask him, a horrific knowing sinking into the depths of my stomach.

Iracara blinks, hard, like the question is unexpected and painful. He swallows slowly, taking his time to say a name that I think he's been afraid to speak for fear she might already be gone.

"My Prophet's name was Nymane."

I nearly choke on my tongue. Nymane, the cruelest of the Councilspirits and easily one of Leumas' greatest opposers. How could someone so kind and loving like Iracara, literally the Altúyur of Compassion, fall for a woman as sharp and as devious as a knife to the back?

"Bhascht was Veltuur's Prophet, Gazara was Dovenia's, and Sungema's was actually—" Iracara stops short, Sungema's golden eyes flashing to him with a frightening warning. Instead, he clears his throat and omits her Prophet's name, but I file that question under the long list of things I plan on demanding they tell me once we're done filling in the Guardians here. "Then there was Wex, Pillox, Virion, and Sudryal. We already know Sudryal died defending Macawna, and Virion disappeared some time before the war, but the others..."

"The others live," I say, breathless. "All of them serve on the Council in the underrealm."

"Nymane as well?" Iracara's eyes sparkle with hope, his lip quivering like it is holding on by a thread and I can either close the scissors around it, or pull them back.

Though I cringe at the sound of her name, and the thought that anyone could possibly love such a vile, bitter creature, I force a smile for Iracara's benefit and say gently, "Even her." I look to Dovenia and add, "Gazara too."

Relief, elation, celebration dances between the three Altúyur, Dovenia and Iracara especially. Meanwhile, I gaze skeptically at Sungema, at the secrets she continues to keep from me. Who was her Prophet? Why wouldn't she want Iracara to mention them? It's possible that something terrible happened to them and it's too painful for her to even hear about it, but Sungema doesn't strike me as someone who actively tries to live in denial, nor is she behaving as though her Prophet had a tragic ending.

"My apologies to interrupt the happy moment. You know I'm not one to pass up a good love story," Belsante says, winking to Aulow beside her. "And obviously, you are all more than welcome here, but I can't help but feel like there's a reason for your arrival that you haven't yet told us."

I shake my head. "We came to free Dovenia. You see, since Veltuur imprisoned the other Altúyur, the only way to free them is by allowing them to witness the gifts they once gave to mankind. Iracara was freed when an act of compassion was performed in his presence, Sungema when someone's memory was restored. We needed a place of peace to bring Dovenia back."

"There is another reason," Sungema calls out behind me, drawing my glare. Is she the Altúyur of Memory, or the Altúyur of Secrets? "If Sinisa is to fulfill her destiny, we need to find the remaining Altúyur and two ancient, powerful relics: the Fate-bringer Pendant and the Blade of Immortality. Although I remember the whereabouts of the Altúyur, I fear the relics will have likely moved since I was last in Tayaraan. We need the aid of one of your Prophets in locating them."

Aulow grimaces. "Then I regret to inform you, that much has changed in the time you've been gone. The Prophets no longer have visions about anything other than the deaths of other Prophets. They foresee the Reapers before they come for them, and with the help of the Guardians here, we save as many as we can."

Sungema shakes her head. "I am confident that there is at least one here who has foretold prophecy unrelated to another Prophet's death. This is where your Prophet resides, isn't that correct, Sinisa? Was she not the one who told you of the key that contained Iracara, of the gate to the underrealm?"

Aulow has to catch her breath. "Miraculous."

"Such is fate," Sungema replies. "May we speak to the Prophet?"

Nodding, Aulow motions to Belsante to leave and retrieve her, and turns back to me with a warm smile. "I'm sure Gem will be excited to see you."

I wish I shared the same assuredness, but I'm fairly certain that once I deliver the news of Hayliel's death and how Acari is still stuck as a Reaper, Gem will likely refuse to see me ever again.

"I think not," Sungema says, halting Belsante in the doorway. "There will be time for a reunion later, but it will have to wait. I'm sorry, Sinisa. But for now, it's best that you not see her. Time is of the essence. We cannot afford to recount all that has transpired again. I will go and aid her in accessing her sight. Please, all of you, stay here until I return. We will need to move swiftly once I know where the relics are."

As Belsante and Sungema leave, Miengha nearly bumps into them on her way in.

"I finally got someone to replace me at the gates. What did I miss?"

11

A PLAN IN FLIGHT

SINISA

"So," Aulow says, slinking across the room to me. She slides down the pillar to lean on it beside me. "I couldn't help but notice the prince's absence as well. You never told us what happened to him."

I snort a humorless laugh. "Haven't you heard? He's a king now."

"We did receive the news. The first Reaper King in all the history of Tayaraan." We sit there quietly, watching Rhet and Belsante fill Miengha in about all that has transpired. Silence stretches between us, but I feel her question coming like a spider creeping up my shoulder. "So what happened with Acari?"

I sigh. "He had unfinished business."

"He chose to stay a Reaper? Did he say why?"

"He wants to prove to his father that he can make a good king. He wants to change the Law of Mother's Love, and he wants his father to be present when he does it." I shake my head. "I can't blame him. That's the least his father deserves for what he did."

Sitting this close beside me, when Aulow nods, her springy curls tickle my cheek. "Perhaps. But I'm not so sure Acari deserves to be the one to bear the heavy burden of revenge, to miss out on so much. Gem will be grown up before he knows it."

"I don't think he plans on waiting that long," I say, glancing at her sideways.

"I'm sure he doesn't. But the Law of Mother's Love will take time to change. Just because he is a king does not mean he can snap his fingers and let it be unwritten. Kings before him have tried. But the law is law. Some monarchs have managed to enact slight change to wording or phrasing, but most fail in abolishing a decree entirely. Even if he were to accomplish such a feat, who's to say he will feel fulfilled in his revenge. Perhaps he'll decide to keep his father around forever, just so he can see his reign."

"Acari wouldn't do that," I snap, my brow bunching. "He just wants to change the law."

"I sure hope so."

I scowl a moment longer, trying to figure out where her such fatalistic thoughts are coming from for someone who has always seemed so optimistic.

Eventually, I realize it doesn't matter. She can have her doubts if she wants, but I know Acari meant what he said. He *will* end the Law of Mother's Love, and he *will* return to Tayaraan a mortal.

At least, I hope he does. If not, well, he only has a short while to succeed.

Nestling back against the pillar, I say, "Besides, once I end Veltuur, I don't think Acari will have a choice. The Altúyur say that defeating him will restore the balance. I think it means there will be no more Reapers. They'll be freed."

Aulow bolts upright, twisting to stare directly into my eyes. She bites her lip, and I grow impatient with the doom she's thinking about but won't just come out and say.

"What?"

She winces, but finally manages to say, "If defeating Veltuur gets rid of the Reapers, I'm not so sure that means they'll be freed."

"You think...they'll just be gone?"

She shakes her head. "I wouldn't know. But it's worth asking these kinds of questions, *before* you dive headfirst into whatever destiny they claim is yours."

"*They claim?* You think the Altúyur are lying? I'll admit, I was overwhelmed by it all myself at first, but now that we've already freed three of them, I don't know. It seems like fate is determined to keep me bound to this path."

"You are never bound to anything you don't want to be. Remember that. Not too long ago, you thought you were bound to the underrealm, but instead you chose to free yourself. You have choices here too. Whatever you do, Sinisa, I just hope you choose love over everything else. Not fear, not duty, not fate, but love. It is the only thing that ever matters and it was the best decision I ever made."

She stands then, leaving me with my thoughts as she returns to the others.

Sungema returns an hour or more later, long after my backside has gone numb against the earth floor.

"Did it work?" I ask, hopping to my feet. "Was Gem able to tell you where we can find the blade and the pendant?"

"She did," Sungema says to me, but she directs her next request to Aulow. "But we need your help if we are to succeed."

Aulow glances to Rhet first before answering, "Of course, Divine Sungema. We will do whatever we can to aid in the safe return of the Altúyur."

"What did she say?" I ask, eyeing the others. The fact that she's requesting them to join us—mortals, Guardians or no—makes me wonder just how dangerous of a task I've undertaken.

Dovenia must sense my unease because she wafts one of her white wings in my direction. I'm aware of what she's doing for only a fraction of a moment before tranquility falls over me like the soft sifting of snow. I should be mad at her for forcing something onto me that I didn't ask for, but I can't fight it. I succumb to the peace she's offered and become eager to hear Sungema's update.

"Veltuur knows Sinisa has freed me. By now, he likely suspects Dovenia is freed as well. The longer it takes us to free the remaining Altúyur, the more likely it becomes that he will stop us or find the relics before we do. I propose that the eight of us in this room split into three groups to cover more ground, an Altúyur and a Guardian in each one. The rest doesn't matter."

Aulow and Belsante step forward, their hands entangled. "We shall accompany you, Divine Sungema, a Prophet and a Guardian. Sinisa is not yet adept with her new powers, so I would suggest another Guardian accompany her. Perhaps Miengha, and the two of them could go with the Divine Iracara. That would leave Rhet with the Divine Dovenia, but he's one of our best Guardians, so I think the two of them would suffice."

Sungema inclines her head. "Your aid is much appreciated. Dovenia and Rhet should go to Kallinei Swamp then to find Quetzi. I believe he has already transformed."

"What makes you say that?" Rhet asks, tightening his belt and making sure everything he usually carries on him—a knife, rope, a coin pouch—is secured.

"Seeing as he's the Altúyur of Integrity, showing him the Mirror of Truth likely would've been all he needed. He has been living a lie and forcing others to do the same. The mirror would've showed him the thing he has been most in denial about: his identity."

"Wait," Belsante says abruptly, eyes bulging. "The Deceptive Serpent is one of the Altúyur?"

Suddenly, it all makes sense. According to Gem's vision, the Mirror of Truth was the only thing that could defeat the serpent. It was the second item Hayliel and I obtained on our quest, and it nearly destroyed us both. The enchanted object preys on the things that the person gazing upon has buried deep in denial. Though I didn't know what to expect of its power, when I used it on the serpent, I was surprised to discover that it actually worked on such a creature. At the time, I didn't have the time to wonder what truth it could've shown to the beast to make it flee the very prey it was set on devouring. But now it all makes sense. If the Divine Quetzi, the Altúyur of Integrity, was trapped inside the body of a serpent that caused mortals to hallucinate on the deceptions they wanted most, were he to catch a glimpse of the monster Veltuur had made him, of course he'd flee.

Sungema gives a solemn nod. "It was, yes. But now I believe he has been set free, although, he is likely disoriented and possibly lost. He will be devastated by the harm he has caused. You two will find him; Dovenia will help bring him peace, and then you will return here." She gestures to herself, Aulow, and Belsante then. "We will seek to free Lorik from the satyr that Veltuur turned him into. Fortunately, the Blade of Immortality can be found alongside him. According to the vision Sinisa's Prophet gave me, it would seem that when Sudryal learned of Lorik's imprisonment, he brought the Blade of Immortality with him when he went to try to free Lorik. Unfortunately, the satyr slew him, and the blade is now in his possession, though I'm not sure he wields it."

Iracara hisses through his teeth. "Lorik killed his own Prophet?"

"*Lorik* did not. The hideous, heinous satyr did," Sungema says sharply. "It was Veltuur's doing, not Lorik's."

It's silent for a while, a few among us looking to the ground and waiting for Sungema to continue.

"So, where will we be headed?" Belsante asks at last.

"The satyr has claimed the Howling Isle as its home."

Belsante's eyes snap to Aulow, who is trembling at the mere mention of the place.

The dark-haired woman takes Aulow's face into her hands. "It'll be all right. We won't go anywhere near the water."

Aulow shakes her head. "Sea. Sinking. Suffocating."

I stare, wide-eyed, at the trembling woman who I didn't even know knew fear. She always carries herself with such control and bravery that to see her quiver so, terrifies me more than anything else in the realms.

Belsante wraps her in a fierce embrace.

"I will go to the Corraeda Isles," Miengha says, stepping forward. "Aulow can take my place on the journey to Ghamaya."

"What about you?" Aulow asks, looking into Belsante's eyes.

"I'll be fine. I'll be with one of the Divine Altúyur and a

Guardian." When the little reassurance she's given doesn't seem to have the desired effect, she presses her forehead to Aulow's. "We will still be able to communicate. It will be like we're not even apart."

Aulow stares up at her dubiously, and I'm inclined to agree. They would be on opposite sides of the continent, Belsante left to face what sounds like a ferocious beast who has already killed at least one Prophet. No one can expect Aulow to agree to this.

I take a bold step forward. "I can go with Sungema. The two of you can accompany Iracara to the Ghamayan Citadel, while Miengha and I go to the Corraeda Isles to face the satyr. Sungema, you said yourself that I needed to reclaim the Blade of Immortality anyway."

"You do. However, I'm afraid it is not an option for you to change course, Sinisa," Sungema says. "Someone else can bring the blade to you once they retrieve it, but you have to be the one to seek out the Queen of Ghamaya. The Fatebringer Pendant awaits you in her hands, and it, above all else, is imperative to your success."

"The Queen," I say, eyes bulging. "Why do *I* need to be the one to recover the pendant?"

"Because once it is in your possession, it is the only thing that can keep you protected while you fulfill the rest of your destiny."

"It's all right," Belsante says quickly, apparently sensing my frustration growing. "Aulow can go with you, and Miengha will come with us."

"What about the rest of the Altúyur?" I ask, still bristled. "What about Pecolock, and Macawna, and Owlena?"

"Pecolock is also in Ghamaya. Once you retrieve the Fatebringer Pendant, you will venture south to free him. Macawna is in the underrealm with Veltuur. She became one of his abyss flies, and though she has likely witnessed the intellect of many, it is the intellect of a mortal that will free her. You won't be able to free her until you confront Veltuur with the Blade of Immortality. Owlena, however...she is no more."

"*No more?*" I ask.

The Altúyur exchange looks, but it's Iracara who says softly, "She sacrificed herself to create the Fatebringer Pendant, so that the Prophesized One might stand a chance in defeating Veltuur."

The weight of that statement hits me like a brick to the gut. She didn't even know me and yet she sacrificed herself just so that I could see this prophecy through... What the other Altúyur must think of me, always asking so many questions, snapping at them when they don't give me the answers I want, all while knowing that their friend died so that I might succeed.

"How did the Queen of Ghamaya come across the pendant? You'd think if it was made to protect me, Owlena would've ensured it stayed somewhere a little closer."

Sungema answers, "The pendant fell into the hands of Owlena's Prophet, Khastyl, gifted to her in order to protect her until she could bear a daughter."

All the breath in my lungs is punched out of me at the sound of that name. My skin runs as cold as the underrealm.

"Did you just say...Khastyl? That's...that's my—"

"Your mother's name."

It's like she's just grabbed the realm by the floorboards and ripped all of Tayaraan out from under me. Everything is spinning. I feel sick to my stomach, confused. My mother has forgotten who she is. Up until a few days ago, I didn't even know she was still alive until I learned about her encounter with the Deceptive Serpent. Finding out she was, was shocking enough. Discovering that she'd forgotten all about me, about my father, was another blow. But this? Learning that my mother served one of the Divine Altúyur, that she knew she was fated to have me and that I would be the one to defeat the Altúyur who imprisoned the others, it's...it's too much.

"My mother...y-you're saying my mother was Owlena's Prophet? That she's been alive for...for... How is that possible?"

"I already told you," Sungema says gently. "The Fatebringer Pendant protects the wearer until they fulfill their destiny."

"I don't understand," I say, head spinning all the faster. Even Aulow's gentle hand on my shoulder can't steady me. My thoughts just rage like an untamed cyclone: Sungema is sending me after an ancient pendant; she's sending me to meet my mother, the mother who I thought was dead, the mother who doesn't even know I exist. I'm not ready. I don't even know what I would say. I don't even know how I'd act. I'm not the same daughter she left behind, and she's not the same mother.

I can't do this.

And for all of Sungema's wisdom and knowing, for her collective memory of history and the battles—physical and emotional—that mortals have endured, she can't seem to wrap her head around the idea that I'm not struggling to understand her words, but the implication.

And so, she repeats herself more plainly. "Your mother's destiny is bestowing you with the Fatebringer Pendant."

"Okay, but," I growl, my anger the only thing keeping me on solid ground. "Why didn't my mother give it to me then? Why is the pendant now in the hands of Queen Miva?"

Despite her usually nearly expressionless face, the pity that crosses her now is undeniable. "Because, Sinisa, your mother and Queen Miva are one and the same."

12

HASTILY PLANNED

ACARI

When the field of smoke finally clears, I find myself surrounded by leaves larger than my head, by bright orange and pink flowers with sharp petals and sticky nectar stems. The small, white rocks crunch beneath my feet as I take in the Forbidden Garden and the new emptiness inside it. With the memory tree gone, the garden is almost unrecognizable. The place no longer feels enchanting as I stroll along the path, but oppressive and taxing beneath the heat that falls down like sheets from the windows above. There is no shade to seek shelter, no centerpiece to tie the room together.

Without the memory tree, the Forbidden Garden just looks like an untamed field of wildflowers that someone just happened to put a path through.

Careful not to let my poisonous skin graze any of the flowers or plants that remain, I make my way to the entrance across the room. There's no telling how long I've been gone, how long they kept me with the Wraiths—days, I think—and I know that I should head to the throne room first, to check in with my adviser and see what I've missed, but I also don't think it would be wise to show up to court dressed like a Reaper.

I nod to the guard at the door as I exit, who I realize with great disappointment *isn't* Borgravid and veer left toward the golden corridor of Aracari Wing.

Once I'm inside my chambers, I slam the door shut behind me. I make for my wardrobe, retrieving a long, golden doublet embroidered with daminila flowers, and I'm about to toss off my Reaper tunic when my father-crow lands atop the wardrobe door. My hands freeze on my uncinched belt, and just before the feather of Veltuur can slip down my stomach and fall to the ground revealing my duplicity, I press my arms against my waist and squeeze the feather in place.

Caw!

"Flightless bird! Y-you startled me!"

The crow cocks its head. I'm probably just being paranoid, but I could swear it's looking at me like it knows that I'm hiding something. One wrong move, the slightest loosen of my grip, a small cough, or a gust of wind blown the wrong way, and this feather will slip free and Veltuur will know in an instant that I have one of his feathers in my possession. As long as my father-crow is around, I won't be able to change, not without outing myself and the task the Wraiths have bequeathed me.

"I need to put on attire more suitable for court," I say, turning my back to the wardrobe. When he doesn't move, I add, a bite of annoyance in my tone, "I can't change with you here. You're my...it's just uncomfortable."

Still, the bird does not move; he doesn't so much as make a squawk or ruffle of his feathers.

The longer I wait, the stranger and more irritating the situation becomes. This crow is my *father*, for crying out loud. If he were still human, he wouldn't loom over me as I dressed, nor would he accompany into my chambers without an invitation. I have servants for that, and even they know when to permit me privacy. But this crow—my father—hovers over me night and day like some watchdog.

I whirl back around to him. "How is it possible that you are even more overbearing and infuriating in your death than you were in your life?"

I glare, waiting for him to move, but still, nothing.

Suddenly, there's a knock on the door. "King Acari. I was told of your return. May I enter?"

Relief floods through me at the familiar voice outside my room. "Borgravid, yes, please come in. I didn't know you were still here. I thought you'd left with Sinisa."

As the door swings open, I realize my father-crow is no longer watching me but the tall captain as he enters. It's a small window, and it's rash of me to try to seize it, but I have no other choice. Releasing the grip on my abdomen, I let the feather drift down to the floor. It lands utterly soundless, like fog creeping over the hills at night. Stark against the pristine marble, it is a black beacon, an ominous, wailing alert that something is amiss.

Borgravid steps around the cherrywood door and closes it behind him. It won't be long before either of them notices the giant feather on the ground. And if I couldn't afford my father-crow discovering it before, while it was still *in* my possession, I certainly can't risk it now. I can't be sent back to the underrealm without the feather to even imprison Veltuur if I had to.

Using my foot, I slide the feather of Veltuur beneath the wardrobe. I'll have to worry about how to retrieve it without being noticed later, but for now at least I know it'll be safe, and at least I can change without arousing suspicions.

"I could not abandon you, my king," Borgravid says, clamping a fist to his chest. His eyes flicker to my foot, but with a sweeping glance around the room, he's able to make it look as if it was just part of a general inspection. "Though, I'm surprised to see the rumors of your return are correct. Will you be staying long this time?"

The bite in his words is unmistakable, but well warranted. Since becoming king only a few days ago, I think I've probably spent more time in other towns and cities, as well as in the underrealm, than I have in Oakfall, let alone sitting atop my throne. But, according to Veltuur, that's all about to change.

"Yes. I'm here to stay. For a while, I believe."

"For a while? What about the underrealm and your duties as a Reaper?"

I pull the red tunic up and around my head. "I've been relieved from all of that, for the time being. I failed them, Borgravid. I was given a simple task, to kill a mortal, and I didn't do it. If I wasn't the king of Oakfall, if Veltuur didn't think I was valuable to the kingdom of Oakfall, the Councilspirits would've locked me away for an eternity. But, since they can't do that, and since they have deemed me unable to fulfill my Reaper duties, I've been banished. Well, banished might be too harsh a word—it was never actually said, the word *banished*, I mean, but...yeah, I think they want me as far away from them as possible until they can figure out how I can be of use to them." A humorless laugh escapes me. "How awful do you have to be that even the underrealm doesn't want you?"

With my chest bared, as I reach back into the wardrobe to retrieve the regal doublet, the scar over my shoulder catches my eye. I still have no memory of how I got it, but given what I know of my final days before initiation, there's no doubt in my mind that it wasn't earned on my quest to save Gem, the sister I also don't really remember.

Don't get me wrong, the memory tree leaves made me remember just how much love I had for her, how I would've rather died than let anything cruel befall her. But I still can't remember her face; I don't have fond memories of us growing up together, nor do I have unpleasant ones. She, like everything before my Reaper initiation, is blank.

And the more I uncover about the underrealm and Veltuur, the more it bothers me that who I had been was taken away from me. But being the *new* me, I am also admittedly afraid of losing who I am now. Would the former Acari have taken it upon himself to change the Law of Mother's Love, or would he have been content running across the Tayaraan realm for the rest of his life? Would he have been brave enough to face Veltuur and the Wraiths, to confront his father even if he was just a pesky bird waiting for death?

"You ask the wrong question," Borgravid says, and for a moment I think I might've accidentally said all of what I was thinking out loud. "It is not about how awful you are, but how good. You were never made for the underrealm. You were made for entertaining foreign dignitaries, making appearances at balls, heeding advice on matters of the state, marrying a young noblewoman. You were not made for killing."

Caw-caw!

They're both wrong though. *I am* made for killing. Quite literally, the day I became initiated into the underrealm's servitude, I was *made* to kill. I am not the Acari who was raised at the palace, no matter how hard I try to be. But Borgravid still sees me as that same young prince, and if killing the king or arriving in the garden to kill Sinisa didn't change his mind, nothing I can say will.

I shrug, securing the buttons down my chest before tying another belt around my waist. My trousers are next, exchanged for a simple pair that are as brown as tree bark, my boots just a shade darker.

"Well," I say, glancing to the ground one final time before turning to him. "What's on the agenda for today?"

He narrows his eyes at me like he's waiting for me to say something else. I catch his gaze drifting to the bird perched above us, before he finally answers me. "Well, I was told that you had interest in reviewing the Law of Mother's Love to see if it was in need of some revising."

"Reviewing the...how did you know about that?"

He tilts his head, eyes narrowing at me. "You told me. Remember? Last we spoke?"

I watch him with suspicious, skeptical eyes. Although my memory before entering Reaperhood is a blank slate, I know without a doubt that he and I have never had such a conversation since. The only person I spoke to about my intentions to change the Law of Mother's Love was Sinisa.

As I assess Borgravid, watching the nearly imperceptible sly smirk that twitches the corner of his lips and flares behind his eyes, I realize he must have spoken to Sinisa the last time I saw him. She must've told him about my mission, perhaps even suggested he remain behind to aid me. It was a generous, kind thing for her to do, but I worry what's going on in my father-crow's mind right now. He's with me everywhere I go and therefore will know that Borgravid and I never had such a conversation.

"Or maybe you didn't have to tell me," Borgravid elaborates. "Maybe I just know you well enough to know that such a thing would be of interest to you."

"It is," I say cautiously. "But I was told it can't be done."

"You might be right. While you were away, I looked into it. It's been a long time since anyone has thought to review the laws that govern Oakfall. The last one that was amended granted female heirs the same entitlement to family estates and wealth as are given to male heirs, and that law has been in place for centuries."

"But it *can* be done then?"

He frowns. "Oakfall's law can be amended, sure. But the Law of Mother's Love is more complex. It is one of the rare decrees that predates the separation of the kingdoms, and therefore our governing constitutions."

"What does that mean?"

Grimacing, he comes closer, taking care to be as gentle as is possible for a man with a voice like an earthquake. "It means that, though the Law of Mother's Love is included in Oakfall's constitution, the statute itself, the original one, was part of the All Truths, the common laws that were accepted by all four of the Tayaraan kingdoms."

If I didn't have a new plan, my stomach would sink. It's no wonder I was told that my mission was impossible. The All Truths are sacred, passed down from the Altúyur as the principles by which we must live. They guide the mortals with decrees of loyalty to the Altúyur, of respect and esteem for the Reapers and the role they play in society...

Although, the more I think about it, the All Truths sound suspiciously biased. Who else would demand loyalty from the mortals but Veltuur? Of course, he'd require respect for his Reapers and demand their roles be utilized—they are his puppets, his instruments.

So it would be him, too then, who created the Law of Mother's Love. What purpose, I wonder, would he have for killing all of the Prophets? Vengeance? Power?

Shaking my head, I clear my panicked thoughts. None of it matters anymore. My best chance at causing any change in regard to the Law of Mother's Love is by freeing Lorik from where Veltuur has imprisoned him.

"All right, I get it. It's impossible. Thank you for the inspiring update. Is there anything else I need to know about the day before I go out there?"

He takes a long time to respond, eyeing me with that hardened look of concern before finally saying, "You have yet to select the couriers to mark the end of the Festival of Wings."

If the festival has ended, it means I was away for at least a few days, since last I remember we were still on day eight. Even still, none of this sounds familiar.

"The couriers?"

"Yes, the couriers." Seeing my confusion only deepen, Borgravid elaborates. "For the feathers that have collected on the altar in the temple?"

I flash him a guilty smile.

He sighs. "At the end of each day of the Festival of Wings, the master of ceremonies places a feather upon the altar, one for each of the Divine Altúyur it represents."

"Like...real feathers from real birds? Isn't that sort of, I don't know, disrespectful to the Altúyur that someone is plucking the feathers from their kin?"

Borgravid plants a hand on either hip and glares, a look that clearly articulates how ridiculous he finds my question.

"Sorry," I say. "Continue about the couriers and these feathers."

Clearing his throat, he begins again. "Upon the festival's end, a courier is selected to deliver each feather to the eight waters of Tayaraan: one to float in each of the three oceans, another three in each of the prominent lakes, one sent to drift through Kallinei Swamp, and the final to be sent down the canals of the Corraeda Isles."

I perk up. "The Corraeda Isles?"

"Yes," he says, frowning at my sudden interest, but he carries on the same. "It is your job to select the ones who will be honored and trusted with such a task. The Ghamayans typically select their own couriers, since they'll be traversing their kingdom, and the Mará-grans are usually permitted to identify one of their own to go to Kallinei Swamp, but that still leaves you with the others. You'll need to make your decision today, review the applicants for those interested in going to Midnight Ocean, Corraeda Ocean, the canals of the Corraeda Isles, and then decide if you'll be the courier for Elashor or Oakfall Lake—"

"I should like to be the one to go to the Corraeda Isles."

Caw! Caw! my father-crow squawks, wings flapping.

Borgravid scowls at me, blinking. "That—it-it's customary for the king of Oakfall to conduct the feather ceremony at one of Oakfall's lakes. Especially given your namesake, the people will see you as the obvious choice to deliver the aracari feather to Elashor Lake, to give them the greatest chance of gaining the Divine Iracara's blessing—"

"You and I both know he's already walking among them," I say. "If the entire Festival of Wings is meant to prove to the Altúyur that we honor them and seek their return, then it's already worked for him, as well as who knows how many others." With my father-crow still screeching on the wardrobe, and Borgravid gaping at me with horror, it's difficult to ignore either of them long enough to get the right words out. "I'm not saying we scrap the tradition completely

—I remember your last lecture about fitting in and proving my loyalties to the people—but anyone can go to Elashor Lake. How long has it been since the royal family has visited the Corraeda Isles?"

Borgravid shakes his head. "I—I don't know, my king."

"Let me ask this: have *I* ever traveled there? Have I ever visited the people who reside there whom I'm demanding loyalty from?"

"No, my king. You were disinterested in travel. But, even so, the Corraedan people have mostly been left to themselves over the years at their own request. They prefer to be as removed as possible from the mainland."

Flicking my hand, I walk over to the vanity. "That won't do any longer." I stand before the mirror, a smile spreading wide as I adjust my new tunic. "They are part of Oakfall, and therefore they are my people. I should know them; I should visit them occasionally and make sure they are faring well."

"I can assure you, they get along just fine without—"

"You say that, but I also hear you saying that we've been neglecting them. You tell me that they requested to be left alone, which means they very well might be considering seeking a more official independence from Oakfall altogether, and I can't be the king who lost part of his kingdom. They've never even met me, so I can only assume that whoever is in charge over there has already considered extrication or, worse, seizing my throne."

"She wouldn't do such a thing. She loves the Corraeda Isles, nothing else."

"You can't know that," I say, letting the truth of my words weigh in the air. "I need to prove to them that they matter as much to me as the rest of my kingdom. What better way to do that than by personally delivering the feather of—which one is it again?"

"The quetzal, my king."

Nodding, I turn my back to the vanity. "What better way to show them I am a ruler worth supporting than by delivering the quetzal feather and participating in the ceremony with them? Don't you agree?"

Caw-caw!

The black bird leaps from the top of the wardrobe and glides over to land on my vanity. But, since his trajectory is fixed, and since there isn't much room on this side of my chamber for my father-crow to turn around midflight, I use the opportunity to walk back toward the wardrobe, widening my eyes at Borgravid once the bird is at my back.

It takes him only a fraction of a moment to grasp my intent.

"Of course, my king. You are right. A visit to the Corraeda Isles has been long overdue."

The bird becomes frantic. He cuts back across the room to land atop my shoulder, his screeching call grating against my eardrums. I can ignore him no longer.

"What has gotten into you?" I ask, feigning ignorance. "You always act like I'm doing something...wrong." My eyes bloom with false horror. "Oh no. I completely forgot. Veltuur said I have to stay at the palace and fulfill my kingly duties. I can't go to the Corraeda Isles."

Shaking my head, I turn to look at Borgravid, making sure he can see my pleading face. It's a long shot to leave so much unspoken and hope that he can follow, but the man did say he's known me since I was a child, and I imagine he's fairly adept at reading me by now.

"Surely, Veltuur will understand," he says slowly, calculating each word like he is balancing one unstable rock atop another. "If you are to fulfill your obligations as king, then visiting your people is among them."

I hide my half-smile before turning back to face my father-crow on my shoulder. "What do you think? I know he said not to leave, but Borgravid's right. If Veltuur wants me to fulfill my duties here, this is one of them. I need to ensure my kingdom is intact, and will remain that way. What should I do?" Then, in a feigned spark of an idea, I light up. "What if you returned to the underrealm to ask him if I'm allowed to go? I don't want to proceed until I know for sure that this won't incur his wrath."

My father-crow cocks his head. His beady, black eyes bore into me like they alone could reveal the lies for what they are. But then, without so much as a squawk or a twitch of his wings, he disappears behind a cloud of gray.

Borgravid wastes no time at all at figuring out what's going on. "The Corraeda Isles? What business do you have there?"

I don't answer him, not right away. I'm too focused on retrieving the feather of Veltuur from below the wardrobe before my father-crow comes back.

The black plume fits snugly inside my new doublet, fully concealed just as it was before. I think about what's to come next, the satyr I'll have to face before then turning around to face Veltuur afterward. I have to wonder if I have such courage inside me, if I'm not the kind of man who would fulfill his own task and then back out of my agreement with the Wraiths altogether. They would never have to know, or at least, I'd never have to face them once they'd figured it out. Once Lorik is freed I can release my father-crow and I never have to return to the underrealm again.

But then I think about what the Wraiths said, about how many of them were there because of the very law I want to abolish. Not many would believe that I, nor anyone, could pull something like this off, but they did. Sinisa, too, seemed to support my decision, even if she had her doubts.

Thinking of her now brings a hollowness to my chest. The last time I saw her, I had been sent to kill her. She must hate me. After all she went through to try to save me, and that's how I repay her, by chasing after her to fulfill her death contract?

But then I remember that she was the only one I spoke to about my intentions, and therefore can be the only way that Borgravid knew of them.

"Did Sinisa ask you to stay behind? To help me change the Law of Mother's Love?"

"No, but she would have if she'd have thought about it. I'm afraid she has other matters vying for her attention right now."

"It's true what they say," I yelp, clutching my chest. "Truth does have a bite."

"I don't remember you having a knack for humor," he says, raising an eyebrow at me. "It should only sting if you're so self-centered that you've forgotten she's trying to fulfill a prophecy."

"You know I haven't, and I'm not."

He crosses his leather-plated arms. "Do I know that? Last I saw, you were in the Forbidden Garden, instructed to kill the very girl you kept asking about when you first became a Reaper. Then, you disappeared."

I glance about the room to make sure my father-crow is still gone. "I didn't want to, but you don't know what the underrealm is like right now. Veltuur has come out of hiding. I had no option but to act like I was trying to do what he commanded me."

"You have another option. You know what it takes to leave the underrealm, and yet you refuse to do it."

"It's not so easy," I snap.

"And changing the Law of Mother's Love is?"

"Maybe? The Wraiths said—" but I cut myself off with a groan, realizing I'm complicating the story more than I need to already. Borgravid is mortal. He has a limited understand of the ways of the underrealm and I need to speak simply if we're going to say what needs to be said before my father-crow returns. "I was told that if I can free Lorik that he could restore humanity's bravery, while Iracara would return to them their compassion. It wouldn't be the same as changing the law, but it would help push everyone in the right direction."

"And the Divine Lorik resides on one of the Corraeda Isles, does he?"

I nod.

With his arms still folded, he bobs his head, eyes fixed on my chest. "And what was that you hid in your tunic?"

"It's...hard to explain, and I don't know how much time we have until he returns, but it's for a promise I made."

A series of slight, measuring nods follow before he finally says, "I'm disappointed in you."

"Disappointed in me? Why? For wanting to change the law? For wanting to create a better, more just system for the people of Oakfall, maybe even all of Tayaraan?"

"For not seeing the flaw in your plan already. What happens once you reach the Corraeda Isles? What happens when we arrive and you insist on heading farther north than is expected for the ceremony? Do you imagine your crow will sit back and let you go on your impromptu search for the Divine Lorik? Do you think he'll sit idly by as you free him?"

I swallow hard. He's right. I haven't thought about any of this. The only thing I was worried about was finding a valid reason to visit the Corraeda Isles. The rest of it I sort of hoped would work itself out.

"What is your plan?"

Hiding my embarrassment at how woefully prepared I really am, I cast my gaze to the ground. "I don't know."

"I see. You know, Sinisa told me about your crow, that it—that *he* is your father, the former king. That means he knows that the feather ceremony is conducted at Illistead Harbor, but you said the Wraiths told you Lorik dwells on the Howling Isle. Tell me, how will you convince your crow to let you go any farther than Illistead?"

"I don't know," I growl again, flapping my arms at my side before flinging myself back onto the bed. "We'll figure it out once we get there?"

"You're dealing with a Divine Altúyur, Acari."

"I know."

"One who has given you implicit instructions to stick to your responsibilities as king and remain at the palace."

"I know," I say a little more emphatically.

It does no good him reminding me what I already know: that Veltuur has my life in his black, tainted, feathery hands. To disobey him means lifelong torment; it might even mean being turned into one of the Wraiths myself. He doesn't need to remind me of the risks because I already understand them, completely. Still, what choice do I have? Freeing Lorik is my only chance at making the realms a safer, more accepting place for Gem and people like her.

After a long moment of consideration, Borgravid finally speaks. "It's been a long while since your father communed with the Corraeda Isles. Maybe we can use that to our advantage."

I push up to my elbows. "What do you mean?"

"It wouldn't be farfetched to discover that the Corraedans have changed the location for the feather ceremony. The whisper wasps gather in the surrounding forest in droves this time of year. Maybe they've decided to move the ceremony to a safer northern location."

A gradual triumphant smirk creeps up the side of my face. "Borgravid, you're a genius."

Ever so slowly, the ruffling of feathers fills my eardrums. Judging from Borgravid's seemingly oblivious, impassive look, my father-crow is still too distant for him to hear it as well, but it's a reminder enough for me that our time for scheming is almost up.

"You should go," I say, shoving off the bed and standing before Borgravid. "Tell the court I'll be there shortly to select the couriers. If you think it will save us grief and argument, inform the Corraedans personally of my decision to deliver the quetzal feather on their behalf. We'll need to minimize outrage from them once my father is present to reduce the likeliness that one of them will slip about the location of the ceremony being the same as it's always been."

With a dutiful nod, Borgravid clamps his chest. "Consider it done."

"Thank you. And assuming my father-crow returns with news of favor, I would like to leave immediately if possible."

"I will send word to the stables to ready the royal horses and escorts."

Smoke blooms from under the bed, coalescing along the patterned marble floor at my feet, gray and ominous. Borgravid looks to the ground, the first indication that he senses my father-crow's impending presence, offers me a brief bow, and exits the room before the bird can fully materialize.

With a flutter of his wings, my father-crow hops along the ground at my feet and squawks like *he's* the one that is awaiting an update.

Glancing from the door back to the crow, I scowl. "Borgravid? I sent him to prepare the court for my announcement. Whatever the message is you have for me, I'll be selecting the couriers regardless. Right? That is, assuming Veltuur hasn't already deemed me in violation of the terms of my stay here?"

My father-crow tilts his head, looking so birdlike when he does that, for a fraction of a moment, I almost forget *what* he really is.

"I guess I can take your silence as a *no, Veltuur hasn't deemed you in violation of the terms of your stay* yet? Or perhaps a better question to ask is: did he give his permission for me to conduct the feather ceremony at the Corraeda Isles?"

He cocks his head in the other direction, and I sigh.

"I suppose the fact that I'm not being summoned back into the underrealm is about as good of an answer as I'm going to get from you, isn't it?"

Caw.

"Great," I say with fake enthusiasm so that he might not pick up on the fact that I am quite excited. When I left Veltuur earlier, never in a million years did I think I'd make such quick work of a plan to get me to Lorik. But here I am, not only having a plan, but dare I say, having a fairly good one. One that is even apparently supported by the Divine Veltuur himself. "All right then, let's head to court."

13

COLD
SINISA

"After your mother's encounter with the Deceptive Serpent"—Sungema explains—"she came to the Ghamayan Citadel believing she was wife to the king who reigned there. That is the lie he forced upon her. She was no longer Khastyl, a woman with a destiny, but she believed herself to be Miva, Queen of Ghamaya.

"Of course, the king had no wife. So, upon her arrival, after days of what the king deemed the mindless rantings of a madwoman, he had his guards seize and imprison her. They feared she might've been sent to Ghamaya with malicious orders to tear the kingdom apart from the inside, or to spy on foreign affairs. They couldn't be too certain, and it was too risky to release her, so she was imprisoned, for a time, while his men investigated her sudden and strange appearance."

Just when I think my heart can't break anymore, one of the already splintered pieces shatters anew. I'm not sure what is worse: dying or imprisonment, but after walking hand in hand with death for years, and given my recent escape from the underrealm, I can at least confidently say that I wouldn't wish imprisonment on anyone, especially not my mother.

To think, all this time, she's been kept captive, much as I have...

"But the longer she stayed in the king's care, the more he became endeared by her," Sungema continues, the story taking an unexpected turn. "She reminded him of a stranger he'd dreamed of often, a woman as fierce as an ocean storm but one who could also be as gentle as a summer breeze.

"He took to her quite quickly. Though there were laws and traditions across the Tayaraan kingdoms regarding nobility and who they were permitted to wed, the Ghamayan royals were often known to make up their own rules. The king wed Khastyl just a few moons after her arrival. Of course, she wasn't called Khastyl then. The Deceptive Serpent took not only the memory of her former life from her, but her name as well."

"Queen Miva..." I utter the words like a dying breath. "She is my...mother."

The rest of our time at the camp blurs around me. As the others prepare for our departures, I'm left to the wanderings of my mind, a place that even I can't seem to make sense of anymore. My mother, a queen. Me, her forgotten daughter. A life we could've had but was taken away from us by Quetzi, by Veltuur.

At the gate, we separate into our respective groups, Dovenia and Rhet setting out first. They take flight, headed for Kallinei Swamp, Rhet's dark body at the mercy of Dovenia's snowy talons. As they ascend up into the clear blue sky, I can't tear my eyes away from the beautiful flowing tail feathers that trail behind them like ripples of the clearest brook or stream.

Part of me wishes I was going with them. Not only did the Deceptive Serpent steal my mother from me—or at least, the version of her I knew and loved—but it also claimed one of the only people I ever called friend. I need to know that their deed is really done, that no one else will fall victim to the serpent lurking in the swamp. And, although Sungema assures me that the Mirror of Truth has done its job, and that Quetzi has almost certainly been released from the torment of Veltuur's imprisonment, I'd feel a lot better if I could see it with my own eyes.

Regardless of my interest in ensuring that Quetzi is freed and Hayliel and my mother avenged, nothing could stop me from being among those headed for the Ghamayan Citadel. Nothing could stop me from seeing my mother.

Belsante and Aulow break away from their embrace, the raven-haired beauty following in Sungema's shadow as she approaches me.

"Safe travels," Sungema says by way of farewell. "Your mother awaits you."

I nod, a simple gesture of thanks.

"Are you sure you're okay with us bringing Avalanche?" Aulow asks, patting the horse's flank. "I don't think I've ever seen you without him at your side."

If anyone else thinks that bringing a horse named Avalanche along on a journey to the tallest peak of the Ghamayan Mountains is just begging for misfortune, no one else says as much and so I bite my tongue as well.

Meanwhile, Miengha smooths a gentle hand along her horse's nose, staring intently into his black eyes. She closes hers and leans in to rest her forehead against him, and I swear the horse leans into her in return. I know that Aulow said all Guardians can communicate with each other via their thoughts, but I can't help but wonder what it would be like to be the Guardian of a horse. Did Miengha have to learn what Avalanche's different whinnies meant, or the day they became intwined did they simply, innately learn to understand each other?

"Iracara cannot fly with the both of you in his talons," Sungema says. "And the Ghamayan Citadel is farther a journey than the Corraeda Isles. The three of us can walk until we reach Illistead Harbor. You, however, will need to journey through a mountain pass and climb to the citadel's bridge."

Either because there's no use in arguing with a Divine Altúyur or because there's no use in arguing with one like Sungema, Aulow does not argue the point.

"It's true. He will be of more use to you on land than he will us at sea. Besides"—Miengha says—"I know he will be in good hands."

With a demure smile, Aulow climbs onto Avalanche's back. "I promise, we will treat him well." Then, with a pat to the horse's wintery mane, she adds with a wink, "He will be fed so many apples."

With a final farewell, Sungema, Beslante, and Miengha head northeast, and Iracara hops into the air, takes my shoulders into his talons, and the four of us head northwest.

On more than one occasion, we have to stop so that I can readjust the new, heavy coat Aulow gave me. The fur will be useful once we start our ascent, but until then, it's so thickly lined with furs that it makes it difficult for Iracara to hold on to me without inadvertently choking me. Or at least, that's how it feels once we're up in the air and I think I'm slipping through it. I don't remember being afraid of heights before, but perhaps I just never truly experienced them.

At my request, we stay low to the ground, hovering just beneath the tree line, with Aulow and Avalanche galloping a short distance behind us.

It takes an entire day, and half of the next, to reach the bottom of the mountain range. The setting sun casts a sheer blue veil across the snowy terrain before us. The fur coats Aulow and I dawned have yet to prove entirely useful, but as the bite of the air shifts from the verdant forest to the alpines, I feel a sniffle coming on.

Our original plan had been to scout ahead, for Aulow and Avalanche to meet us once they'd arrived. But there's a darkness looming over the mountains that feels alive and malevolent. Concerned by the wailing winds, and of getting separated, Iracara and I opt to walk alongside Aulow and the horse instead of flying.

As we begin our ascent, I hike my coat up higher around my neck, burrow into the ring of black fur there that I think belonged to a bear, and settle into the silence of hiking and turn inward to the roaring of my mind.

None of this feels real. When I became mortal again, I'd expected to return to a normal, quiet life, like oh so many whom I have met. Cobblers and blacksmiths. Innkeepers and bards. Bookbinders and candlemakers. But never would I have guessed that I'd be setting out across the realm on a quest to ensure the release and return of the Divine Altúyur.

And you'd think that would be the strangest of it, but as someone who's spent three years in the underrealm, communing with Councilspirits, Shades, Reapers, and crows, it's not.

The thing that feels most surreal is the knowledge that within a few days' time, I will get to see my mother.

I don't even know what I will say. I imagine most reunions between child and mother are spent catching one another up or agonizing over time lost. But I neither want to revisit those disconnected years with her, nor would I want to guilt her for leaving when she has no memory of it. No memory of me.

The winds only intensify the higher we climb. It's like every step we take enrages the mountains, and they lash out at us with everything they have, gales of sleet and snow and hail.

"As miserable as this all is," Aulow yells over her shoulder. "I just keep reminding myself of the gift that's awaiting us at the top of these peaks!"

"Gift?" I yell back, peeking my mouth out from the furs only long enough to respond before turtling back inside.

"Your reunion with your mother! And of course, obtaining the Fatebringer Pendant. To think, we will carry the honor of restoring the realms to their rightful ways and aiding the Divine Altúyur in their glorious return."

At the end of the first day traversing up the mountain, we set up camp. There are two parts to our camp: the first is a modest thing, an enclosure dug from snow with just enough space inside for us to sleep shoulder to shoulder. Then, there is the giant snow cave we built for Avalanche, with a wide opening so that he can come and go as he pleases—according to the information Aulow was able to glean from Miengha by communicating with Belsante, horses are wild, unpredictable creatures with a predisposition for autonomy. Miengha, having come from Ghamaya herself, and having some experience with traveling by horse through the alps, guided us on how to create a cave tall enough for him to fit inside, with enough space to protect him from the weather, while also allowing a large enough opening for him to come and go if he needs. Admittedly, I was disappointed to find out we wouldn't be sleeping with him. Less bodies in our igloo meant less body heat. Then again, I can't say I was too excited by the idea of bunking with a creature that has no qualms walking through its own excrement.

By the time we're done building both structures, our gloves are nothing more than puddles. Despite my leather boots, my socks, too, are soaked through. I spike two sticks into the ground and hang the damp things atop them in hopes that they might dry easier in the open air, and that my feet might have a reprieve from pruning. As I sit on the compacted snow, I wrap myself tighter into my coat, only to find that the hem of my skirt is utterly drenched as well.

Woefully, I glance to Aulow. She flashes me a commiserating smile. "It could be worse."

My laugh is cynical. "Yeah? How?"

She strips her wet socks off, laying them out across her boots, before plopping to the ground beside me. Pulling her hood up, she sinks deeper into what little warmth it can provide her. "Well, we could have left without coats. We could've not had Miengha's aid and expertise in creating shelter for the evening."

Iracara ducks in through the entrance then, catching enough of the conversation to add of his own accord, "We could've forgotten to bring food. Just think how miserable that would be after such a grueling journey."

Finally, I smile, forgetting if only for a moment about the ice that has seemed to crawl beneath my skin.

In Iracara's hands, he holds a steaming tray of freshly roasted eggplant and carrots, a few rolls that have flattened from where they rested in our packs, and some dried fish. "Hungry?"

"You gave Avalanche his share already?" Aulow asks, reaching up for an offered roll.

Iracara nods. "Of course. He ate almost half of the carrots we brought with us. But don't worry. I made sure to save some for us."

When he dips the tray—which I realize is just a long chunk of shale that he likely collected from the mountainside—I count only three carrots among the assortment of delectables.

Expressing my thanks, I grab one of the roasted eggplants and make work of peeling back the charred skin. Even though the fish looked delicious, glistening with a tacky glaze that smelled of oranges and sugarcane, I'm still not ready to eat meat again. It's practically all I ate over the last few years, whereas I have a difficult time even recalling the last time I sank my teeth into eggplant. It would've had to have been before my time at the orphanage, because nothing so decadent was ever served there. It was likely something my mother made, or perhaps my aunt Theffania who loved hosting us for meals that, not only allowed her to serve up her day-old breads, the potatoes that were about to go bad, and anything else she had lying around, but also brought our family together, like she knew our time was limited.

I notice Aulow forgoing her helping of fish as well, and it reminds me the fear that flashed before in her eyes when Sungema mentioned going to the Corraeda Isles.

"Does this mean I'll never grow accustomed to eating meat again?" I ask her, nodding to the tray that Iracara sets at our feet before sitting beside me.

She smiles, but it doesn't reach her eyes. They're too clouded by dread, by shame.

Hayliel would have the heart to apologize, to reassure the woman that she meant no offense and that she has nothing to be embarrassed about. But for all the strides I've been making in acclimating back into a mortal life, there's something too uncomfortable about uttering an apology.

Instead, acting like I don't see her confliction, I focus the conversation back on my own shortcomings instead. "I guess I can live with that. Maybe it can be a sort of repentance, a declaration of paying for some of the lives I am responsible for ending. Most of them were livestock anyway."

"I'm sure your appetite for meat will return in time," she says quietly, head lowered. "But, for some of us, there are certain things that cannot be overcome."

"Like whatever happened on the Corraeda Isles?"

Her eyes flick to mine, terror ravaging them before she's able to take hold again. "Yes."

Iracara bites into his bread roll, yanking it from his mouth with audible, dry smacking.

I glare at him. Though I'm not one to typically enforce meal-time etiquette—I'm not even sure I can claim to be versed in it anymore—I'm at least aware enough to realize how rude it might seem in this circumstance.

He stares at me, shrugging before glancing to Aulow with a guilty swallow. "I'm terribly sorry. I saw food and suddenly nothing else existed. Please, ignore my impoliteness. Continue, continue."

Before his invitation to do so, I'm not sure she had planned to. At least, I don't think I would've if I were in her place. The pain looks too gripping, too immobilizing for her to want to even speak it. It's a feeling that I can relate to all too well.

But Aulow isn't me. And though I spent three years in a forgotten fugue with no sense of who I was or what battles I had fought, Aulow has spent those years living in Tayaraan, surrounding herself with friends and allies, and healing.

She clears her throat. "That was my job, when I was a Reaper. I had a weekly assignment on the Corraeda Isles, in Newhaven actu-ally, to help the fishermen with their weekly catches. I always thought, if I ever lived a different life, I'd live there. I loved the vibrancy of the oceanside town. Loved the salt in the air. But...no matter how many years I put between me and that time of my life, I still can't stomach the smell of fish."

"That's all?" I ask. Realizing I sound like an insensitive jerk, my eyes bulge. "I just mean, you seemed so afraid. I understand needing distance from the smell of fish. I might feel the same way about the meat market I visited often. But I don't fear the place."

"No, you're right. I don't fear fish or the Corraeda Isles in particular. I fear water. It is what brought me to my servitude in the underrealm." She pauses to look up at us, sees she has us both captivated, and continues with a sigh. "I had a choice: save a drowning girl, or save a drowning boy. I chose the girl, and I was punished for the boy's death. The Councilspirits—or, Veltuur, I suppose—makes no distinction between intention and happenstance. Since I could've saved either of them, I therefore condemned the other."

Iracara shakes his head. "It was one of the many reasons we didn't approve of his Reaper process. Good people were forced to suffer as vessels of death just because he was angry that we created Guardians."

She lowers her head.

"So," I say. "You don't like to be near water now."

"I don't trust it. Lakes and rivers and oceans by nature are wild and reckless things. Water flows whether someone wades too deep. Rapids pulse whether someone has lost control of their vessel. Waves crash whether someone is standing on the beach."

Her last words make me think of Rory, of the swell of the tide that shoved her into the cave's mouth. The surge of the ocean didn't care if we were inside; it walloped against us, splashed over us, tried to course straight through us. It claimed Rory's life, and came very close to claiming mine as well.

"It lures people in with its serenity," she continues. "With it promises of cooling those on a hot, summer day, or offering a blissful moment of splashing about with friends. The water lies though. It doesn't know how to control itself, and therefore it cannot be trusted."

Aulow tears off a piece of her roll and nibbles away at it, thoroughly concluding story sharing. It's just as well, as I'm not sure what to say anyway. Her fear of water, although slightly irrational, can hardly be argued against. As Guardians, we live with the knowledge of what life can be like should we be taken by the Wraiths. We know what we'd be giving up. We know what our life would become. And I may not know her well, but I would bet that she is as determined as me not to return to that life, but there is only so much we can do. Accidents happen. An unjust system could find us at fault for something we couldn't have changed.

I don't blame her for wanting to avoid going to the Corraeda Isles, or anywhere near a body of water for that matter. Come to think of it, I'm slightly relieved not to be accompanying Sungema now. The mountain has been bitterly miserable, but at least I have a little more control in my demise here. As long as we are cautious, and follow the paths Miengha told us about, death and blame should not become us so easily.

"But that's enough about me and the obstacles I face," Aulow says at last, already sounding like her usual cheerful self, and with ease. "The beauty of it is that once we complete our tasks, once we set free the Divine Altúyur and you put an end to Veltuur, I will have nothing more to fear of water, but the same thing every mortal has to fear: death. But even that doesn't seem so scary if I know the realms have been put back into balance."

Blinking, I'm surprised that I can't find the same comfort in her words that she seems to. Death is not something I've had much time to consider. I'd almost forgotten that it is a part of being mortal, but she's right: every breath I take, every moment, could be my last, whether Veltuur has his feathers in it or not.

"And you will be reunited with your mother. I bet you're over-whelmed with joy about that." Aulow flashes me a lopsided smile, one that I try to return. "Tell me, what was she like when you last knew her?"

I like the way she phrases it, a quiet acknowledgment of how much time has passed and how very different she will likely be.

A sad smile bleeds into my expression. "My father would always say that my mother was unyielding steel on matters of decision, and drought when it came to expressing any emotion. I guess I remember those sides of her, but more than anything, I remember the fierce pride reflected in her eyes when I stoked my first fire, or the patience she took to teach me how to patch my father's trading clothes. She could've completed such a task in half a day, but instead, she insisted he wait so that I could have the opportunity to learn.

"She wasn't cold and cruel as steel or drought. She was...intentional, in everything she did. She was proud of her family; of the life she and my father had created for us. And looking back on it all now, I think it amazes me even more to know that she lived for centuries and still was able to look at her family's meager existence with such a sense of fulfillment."

Silence fills the small, snowy structure. Nothing but the wailing of the winds outside, and the occasional snort from Avalanche dare break it for a long, long while.

But finally, Iracara reaches across to retrieve another helping of fish, and as he settles back beside me, he stares at the assortment as he says, "I can all but assure you that Khastyl will still be herself. Even the Reapers retain some of their former selves, their deepest personality traits, when they go to the underrealm."

"It's true," Aulow says. "I've heard stories of Queen Miva. I've maybe even heard similar comparisons made between her and stone, ice, steel. But I've also heard she cares deeply for her people. She won over their hearts almost instantly, and no monarch takes greater pride in their kingdom than she."

With a crack in my heart, I nod a silent appreciation to them both and lay my head back against the cool ground. And as I let my eyes flutter closed, staring up at the compacted snow that seems to glow overhead, I can think of nothing but my mother. I try imagining her as I remember—dark, flowing hair, her fierce and loving heart—but it's her eyes that my memory can't do justice. Though I should find comfort in knowing that I will soon have a new memory of her to draw from, I have the sudden dreadful suspicion that the eyes I knew are long gone, and I wonder who I might see reflected in her gaze when we meet next.

14

AVALANCHE
SINISA

I spend the night nestled next to Iracara, savoring the warmth his thick feathers provide us all. Under normal circumstances, it should be uncomfortable to lay so close to him, to any man—even one who *isn't* entirely human. And, at first, I suppose it was. It's difficult not to think about the only man I've ever laid beside, the one who made my bed feel like it was my own personal prison, an island of isolation and abuse.

However, the moment Aulow's and my teeth started to chatter, Iracara offered us each a wing and it became a little easier to remind myself that he, the Altúyur of Compassion, would never harm me in such a way.

The next morning, we set out at first light. Fortunately, whatever storm was raging this mountain range has mostly subsided. It's nothing but clear skies, a bright sun, even if the altitude still seizes my lungs. By the time we feed Avalanche and ourselves, and leave our makeshift camp, my toes had almost regained most of their feeling. But with each step we take, scaling up the snowy mountainside, my boots sink midcalf into the snow. I doubt the feeling, nor the dryness, will last very long, and I try not thinking about what it will be like to sit before a warm hearth or soak into a steaming bath.

"You two should take to the air today," Aulow says, catching me breathing into my hands. "It's not as windy anymore, so there's no danger in flying. You could reach the peak far earlier than we can on foot. You could head to the citadel and I can find you later—"

I snap around to face her. "We're not just leaving you."

Despite that being our original plan, it feels inhumane now to just abandon them on the mountainside. I'd rather us stay together. It feels safer that way. That, and the longer it takes us to reach Ghamaya, the longer I have to figure out what I will say upon seeing my mother.

The smile Aulow fixes is flawless, practiced, believable. "I am not the important one among us. You have a task to complete. I'm just extra weight. Besides, Avalanche will keep me warm, as will my cloak until we reunite with you at the citadel. It can't be more than another day's journey, but the two of you could make it there before nightfall if you flew."

"I'm not leaving you," I say again, clenching my jaw.

Aulow's lips are still chapped from the wind yesterday, but her smile grows wider. "What did I tell you, Sinisa? It's not about duty or loyalty. Love is all that matters. You have the chance to see your mother again. Go to her. I promise, I will be fine, and I will find you and Iracara once we arrive."

"She's right," Iracara says to me. "I think. I mean, we could be there before nightfall. Let the two of us go ahead. I, too, believe your friend will be just fine on her own. It's not too far away now. It's as Sungema said, retrieving the Fatebringer Pendant is of the utmost importance. Now that the skies are clear and the tempest passed, this part of the journey doesn't need to be long. Besides, there is still so much we need to accomplish. We still have to find Pecolock. You have to obtain the Blade of Immortality. The longer we wait, the more time Veltuur has to seek the Altúyur and take them somewhere we will never find them."

My eyes never leave Aulow's. The verdant green of her irises have already started to dim up here, like the farther away from the forest they get, the more they are drained of the very essence that runs through her. She keeps her hands at her sides, surely fighting the urge to rub her shoulders, lest proving to me just how deep the bitter cold has bitten.

Glaring at them both, I dig my heels in. I don't want to leave her. We've already come this far together, and I'd feel more comfortable if we stayed that way.

But the longer I glower between them, the less I'm able to deny the logic they're making. The only reason Sungema sent another Guardian with us was because she thought it might be helpful to have multiple perspectives once we set out to free Pecolock. But that will come later. This part of the journey, the one in which I confront my mother after nearly seven years of absence and retrieve from her an heirloom created from the Divine Altúyur of Fate herself, this part I suppose I really don't need her for.

"I doubt taking a half day longer would change much," I say sheepishly. "But I understand what you're saying, and I respect your input far more than I should of someone I barely know."

With a soft smile, she shakes her head, red curls vibrant against the gray mountainside. "I believe you and I are linked by destiny, which means we are no more strangers to each other than the sun is a stranger to the sky."

"If we are linked, then we should stay together."

"That is not always how it works. People's paths veer and reconverge all the time. Like you and Acari have. Like you and your mother will soon."

The mention of both of them sends a spear of pain through me, each more powerful than the last. Seeing Acari again is something I have barely had the time to even hope for, and my mother... It seems like every other second I grapple with whether it's possible or that I even believe that she could still be alive, and queen of an entire kingdom, at that.

"Why would Sungema request your aid if we were just to abandon you on this mountain? We've already wasted time standing here discussing this. Can we please go together?" I say, looking between the two of them, but I focus my gaze on Aulow at last. "And not because of duty or loyalty, but because of that other thing you keep talking about."

"Love?" Aulow giggles.

I roll my eyes but make sure she catches the faint smile burgeoning behind them. "I know I don't know much about love, but I know it isn't just about family or doing things for your own gain while abandoning your friends knee-deep in snow. Love *is* loyalty, it's commitment and sacrifice, and the three of us"—at Avalanche's whiney, I correct myself—"*four* of us, are in this together. Maybe your roles haven't been deemed important by prophecy, but having you by my side is important to me. Please."

The two of them exchange a wry look, but they both look far too proud of my show of heart to argue.

We start walking again, the snow deepening with every step. The tips of my fingers and my nose have joined my feet in their numb state, no matter how much I rub them or breathe steam onto them.

Aulow and Avalanche take the lead, but when the path narrows, we're forced to march single file. The horse and Iracara struggle the most. On more than one occasion, Avalanche whinnies and starts walking backward the way we came, almost knocking me off the ledge. We must've gone the wrong way at some point, missed a turn that Miengha had said to take.

"Bels says Miengha thinks part of the path might've been lost," Aulow says, apparently having wondered the same thing. She rushes to soothe Avalanche before he can cause a disaster, stroking his nose. "She says, if we can, we should keep going, that she doesn't know of another way up that doesn't take two days longer."

Both Iracara and Aulow look to me.

If the path stays this way, we can still make it. But even now, it is so thin that it would be difficult for Avalanche to turn around. We don't have any choice.

"Then we go on. If it gets too dangerous...we'll figure something else out."

With Aulow's hand gripped tightly around Avalanche's rein, the leather wrapped around her wrist, she's able to encourage the horse forward again. She guides him along, a slow and careful gait, even as the path continues to dwindle.

Not a one of us dares to speak. We're too focused on our footwork, on staying upright instead of tumbling over, on surviving.

The winds return shortly after midday, the sky turning gray as clouds roll in overhead. As they howl around us, echoing throughout the gorge, I can't help but feel like they are intentionally trying to knock us down. The creaking of the heavy snow is ominously peaceful. We stay as close to the craggy wall as we can for security, though it provides little. My fingers burn as they clutch the sharp edges visible to grasp, the rest buried in snow. My legs wobble as I slide carefully along the ridge, and on more than one occasion, I feel Iracara's feathered hand at my back, ready and solid.

As I'm muttering my thanks to him for the dozenth time, suddenly Aulow shrieks.

I jerk forward, the path giving way beneath her. Rock and snow tumble down the steep wall, taking her body with it. The horse neighs, rearing in fear as the path collapses beneath it as well, but with Aulow's hold on the reins, it can't back away in time. She weighs him down, and the horse falls with her.

I scream their names, clutching to the snowy mountainside for fear I might be next. With my face buried, all I can hear are the sounds of their bodies tumbling down the cliff, the puffs of air forced out of Aulow's lungs on each impact, until they both land with two heavy thuds.

Pressed against the icy rock, my face is wet from snow and tears alike. I can't lose another friend. I can't be the reason that another beautiful soul was lost to the realm because of a dangerous quest I embarked on.

She shouldn't have even been here. We should've sent her after

Pecolock instead. We should've turned around when the path became too treacherous—

"You have to lean back!" I hear Iracara yell over my deprecating thoughts.

"What?"

"We have to go to them. We need to see if they're all right. I can't grab you while you're pressed against the mountain. Lean back and create space between you and the wall."

I dare a look over my shoulder, see Iracara's magnificent, sable wings flapping amid the pale landscape. Without putting much thought to it, surrendering myself to him and his plan entirely, I press away from the wall.

He grabs me into his talons and lifts me from the mountainside, and we plummet. It feels like we dive forever, snowflakes pelting into my face like shards of glass, wind howling past my ears, my hair whipping all around me. Surely, no one could survive a fall like this, not with a pit of jagged rocks waiting at the bottom of the cliff to break their fall.

We reach the ledge below us, the snow already stained red, and stare at the writhing bodies of a young woman and a stallion.

Avalanche's back leg is twisted, his front half thrashing to stand on the hind legs that won't support him. He neighs weakly, throwing his head back in a jerk to reveal a deep, crimson gash where a rock sliced into his thick neck. Blood gushes and spurts. It's mostly responsible for the red snow, but I know he is already too far gone for me to do anything about it.

I run past Avalanche, sliding to Aulow's side.

A splatter of red bursts from her lips. Her blue eyes blink back tears, pinpricked and bloodshot. She's so still she could almost be dead. I examine the rest of her, searching every inch to find a seeping wound, a shattered limb, or entrails. As I do, I also search the sky for a crow. Where there is death, there should be a Reaper.

I'm not sure how she managed, but I see no major wounds or broken bones. Still, I know enough about death to know that mortals don't just gurgle blood for nothing, and if this continues, she will be claimed in no time.

With a whimper, Aulow pulls her gaze from the clouds and glances down her supine body, to her hand lying palm-up in the snow, and I realize she's trying to move it, but it won't budge.

A broken spine. A death sentence.

"No," I whimper, taking her ice-cold hand into my own. "You can't die. Not you too."

She blinks, and when a tear falls down either side of her face, two run down my cheeks as well.

Iracara's winged hand rests on my shoulder. "Can you heal her?"

Blinking away my grief, I look back at him, confused. "What do you mean? I'm no healer. And if I was, you saw my bag. I didn't bring any herbs or bandages—"

"You're a Guardian, are you not?" he interrupts, gentle as rain. "It's one of the gifts we bestowed upon your kind: the gift of restoration."

With a newfound sense of hope, an ironclad sense of determination, I wipe the wetness from my eyes. "How do I do it?"

Aulow's grip on my hand tightens, and I shift my attention to her. Her lip bobs with every effort it takes to speak, a breath barely heard over the moan of the wind. "None...can heal...anymore."

I twist back to Iracara. "How did they do it? How did the Guardians heal back in your time?"

"I—I wouldn't know. I am not one of them."

"But you made them. You must know how it works!"

"I only offered a small fraction of my own self; I did not mold the Guardians alone. But all power comes from the soul. If you search inside yours, perhaps you'll find the answer you seek there."

Growling, I ball my free hand into a fist. "You're useless! What good is a Divine Altúyur if you can't even help her!"

Iracara straightens. A darkness rolls through him that I've only ever seen once when he was reliving his memory of the day Veltuur trapped him. "I am not the Altúyur of Life or Blood or Regeneration. You are lucky I reign over compassion, and so I am able to have some for you in this moment of great heartbreak. But I will leave you to say goodbye to her in peace and remove myself from your outlashing." He pauses, thoughtful, before adding, "You used your power when we were at the palace. Whatever you used to reach out to it then, you can do the same now, just with a different skill."

Before I can say anything else, he turns on his heels, taking a seat beside Avalanche and running a hand over the horse's barely breathing velvet body.

I turn back to Aulow, to her blood-soaked ringlets and shallow breaths. Iracara's words are like stigrees buzzing in my mind. They burrow into me, insistent and niggling, until I have no choice but to face the fact that he's right. *I* am the only person who can use *my* power, and I've already done it before. Not *this* power, but maybe that doesn't matter.

"I'm not letting you die," I vow, staring down at her paling face, her fluttering eyes.

I draw my focus to her breathing, to the spine I know that lies just on the other side of her body. If Iracara is right—and his advice is the only thing I have to work off right now—if I recall what I did back in the Forbidden Garden, I might be able to find the power I need to heal her.

I hover my hands over her body, one over her abdomen, the other over her chest, and close my eyes. I think about what it was like to see Nerul and Acari working together. I remember my head still spinning from all the history Sungema had just unleashed upon us, and though I wasn't yet sure if or how I would help, I knew *I* wanted to be the one to make that decision. Not Acari. Not Nerul. Not Veltuur.

Necessity. It was pure, raw need that fueled me. I needed to protect us long enough to make sense of it all. I needed to make Nerul and Acari think that we were gone and unreachable. I needed Veltuur to know that I wouldn't be taken again so easily.

Opening my eyes, I hopefully scan Aulow's body in search of

any signs that it's working. I scan myself, too, looking for light or smoke or streams or whatever healing magic might look like, but I find none.

I think harder, strain my inner voice until it is screaming inside my head: *I need her to survive. I need to keep my friends safe. I need to stop pulling them into danger.*

Another peek. Another letdown.

This isn't working. Aulow drifts closer and closer to death, and I'm just kneeling here beside her watching it happen, doing nothing.

Something else Iracara said strikes me, something about finding the power inside one's own soul.

My thoughts travel inward again. I think about what my soul has become, who I am, who I was, all I might be. Not too long ago, I was a shattered and frightened child. I belonged nowhere and trusted no one, until the day I became a Reaper and I found my place and forgot my past. I think about the day I was sent to claim Gem's soul, the day I was bested by a bumbling prince and his toddler sister. I consider the path that led us to discovering the Guardians, and my salvation from the prison I didn't know I was contained in, the strength it took to leave the underrealm behind, to embrace the person inside myself that I'd lost. I think about the friends I've made since then, both the living and the dead. Of Hayliel, of Rory and Dethoc, of Belsante, Aulow, and Iracara.

Of Acari.

Of the mother who awaits me.

Of love. So much love that I never expected to find again. It warms my heart, my chest, my torso, until I can't contain it anymore.

I channel the feeling outward, a warmth that spreads, gentle and quick. I feel it course its way out from my heart, feel it crawl across my shoulders, and down my arms until it reaches my fingertips. My hands illuminate like they are made from the stars. Like the morning sun, the blazing and blinding light erupts from my hands until Aulow disappears behind a white flash.

But I hear her scream all the same. I feel her nails dig into my wrist as she arches into the power blasting from my fingers.

I want to stop. I want to make sure she's okay, but I can't. I don't have control here. Heat pulses through me in tidal waves until I am shaking and depleted.

Only once I'm thoroughly spent do I fall forward, the light dimming at my palms. I collapse face-first into the snow, hunched over Aulow's still body. I lie there, panting and sweating, wondering whether I just killed her, and how long it'll take for the Wraiths to come and collect me.

"You...did it..." comes a harsh voice beneath me.

Though every muscle inside me has surrendered to exhaustion, the sound of her voice rejuvenates me. Slowly, aching in every bone, I push myself up off her and lean back onto my knees. "Aulow? Are you...are you..."

Weakly, she nods. "I can move again. You...you healed me."

I dive forward and envelop her in my arms. Pressed against her matted curls, I smell the scent of pine still lingering from our journey through the woods, feel the warmth of her cheek against mine. She's alive. She's alive.

And I saved her.

But it's at that moment that I notice the shadows beneath her body are darkening, and only then that I remember that she wasn't the only one in need of saving.

15

SHADOWS COME

SINISA

I bolt upright, twist to look behind us, and find Iracara kneeing
beside the fallen horse. Its chest rises and falls with a shuddering pulse and relief floods through me. I haven't failed
Avalanche yet. There's still time to save him.

But the white stallion doesn't take another breath, doesn't blink,
doesn't move.

Iracara leans over him with a sob. He rests his forehead on the
beast's flank, and I sink back onto my heels, my frightened gaze
dragging to the growing shadows around me.

They drip from the crevices of the mountain, sleek and tenebrous, pooling at the ledge I'm kneeling on. Aulow meets my eyes
as they stalk closer, but I tear mine away in shame.

I've failed her, failed Gem and Acari; I've failed everyone. And
possibly worst of all I've failed myself. What point was there in
clawing my way out of Veltuur's clutches, if this was to be the
outcome? Why did we come all this way if I was *fated* to fall here
and now? If we had just stayed at the camp, Avalanche would still
be alive. If I had stayed a Reaper, Hayliel and Dethoc and Rory
would still be breathing, and Acari would still be mortal.

It's the sound of the birds cawing around us that draws Iracara's glistening eyes to me. He watches the darkness encroaching with uninhibited fear, and it's then that I realize this is it. The prophecy was wrong. I wouldn't defeat Veltuur. I wouldn't meet my mother again. I wouldn't free the Altúyur.

"No!" Aulow shrieks. As if she wasn't just brought back from death's door, she launches herself at me, wrapping me in an unbreakable embrace. "You can't take her. She didn't do anything! She saved me!"

It's not until the sob breaks through her that I remember the story she shared of how she became a Reaper, the person whose death was shifted to her shoulders simply because she made a choice to save the other person. It dawns on me then that the reason I could find no crow earlier was because, not only was Aulow's time not up, but Avalanche's soul wasn't for a Reaper to take.

It was for a Reaper to be born.

I suppose I should be grateful. Having Avalanche as a crow will be far better than the last hand I was dealt.

Besides, perhaps this is how it's meant to be. Since becoming a mortal, I haven't exactly lived like one. I've spent my days amassing the deaths of my friends, trying to break into the underrealm, and frequently running into Shades and Reapers alike. I never fit in here in Tayaraan. The underrealm, though, that always felt like home.

Maybe this is for the best. Maybe the realms are already as balanced as they can be. Now that Sungema is free, as are so many of the other Altúyur, I have no doubt that they won't find a way to free the rest of them, and, in time, even arrange a meeting with Veltuur to negotiate the realms back to the way they were.

They don't need me. Especially not now that I've proven I'm not fit to fulfill this task anyway.

Gently, I shove Aulow away. She blinks up at me, eyes wet and frightened, as I stand tall to face the Wraiths. The shadows wrap around my ankles and coil up my calves, and it's like I'm thirteen again. Only this time, I know the darkness that awaits me. The isolation. The scorn I'll receive from the mortals.

Perhaps I'll see Acari sooner than I thought.

As the obscure darkness breaks farther through the mortal realm, the claws become more solid against my feet. They puncture my leather boots, sharp and possessive. With nothing left to do but accept my fate, I hold my head high.

Iracara's brown, pleading eyes await mine, but I don't find helpless acceptance reflected in them. I find calculation, frantic and hopeful.

With a wave of his black wing, a gentle breeze blows over us, me and Aulow, over the Wraiths. In it, a soothing warmth wraps itself around my fractured heart. It seeps into the very cracks of me, the ones so dark and full of fear that I thought that they could never be repaired, never filled. But Iracara's magic is profound.

Feeling the grip loosening around my ankles, I look down to the ground. The Wraiths are retreating. They don't slither all the way back to the underrealm, not entirely anyway, just far enough to release me and stand close guard.

With his winged arms at his hips, Iracara strides forward. "You have been tasked with the duty of claiming murderers from Tayaraan and turning them into Reapers who serve Veltuur."

Though none of the shadows have faces or heads, the amorphous tendrils and slivers seem to look among themselves in answer.

Iracara continues. "But you have come for the wrong person. This young woman here, Sinisa Strigidae, did not commit murder." He points behind him to Avalanche, snow already beginning to accumulate atop the horse's corpse. "He fell from the mountain. It was no one's fault, the path simply gave away. Aulow fell too. By the time we arrived, they were both already dead. But Sinisa did the impossible. She saved the woman from meeting her end before it was time.

"She is no murderer, and she has no place in the underrealm. She is a savior. Surely, you can see that now."

The Wraiths glance between themselves again, and there's a frightful moment when I realize it's not the whispering of the winds that I hear, but that of the Wraiths. I gape into their darkest pools, wondering whether compassion is enough to save me.

But after a few moments that pass as slowly as snowfall, the dark shadows start to lighten. The claws and branches of black retreat, climbing back the way they came, from up the mountain, beneath Aulow's body, beneath my boots, until all that's left are shadows, normal ones, unfrightening ones.

I loose a shuddering breath, one I didn't even know I was holding. "You didn't... I can't believe... You... Thank you."

Iracara grins, a proud, lopsided thing, and nods.

My exhaustion resurfaces, reminding me of all of the traveling, all of the hiking, all of the shrieking and loss, of me using my power and then turning around to evade my greatest nightmare. I collapse back to my knees, Aulow doing the same beside me as she lies back in the red snow.

"I forgot to tell you," she says, breathless. "Bels says that when she sees you again, she's giving you a big fat kiss."

Despite the tears in my eyes, I smile at her.

16

WHISPERS

ACARI

"You smell that?" Borgravid asks from atop his horse.

I tilt my nose skyward, quickly, before returning my full attention back to the reins in my hands and the sway of my body. "No. What is it?"

Though I could've opted to take a carriage, Borgravid assured me horseback would be our fastest route to the Corraeda Isles. He insisted it would give our small entourage—which consists of Borgravid, myself, and about ten guards—easier maneuverability through the forest than a carriage would provide.

Still, traveling by horse comes with its own challenges. We had to cover the poor creature beneath me almost entirely with leathers and padding, just to ensure that my Reaper power doesn't accidentally find its way through to the horse's skin. You would think it would be the beast that's afraid of me and not the other way around, but the longer we ride, the less I can shake the constant fear that my steed has a mind to rear me off and bolt as far away from me as possible.

Borgravid snorts. "You lived such a sheltered life at the palace, you can't even smell the ocean in the air?"

"Oh, *that* smell. Sorry, it's hard to get a good whiff of anything over the stench of hay and, well, something far worse that seems to be permeating from the creatures *you* insisted we take."

His grin is almost imperceptible beneath his moustache and beard. The only reason I notice it is because of the amusement that flashes in his eyes. "We're getting close. Once we arrive to Illistead, we can hire a boat to take us to the Howling Isle, and then it's no more horses."

I feel my father-crow's attention fall to us. Though we've already made a point to say this a dozen times, I add again hastily, "Right. Because the Howling Isle is where the Corraedans host the feather ceremony now, correct?"

"Yes, my king," Borgravid says a bit stiffly, casting me a glare out of the corner of his eye.

I'm worrying too much about my father-crow figuring the truth out, and that fear is making me act foolishly. I have to remind myself that, at least so far, everything has gone as planned. The more conspicuous I am, the more likely it is that this will end poorly.

"It's just as I've said," Borgravid continues, apparently giving into the worry as well. "The Howling Isle was a place of fear and hatred for years. The Corraedans believed that treating an island so poorly, abandoning it almost entirely, went against everything the Divine Iracara stood for. So they relocated the feather ceremony as a way to make amends for their past misjudgments."

Making sure my father-crow is ahead of us so as not to see, I give Borgravid an appreciative nod.

But without warning, my horse's hoof plummets clean through the ground. A rotten log swallows it all the way to the knee and the two of us sink into the earth. We might've noticed the fallen tree if it hadn't been covered by overgrowth, moss, and grass.

The horse whinnies, jerking its neck upright and I hold tight. If there's one thing I fear more than being atop a horse, it's being flung from one.

With a few lurching motions, my horse is able to pull its leg free. But the sudden burst of excitement leaves the creature jostled and frantic. Even once its hooves are back on solid ground, it can't seem to settle. It bounces around, head swaying, coarse hair whipping to and fro, and just as it starts to rear, Borgravid trots beside us and lays a calm hand on the beast's neck.

"Whoa there. Easy."

There's no way the horse can feel him through all the extra layers, but once Borgravid hops down from his own horse, hands splayed out in a gesture of goodwill and trust, the creature does finally start to settle.

"You're all right." Borgravid reaches up for the horse's muzzle, the one part of it that isn't completely covered since I had no intention of putting myself in front of the large thing. With slow, gentle movements, Borgravid rubs the length of the horse's nose until it finally stops clopping around.

Beneath me, I feel its breathing slow back to normal.

But in the quiet, we finally hear it, the low rumble that almost sounds like an entire town is whispering from somewhere down below us. I tilt my head toward it, eyes fixed behind me to the hole.

Some of the other guardsmen do the same, until one of them finally cries, "Whisper wasps!"

My heart leaps into my throat. There is still much I don't remember from my life before, but I am quite familiar with the creatures that the underrealm works through. Whisper wasps serve only one purpose: to kill.

Eyes bulging, I spin back around to look at Borgravid. He's backing away from my horse, peeking over its backside to the hole.

"Go!" he yells, swatting my horse's rear.

As the mare takes off, I glance over my shoulder just in time to see the swarm of wasps rise from the ground like a plume of smoke. They hover there, calculating, determining their mark. But whisper wasps are not single-minded. They only strike as one if there is but one threat. But here, spying a small militia having surrounded their underground hive, surely all of us will be deemed dangerous, and therefore they will not charge as one, but as many.

The colony begins to break off into smaller swarms, but each one still has to have thirty or more wasps in it. They hold nothing back, and charge.

I'm still looking back over my shoulder as Borgravid swings his leg up and over his saddle. He bolts after us. "To the harbor!"

When I turn around to watch where we're headed, low-hanging branches swat against my face and arms as we gallop through the woods. I don't spare a second thought at their inevitable deaths. Instead, I ride. My body slams against the horse's back, the sound of hooves is thunderous in my ears and thankfully drowns out the buzzing of the whisper wasps. I squeeze my eyes shut and kick my heels into my horse's flank, and ride as hard as I've ever ridden.

Behind me, people start to scream. Even the horses can't outrun the whisper wasps; the trees are too dense for them to gain much momentum. I can't pick Borgravid's cries out among them, but seeing as he had been one of the closest to them, one of the last to flee, I'm sure he's one of the many who the whisper wasps have already began attacking.

I look back over my shoulder again. Cloud after cloud has surrounded a handful of my guards. Some of them have jumped off their horses and started running. Others have curled themselves against their steed's backside, condemning both beast and man to the onslaught of stingers and venom.

For a moment, I wonder why no one is swatting the whisper wasps away, why they're not at least smacking them off their bodies. But then I remember the curse that the mortals must live with. None of them can kill—not another mortal, not even a whisper wasp, unless they want to become a Reaper.

Their only choices are to endure the assault of stingers, succumb to the venom and die, *or* make it to the water before it's too late. Even if the ones who are still atop their horses could make it that far though, there's still no guarantee. Whisper wasps are creatures of imprint. Once they believe someone has meant them danger, they will be on the hunt until either the wasp or their target has died. It's why they've made such great allies to the underrealm; they are just as focused as any Reaper in their killings.

Unlike my mortal guards who are defenseless, I, on the other hand, *am* allowed to kill them. Typically, by contract only, of course, but it's not like if I kill them I will become even more of a Reaper. And though I'm sure the Councilspirits and Veltuur would be enraged to discover one of their Reapers killed an entire swarm of whisper wasps, Veltuur already okayed this journey. He knew the risks of me being in Tayaraan. He told me to do what I must to fulfill my role as king.

Up until now, that's meant traveling to the Howling Isle to conduct a falsified feather ceremony.

But as of this very moment, it means saving my sentries.

I pull back on the reins until my horse kicks back to a halt. It's a clumsy, shaky descent, but once I'm back on solid ground, I swat the horse's rear, the leather stinging my hand hopefully more than it stings her, and I let her run. Whisper wasps don't care if you're human or animal. They'd come for her too if I let her stay. Hopefully, she hasn't been marked as a threat. Hopefully, she'll make it.

Shakily, I turn around to face the direction of the screams. Horses barrel past me on either side. I'm grateful to see that most of them are not still swarmed by the wasps, which means they should be safe once they leave the forest, if not frightened and lost. But through the occasional clearing their large bodies offer, I see the swarms they've left behind. Two, three, four mortals are curled up on the ground now, surrounded entirely and screaming in agony.

Caw, my father-crow squawks from a tree above me.

"Shut up. I don't want to hear it," I snap. Though I can't really understand him, I know exactly the kind of thing he's likely saying. For someone like him, someone who would let his own daughter die just because of a cleft in her lip, no life is as important as his own. "I'm not going to let them die when I'm the only one that can kill these things."

Perhaps it's my father's disapproval, or the truth of my words, but suddenly my apprehension fades away. I charge the nearest person at full speed. I hold nothing back as I swat at the swarm of wasps surrounding them. At first, nothing happens, except that the ones I manage to touch die instantly just like anything that my Reaper power comes in contact with. But the more wasps I kill, the more that those remaining reassess the situation. They pull back from the swollen man on the ground and discover a new, more formidable threat.

They aim their collective at me, a deadly vibration rippling through the air.

"Go," I tell the man, backing away as the wasps aim themselves at me. "Try to reach the harbor if you can."

Then I'm running again, bolting for the next downed guardsman.

She's sobbing, shaking violently, and I'm not sure if it's already too late for her, but I start smacking the wasps out of the air again.

The first swarm reaches me and begins launching their assault in return. The first one stings me on my neck. Heat flares through me like someone's just set a torch to my shoulder. The next wasps gets one of my hands. Another my eyebrow. But I keep attacking, keep killing as many as I can until the second swarm finally turns on me too.

The vision of my right eye starts to blur from another sting, but once I mutter to the woman to head for the harbor, I charge toward a third person.

I reach her only a fraction of a second too late though. With a powerful roar, she chops her hand through the air, knocking a handful of the whisper wasps down before squashing them in the dirt with her boot.

The shadows waste no time in coming to collect her.

Her death twists through me unexpectedly, but with the wasps pummeling into me over and over, their stingers stabbing into me like pokers pulled from the fire, I waste no time in rushing to the fourth and final man.

Borgravid sits in the dirt with his cape wrapped up and over his head like a shield. As I draw nearer, I see him flinching periodically, but for how many wasps are diving for him, it's obvious few of them are landing their blows. The protection he's built around himself is working. At least, for the time being. If no one intervenes, if I don't pull that swarm off him soon, they'll attack him for the rest of their lives, which admittedly is short, but will most likely be longer than it takes for enough of them to reach their stingers through the fabric before the poison takes its hold.

Teeth bared, I charge forward again. My hands rake through the air, killing a dozen wasps in one swing. A dozen more jam their stingers into my skin, also dying in an instant, but not before they release their toxin.

Every inch of me is bloated and on fire. The pain sears through me in flares, like I can feel each individual strike. I would've expected the opposite, to start to numb to it, but I don't. They attack with their lives, and I feel every. Single. Jab.

Once I have every last wasps' attention, I start stumbling away, leading them in the opposite direction of Borgravid and the others. If I am to die, hopefully it'll give them enough time to escape, or hopefully the wasps will keep attacking me even after death, until my Reaper power has killed every last one of them.

My steps are no longer the powerful strides of an invincible immortal. My calves and thighs swell as I stagger until finally, I can take not another step.

I brace myself on a tree before it too dies beneath my touch. As it withers and decays, I lean against it, taking sting after sting from the hundreds of wasps I have accumulated.

My skin is fire. It is the molten surface of the sun, and I feel myself melting away.

My eyes become so enflamed that my vision disappears entirely, followed shortly by my hearing.

I am only faintly aware that the constant stinging finally dwindles as the last of the whisper wasps die out and I succumb to darkness, my mission fulfilled.

Awareness is a strange, dreamy thing. I feel heavy, sunken into the bottom of a gray ocean of nothing. Sound is muffled beneath the swaying waters. But as I start to rise to the surface, as I float back into my body, I start to discern a voice.

"Acari?" a man asks, concern edging his tone. "Acari! Are you with me?"

My eyelids flutter open. Branches weave through the blue skies above me. I stare through them, beyond them, unaware of where I am, how I got there, or why I'm most certainly lying on my back in the dirt and not floating out at sea.

A bearded man leans into my view. "Flightless bird, when did you become so reckless and brave?" And with a quirk of his lips, Borgravid adds for good measure, "My king."

Weakly, I smile back at him, realizing my face isn't too swollen to do so anymore. In fact, none of me seems to be. My elbows are still a little stiff, but I bring my hands up to my cheeks, to the eyes that had become so puffy that they had completely closed, and find that my face feels normal again.

"I'm...I'm okay," I utter, breathless. "I survived. How did I—how did I survive?"

Borgravid grabs my forearm and helps me up to sitting. "Once the whisper wasps were dead, your crow fazed you to Veltuur, just in time apparently because when he brought you back, you were healed. I wish I could say the same for the rest of us."

As Borgravid indicates to the others, I notice the bulge of his cheek, the awkward way he's elevating his ballooned hand. I glance over my shoulder to the rest of our party to find them kneeling and scattered throughout the woods. There are fewer than there should be, even though I only saw the one woman taken by the Wraiths. The rest I assume—almost half of our group —must've made it all the way to the harbor, just as they were told.

Those who remain here have suffered greatly, some worse than others, but all at alarming levels. Faces reddened and oozing with poison.

"We need to get everyone to a healer," I say to Borgravid.

But before he can respond with what I'm sure will be a protest to send the others to a healer while he helps me stay on our path, a voice calls out from the trees.

"Very interesting sacrifice, Reaper King."

She draws our attention to her like moths drawn to flame. At first glance, I mistake her for a child, so small beside the bushes from where she emerges. But she carries herself with the grace and poise of a queen, and the closer she approaches, the better able I am to tell that the green drapery cascading down her back that I mistook for a cape is actually a pair of wings.

She is no queen, but a divinity.

"S-Sungema..." I stutter, searching the trees for my father-crow. "What are you..."

It's then that I remember who was with her the last time I saw her.

Desperate and eager, I search the tree line for Sinisa, hoping to see her emerge next, just as Sungema before her. But no matter how long I stare, no matter how far I scan, or how high I stretch to the tops of my toes, she doesn't come.

Of course she isn't here. Like all of my contracts, I'd be able to sense her presence if she was nearby, but I sense nothing. Not the tug of our souls as hers beckons me toward her. Not the static in my stomach that seems to be inspired by her presence.

Unless I'm no longer contracted to kill her, I muse. Maybe Veltuur has sent someone else after her, someone who won't fail him to complete the job. I thought I'd feel it though, the severing of the ties that bind us, but perhaps I wasn't meant to. Maybe this was meant to be my punishment? Or maybe not—I don't know! I don't know what to expect from Veltuur because—

Suddenly, I remember myself. I glance nervously to my father-crow, to my keeper and watchman. His black eyes are trained on me like any second now he's about to sound an alarm. In fact, I'm surprised he hasn't already.

Despite my eager appearance, maybe I still have time to convince him and Veltuur that I am loyal and that they don't need to send me back to the underrealm. Not yet.

"Veltuur wants you dead, Sungema," I say, trying to steel my voice to sound just as convincing as I hope I am intimidating. "I will have to—"

"You will *have* to do nothing," she says airily. "Veltuur does not desire us slain, but captured. Though misguided, he holds balance above all else, and to murder any of the Altúyur would be to disrupt that balance. Suppose you were to capture me though; might I suggest you do so after we provide you aid?"

"We?"

Just as my sluggish eyes scan the surrounding trees again, two others step forth from the foliage. Once again, hope flurries through me that one of them might be Sinisa, that I might have a chance to see her and explain myself again.

But neither of Sungema's companions I recognize.

The first is a woman who the Law of Mother's Love should've claimed long ago for the birthmark that covers most of her cheek. Even it can't conceal her beauty though, her raven hair and eyes alluring to the point that I almost can't look away from her.

The second is a blonde Ghamayan with twisting braids down her back. Her eyes are tinged red like she's been crying or hasn't slept in days, and there's a bow slung over her shoulder. I'm surprised she's not aiming it at us, until I notice the runes on her hands, the same ones that Sinisa has, the same ones that give her and anyone near her protection from a Reaper with a single blast of power. She has nothing to fear from me, and she knows it, and seeing her runes and the commonality she shares with Sinisa makes her feel more like a friend than foe, even though to her, I'm sure she sees the opposite.

"So may we?" Sungema asks.

Dazed and unsure, I glance between the three women. "May you what?"

"May we aid you?"

My first instinct is that it sounds like a trap. But then I look to my guardsmen, to the sorry states they're in, and I'm not so sure Sungema and her friends need to trap us if they wanted to harm us in some way. Half of my guard will die within the hour if their wounds are not treated with the proper herbs. Some may die still. And the longer we stand here, the more confused I am by why I'm being allowed to remain. My father-crow should've taken me back to the underrealm by now, the second Sungema even appeared, let alone the moment she suggested we work together and I left her unharmed and didn't disagree.

"What aid can you provide us?" I ask finally, hoping that, even if my father-crow does take me away, at least maybe my men can find the care they need.

"You said you needed a healer. Miengha is one."

Sungema gestures to the Ghamayan woman. Bow around her shoulder, she steps forward slowly. She's cautious about removing the satchel slung over her other shoulder, careful still as she pulls out three small glass jars and holds them up for me to see.

I know nothing of healer's medicine, but my men don't have much choice but to trust her. With no other real choice, I nod, inviting her closer.

Miengha sets about her work grinding herbs with oils and applying them to each sting. There are many, so it takes a while for her to attend to everyone, but she's surprisingly quicker than I expected. As she works, the darkness under her eyes seems to fade, and whatever anguish she was experiencing diminished, at least as long as she is distracted.

She makes a tonic next, one that's milky white and has a flowery aroma that I can't place. Each guard is given a small sip and told to chew on a leaf she provides them next.

As the poultices set, pulling the toxins from the bloodstream, I venture toward Sungema.

"Where is Sinisa?" I ask, trying to sound casual. "Last I saw her, she was with you."

Sungema tosses her hand. "She seeks another, but will return to us once she is finished. Where, might I ask, is the king of Oakfall headed today?"

From where he sits against the base of an oak tree, Borgravid glances warily in my direction. I, too, worry about why she's asking. Though she is not *my* enemy, she doesn't know it. We are on opposing sides of this feud, and therefore we have no real reason to trust each other, nor to answer each other honestly.

Still, despite my apprehension, I decide I have no real reason to lie to her either.

"We're headed to the Howling Isle."

She pins her golden, glowing eyes on me, and I become entranced. Trapped. Stuck.

Finally, my nervous gaze pulls away only to fall to my father-crow. He's perched above us, feathers ruffling, head twitching with every word that's spoken between us, like he's just waiting for me to say something truly incriminating. I worry that I already have.

"You fear him," Sungema says.

"What?" I say blinking, turning back to her. "No, I don't. I—He's a crow."

"Not only a crow though, but you already know that."

My eyes find hers, wide and unblinking. The golden rays burn into me.

"You should not fear him. Veltuur has little hold over him while he is in Tayaraan. He acts on his own behalf, as do all the crows when in the mortal realm, and he has no intention of stopping you on your quest."

A scowl folds over me. "Wait. Do you mean that you can...you know what he's thinking?"

She looks up to my father-crow, stares at him like they're deep in conversation. "Yes, I can understand him. It is the way of the Altúyur."

Though my gaze flits up to him, it is brief before I instead look to my hands. "So...he knows the real reason why I'm going to the Howling Isle?"

A sharp, humorless laugh. "He does. He does not agree with your desire to change the Law of Mother's Love, but he has enjoyed watching you grow into the crown. He feared you wouldn't be able to, that the burdens would be too great for your delicate heart. But now he sees that your compassion is fierce; it is not a weakness. He says that he has never been prouder of you."

Tears well in my eyes. The more that they fall to my hands, the more I quiver. All this time—which I suppose really hasn't been very long since I've only been on this quest for a matter of days, but I guess somehow, somewhere deep inside me, I've known that a lifelong quest of mine has been to obtain the approval of my former father. Upon his death—upon his *murder*—I remember feeling like I could've been a better king than him, that we could've been a better family if he had just let us. I knew that I wanted his approval, but that I would never get it. But now? It makes no sense for someone who barely even remembers him, but having his approval now means more to me than I can even fathom.

"He also knows that the feather ceremony does not take place on the Howling Isle, so he is not sure how you will rewrite the Law of Mother's Love by traveling all that way."

A faint, crooked smile springs up my cheek. Lying any longer seems futile, like wasted energy. "I go because I seek the satyr."

"How fortuitous. We seek the same creature," she says coldly, but there's something in her voice that's different than the usual chill of her tone. Something darker. Something more frightening. "What are your intentions with the satyr once you arrive?"

Ahh. She's defensive. Of course. She is still unsure if I can be trusted, and I don't blame her.

"I... Well, my plan is... I need to..."

Despite everything Sungema has said about my father-crow, I'm still not sure that I should be that open in front of him. If Veltuur found out I was trying to free the Divine Lorik, well, let's just say I'd learn a whole new meaning to the word *enraged*.

"Spit it out already," Miengha growls. "Do you plan to kill the satyr, or have you finally joined us in our cause?"

My wide eyes flit to the crow in the branches. It, too, awaits my answer.

"You do not wish to say because of your father's presence," Sungema says. "And that is answer enough. We shall travel together then. Perhaps between all of us, someone will be brave enough to face him."

Borgravid snorts. "Did you see the way the king threw himself into the swarms of wasps to protect us? I'd say he's already proven his bravery."

A sliver of a smile curls Sungema's lips, like a crescent moon in the night sky. "Perhaps, but only the satyr will be able to decide who is worthy. Besides, I imagine even as the king protected you all, he feared he wouldn't succeed. It will take true bravery to free the Divine Lorik." She glances over my shoulder to Miengha, a silent appraisal on her progress. The healer nods, and Sungema continues. "Come, then. The poultices have sat long enough. We must continue on our paths. Will you join us?"

I examine the guardsmen among us. The swelling of Borgravid's hand is already dwindling. The ashen color of death that had sheathed itself over another guard is brightening. Of those whom Miengha has treated, all seem ready to be back on their feet, even eager to be, especially if it means following the Divine Sungema herself. I forget how much the mortals worship the Altúyur. Seeing her now in the flesh is likely a beacon of hope for them, a calling. Even if I decided to set out on our own, it's likely many of my remaining guard will still choose to follow her instead.

"We will," I say at last. "Our chances of success increase with numbers."

Sungema bows gracefully. Though it is true that allying ourselves with one of the Divine Altúyur gives us an advantage when facing the satyr, I'd be lying if I said that was the deciding factor.

On top of being worried to lose any more of my guardsmen,

Sungema said Sinisa would return to them once she was finished with her current task, and I want to be there when she does to set things right, to make her understand that I *am* grateful for everything she's done for me, and to make sure she knows that I know she is a good friend.

"Gather your belongings and the horses we can find," I shout to the men. They scatter at my command. "We set out for Illistead Harbor before nightfall."

17

QUEEN OF GHAMAYA

SINISA

We spend the next few hours burying Avalanche in the snow, and I might've found the irony in that at one point in time, but I'm too drained now, too emotionally beaten to be able to summon whatever's left of my morbid sense of humor. This mountain shouldn't be Avalanche's final resting place. Come the next rise of the sun, the wolves or a mountain lion will come and dig him up to feast on his flesh until nothing is left but bones. But burying him now was the least we could do for him, for him and Miengha both.

"You know you have to leave me now, right?" Aulow asks, taking a seat on a nearby, snow-covered rock.

I glare at her. "We've already had this conversation. If I wasn't going to leave you before, I'm certainly not doing it now."

"You have no choice. Look at us. Look at where we are." Aulow scoops her arms out wide. "We've fallen off the path. We have no way of knowing where we are, or how to get back to where we were."

"Not to mention," Iracara adds. "The path we were trekking was a bit dangerous, don't you think?"

Scowling, I chew on my lip and examine the area around us. We are perfectly wedged between an impossible climb up ice and another deadly drop. There is no path, only deep snow and jagged cliffs.

I tilt my head back, stare up at the ledge where they fell. It's too far a way to climb, but even though we are accompanied by someone with wings, Iracara is right; the path we'd taken was leading us nowhere but peril.

The only way out is in flight, and Iracara can carry only one of us at a time.

"Fine," I say, and with a bounce of my shoulder, I begin shrugging my cloak off. "Take this then."

Aulow puts her hand up. "No. I'll be all right."

"It's freezing," I roar. "Just take it."

"No," she says again, gentle, but firm. "You need it just as much as I do. Iracara will be back soon. Until then, I'll stay dry. I'll talk to Bels and the sound of her voice will keep me warm."

I'm still glaring at her, prepared to take my stand on this, when I feel Iracara tugging my cloak back over my shoulders.

"She's right, you know. It'll be even colder in the higher altitudes. Keep your cloak. I will be as swift as I can to make sure Aulow isn't left here for too long."

Because I know they're both right, and because just that little bit of exposure to the cold has already seeped into my bones, I don't argue. The sooner we can get this over with, the sooner Iracara can return for Aulow and bring her to safety.

"Are you sure you'll be able to find her again?"

Iracara looks offended. "Of course! You think one of the Divine Altúyur has difficulty with directions? Besides. She stands out like fire up here in these peaks. I'll be able to find her."

We leave Aulow where she is with little discussion more about it. As we soar high, I keep looking down at her, watching as long as I can until her red curls become so distant that they finally blend in with the landscape of white and gray. I just hope Iracara is right, that he has some keen ability to navigate all of this because the more we climb, the more it all starts to look the same to me.

To my surprise, it doesn't take us long to reach the top.

"You're sure you're all right to do this alone?" he asks, releasing me onto the stone bridge that crosses to the citadel. "I'll be back with Aulow in half a day at most. We could accompany you."

I stare down the bridge that stretches forever, take note of the decorative archways piled with snow that have stood the test of time.

As a young girl, though my father traveled here on a few occasions, he never brought his family with him. The journey was too dangerous, as I can now attest. But he always returned with enchanting stories of the gothic city steeped in snow, and I'd sit at the hearth wondering what it would be like to be that high in the sky.

Though, as a Reaper I was sent to the Ghamayan Citadel on a few occasions, I'd never set foot on the Bridge of Evermore. I fazed inside the stone walls, beyond the gates, and left the same way I'd come.

Since my trips here had been limited, I'm not as familiar with the layout of the city as I wish I was for what lies ahead. Regardless, embarking on this part of the journey on my own is actually preferable. A private reunion. Just me and my mother.

"I'll be fine. Sungema's instructions were clear. If I can't find the queen or if I come across any issues, I'll find you both and we can do this together."

His face twists like he's about to protest.

"Go. Return to Aulow before she freezes to death."

With a dutiful nod, Iracara readies his wings and says to me before launching into the sky, "Travel safely. We'll find you in half a day."

Though the Bridge of Evermore is far less populated than it was during Sungema's retelling of history, Iracara draws the attention of the few people who were coming and going. I leave them with their heads tilted up to the gray sky, whispers of wonderment on their lips, before they can turn to me with their questions.

Wrapping the furs tighter around my shoulders, I trek across the Bridge of Evermore, the pillars of the Altúyur coming into view up ahead through the misty fog. All but one of them, that is. Just as I'd seen in drawings and books as a child, there are only eight pillars that guard the Ghamayan Citadel: Owlena, Pecolock, Sungema, Macawna, Lorik, Quetzi, Iracara, and Dovenia. It's no wonder no one has ever wondered about the stub of the ninth pillar though, for even as I look down over the edge of the bridge, the bottom of the chasm is obscured by the densest haze I've ever seen. It's like the bridge towers over the clouds, the haze having settled at the bottom of the chasm like a sinking omen. I cannot see the base of any of the statues, let alone of Veltuur's, which seems to have been broken some time ago.

Once I'm on the other side of the fortress walls, my eyes scan the dark, damp paths that wind up the mountainside and my thoughts drift back to what Sungema told me about my mother's time as the king's captive; how the Deceptive Serpent imbedded a lie in her mind, one that neither I, nor my father, could break; how she has spent all this time here in Ghamaya not knowing anything about her past, just as I had spent my time in the underrealm not knowing about mine.

"I will find you, Mother," I say to no one but the crisp, mountain air. "I will find you, and I will return to you what was stolen."

By the time I climb all the way up to the castle, I'm breathless. My feet are still wet from the day's journey. My bones feel like they will never warm again. And I am weary. Fatigued. Nearly entirely spent.

And things are about to only get worse.

They have an open-gate policy, though it is customary for visitors to be invited or to announce their arrival in advance. You will have done neither.

"E-excuse me, miss?" the guard at the gate stammers as I walk through the castle entrance without so much as a nod in his direction. He fumbles with his black leather belt, an attempt to appear more official and imposing I guess, but when I don't stop, he yells louder. "Excuse me!"

I bolt. The castle blurs around me, a drafty labyrinth of stone corridors and torches.

This is where Sungema's instructions cannot fail me. I don't know the winding layout of this place. I don't know where I'll find dead ends, nor the rooms that are typically full with people who will ask questions about a girl racing through the halls, and I only have Sungema's word to guide me.

"Stop!" the guard shouts.

Around the corner, I draw the attention of two more guards. Having apparently heard the first man shout, they're a little more ready on their feet to intercept me, but still uncertain enough that I easily barrel through them. Our bodies crash to the stone floor, but I don't give up my momentum, and try desperately not to lose my bearings.

One left, then follow the hall until the third doorway on the right.

At each turn, I look for the landmarks she gave me: an iron chandelier big enough to hold a hundred candles, a room guarded on all sides by more stone sculptures of all but one of the Divine Altúyur, the wide staircase backlit by panel after panel of stained glass of every single color imaginable.

Finally, after shoving and clawing my way through what feels like every hallway in this place, the guards pawing at my cloak the entire time, I burst through the carved doors Sungema described and hope that I have finally reached the throne room.

"I need to speak to the queen!" I yell, hoping she's inside.

My throat catches at the sight of her. My mother sits atop the white throne, a gown of jewels dazzling against her body like dew. When she stands, her dark hair falls from her shoulders, cascading in waves down her taut, slender back.

It's like these mountains have frozen her in time. Though years have passed, she doesn't look a day older than the last time I saw her in our cottage on the Coast of Dreams. Everything about her— her prominent cheekbones, her honeyed eyes, hair black as coal but as soft as silk—is exactly as I remember.

The only difference now is that she is a queen.

And I have to admit, staring up at her, power and confidence radiating off her like sunshine beaming down upon me, it's a crown that suits her quite well.

Everyone quiets in the room, including the guards chasing me, as Queen Miva makes her examination of me, chin pointed out, eyes cast down.

Finally, she sniffs. "Take her away. And the next time you allow some churl off the streets this far beyond the palace walls, you'll be flogged."

"Yes, my queen."

A guard seizes either of my arms. They start dragging me back toward the giant double doors, and I'm too stunned to fight against them. My mother is exactly as I remember, cold and unrelenting, powerful, beautiful. For the first time in years, I am seeing her in the flesh, and if they succeed in pulling me out of this hall, I will never see her again.

I can't let that happen.

"Many years ago," my voice echoes as I yell across the expansive room. The guards keep pulling me, but I keep spewing words, desperate to make her stop them. "You found yourself wandering in the Kallinei Swamp and you didn't know why. You knew you belonged at the Ghamayan Citadel, but once you arrived, no one knew of you. I, alone, know the truth. I am the only one who knows how you ended up in the swamp that day!"

We reach the entryway, just moments before they're about to turn and drag me down the next corridor, when I see my mother stand from her ivory throne.

"Stop," the queen says.

We halt just outside the double doors.

The wooden heels of my mother's boots click as she makes her way down the stairs and across the walkway until she's standing over me. "Only a few know of my experience in the swamp, and I do not remember telling you."

"You didn't, M-m—" I stutter, only just catching myself before almost accidentally calling her mother. "Your Majesty."

"Then, wings tell, who are you?"

"My name is Sinisa."

"I have no use for your name," she barks. "What brings you here, girl?"

Fortunately, I've had a few days to think this through. If I tell her the real reason that I've come all this way while the others in the room listen in, she'll have no choice but to deem me deranged and send me to the dungeon.

I have to get her alone if I'm to reveal to her the past that she's forgotten.

"King Acari has sent me. I am to have a word with you in private—"

The hard edge of her eyes softens with something like curiosity. "The Reaper King? What business could the two of us possibly have?" Then she adds quickly, "Let me see his summons."

I show her my empty hands. "He...didn't send one."

Her eyebrows twitch with suspicion and I know my time is running out. Like me, my mother has never known how to summon patience. If I don't convince her that I'm harmless—useful, in fact —and soon, then she'll have me thrown out of here faster than a Reaper's touch kills.

"He is a little unorthodox," I say to her, trying to sound convincing, like I believe the lie pouring out from me as much as I want her to believe it. "As you can imagine, being a Reaper, and all. But I assure you, his message is safe with me."

"And I am to simply take your word for it? A nobody?" She leans closer, taking my chin into her hands. "Though I'll admit, there is something familiar about you."

I swallow hard. "I believe we might've met once or twice."

She stares into my eyes a moment longer, the golden-brown

pools making me sink into them like honey. When she finally releases my chin, she addresses her guards. "She is without any weapons?"

"Yes, your Majesty. We only found this on her." The man hands her my pouch.

"It is part of what I've been sent here to discuss with you, your Majesty," I say.

She ignores me and continues her line of questions to her men. "And she came alone?"

"Yes, your Majesty."

The queen crooks an eyebrow, returning her focus to me. "Very well. Release her and leave us."

The guards give her a dutiful bow and do as they are instructed, not a single question asked. My mother has always had that influence on people though. It's no surprise to me how naturally she has fit into her royal life.

As the guards close the doors behind them, the queen turns on her heels and returns to her throne. She sits down on the rigid slab, pouch still in hand, and pulls back the drawstrings.

With a peek to the contents inside, she asks, "Well, do we have matters to discuss or have you lost your tongue?"

I take a few cautious steps forward so that I don't have to shout, but I don't approach too far. I don't want to make her feel unsafe or regret her decision to allow us privacy.

"You're familiar with the last known memory tree in Tayaraan?"

"I am. King Renaudin never would shut up about what a privilege it was to oversee the conservation of it."

"Well, your Majesty, what you're holding in your hands are all that's left."

Her eyes snap up to mine. Rather than concern, distrust reflects in them, like she still thinks I'm trying to trick her.

"What happened? Where is the rest of Oakfall's prized possession?"

Swallowing hard, I caution another step. "It is not an easily believed story, your Majesty."

"And I am not an easily fooled woman. If there is truth in what you say, I will know it. So, deliver the message that you've come here to deliver."

I take a deep, steadying breath. "The mortals have believed—"

"The mortals?"

My mouth hangs open. I clear my throat and try again. "We have believed that the Divine Altúyur have been absent from the Tayaraan realm for generations. However, we've recently discovered that that's not true. A few days ago, the memory tree changed. Its branches shrunk down into two arms, its roots became two legs, and the trunk became a body. Where the memory tree once stood was now Sungema, the Divine Altúyur of Memory. I might not have believed it, if I hadn't seen it with my own eyes, but it is true."

When the queen doesn't say anything, I take it as a sign to continue.

"Sungema told us that the other Altúyur share similar fates. They have been trapped all this time, and now we have set out to free them and restore the balance they once brought to the Tayaraan realm."

Suddenly, the queen stands, her eyes as wide as disks. Her words are breathless, nearly inaudible with the wind gusting outside against the windows. "You are telling the truth."

I nod. "I am."

She takes a few more moments, eyes blinking rapidly like she is still processing it all. But even in her shock, she remains more composed than most, and when she finally fixes her attention back to me, all indications of amazement have vanished. She is resolute, solid once more.

"Then rest assured that I will do what I must to aid in the return of the Divine Altúyur. Tell King Acari that he has the aid of Ghamaya—"

"Forgive me, but that is not why I am here."

She squints at me, but when I am too slow to respond, she looks to the pouch in her hand again. "These leaves, they restore memories, do they not?"

"They do."

"And you have brought them to me because you need me to remember something I have forgotten?"

A proud and sad smile sneaks up the side of my face. She always was so quick, so clever, so intuitive. I would've loved to have grown up with her, to watch her through the doting eyes of a child who aspired to be just like her.

"Tell me," she says. "What memory will I uncover from the leaves?"

"Your Majesty, I think it would be easier to see it for yourself, rather than to have a stranger tell you—"

"You yourself said that you were not a stranger, that we had met, *once or twice*." She walks down the steps once more, gown of crystals trailing behind her. "Perhaps you do not truly know me though, for if you did, you would understand that I do not do things recklessly. I prepare. I plan. I assess."

Another small smile escapes me, and I avert my gaze to the floor. "You're right. I should've known." I take a deep breath before bringing my eyes back to hers. I want her to be able to see me when I say it. "According to Sungema, you were there when the Altúyur were imprisoned. The Divine Owlena foretold a prophecy, one in which you would have a fated daughter who would free the Altúyur from their chains. She gifted you an item that would keep you alive until you fulfilled your destiny. A pendant."

Reflexively, her hand floats up to the large, blue gem hanging around her neck. She traces a finger over the metal that twists around it.

"I never could bring myself to get rid of this thing. It was all I had from whatever life came before the one I live now. Though I did not know the reason, I knew this pendant was important somehow. I thought it was just a sentimental trinket from my past, something that one day someone would see and recognize and be able to tell me who I was and where I came from. I suppose all this time, I've been waiting for you."

Heat rises to my cheeks and I clench my jaw tight. I don't know what to say. I don't know what she's thinking. I'm too afraid that anything I could do might ruin whatever hope for a relationship with her I have.

She releases the pendant, letting it rest once more between her bosom, and reaches her hand out to me instead.

"I see it now, the reason you looked so familiar. It's your eyes. They are the same crystal blue shade as the man who was with me in the swamp."

I barely register that she called my eyes blue when they are gray because I'm too busy thinking about my father's and mother's final moments together. His wife lost all memory of him, right before his eyes. She was tricked into believing that she was some queen of Ghamaya, and despite trying to convince her otherwise, he could do nothing but let her go so that he could venture to Pyrethi Tower, find the Mirror of Truth, and hopefully, restore his wife and family once again.

"Arik," I croak. "His name was Arik."

Thoughtfully, she nods. "Yes, I remember. A woman does not forget the name of the man who insisted they were married, the man who roared and roared as I ran away from him toward the life I believed to be mine in Ghamaya." She smiles, a sad, bitter thing. "It's not just your eyes though, and it's not just him I see in you. There is me as well. You are the daughter that you said Owlena thought I would have," she says it like a statement, but I sense her question still.

"I am."

"Why have you not come for me sooner?" There is no hurt in her voice, no accusation. Her brilliant mind simply seeks to understand the intricacies of it all.

"I believed you were dead. Miva was not your name when I knew you, so I had no way of knowing that you'd become...a queen."

Her scrutinizing gaze never wavers. She is steel and stone and ice. She is unbreakable, and I keep waiting for her to disbelieve me, but she does not. Perhaps fate protects this moment, as well, because she has every reason to doubt me, a nobody in her eyes. And yet, she doesn't. It's like everything I tell her fills in a blank space of the story of her life, the one she's likely been trying to fill since the day she fled the swamp.

After a long stretch of painful quiet, she raises her chin high, every ounce the regal queen she has become.

"You need the pendant from me to finish freeing the Altúyur."

I nod.

"Then I have decided. Forgive me, I know what a monster this will make me appear to you, but I shall not take the memory tree leaves. I do not need them to do what needs to be done."

"But why?"

Something like a blade twists through me. Before I became a Reaper, all I wanted was to see my father and be held by my mother. If she doesn't take the memory tree leaves, then it's like my mother never existed, and I will never get that moment with her.

"You said the pendant has kept me alive all these years, until I can fulfill my destiny of gifting it to you. You said that for generations the Altúyur have been missing, which means that I am lifetimes old. It seems that once I bestow the pendant to you, my life will no longer have protection. I believe I will die."

I frown. "Die? No, y-you wouldn't. That can't be…"

No matter how much I deny it though, what she's saying makes frightening sense. I do not know what will happen to a person who has lived for centuries once the magic keeping them alive is removed.

She reaches out, cups my cheek with the softness of her hand. "I do not lament such an end. If it is my destiny to aid you in returning the Divine Altúyur to Tayaraan, then it is a good destiny to have. But I would like to do so as I am, with an untarnished memory."

"Your memory *is* tarnished," I grit out. "You encountered the Deceptive Serpent while you were in Kallinei Swamp. He took every memory you ever had so that you would believe a lie he'd spun."

She holds up her hand. "It does not matter to me what was a lie then when the life I live now is not one. I have a family now, here. I have three sons and a kingdom of people who love me. I would like to say goodbye to *that* life. I'm sorry for the pain that may cause you, but that is *my* choice."

Queen Miva brings her hands to the back of her neck, behind the heavy, dark waves of hair that fall there.

"No," I say, grasping her wrists and holding them in place. Tears sting my eyes. "I just found you. I can't lose you again."

Queen Miva pauses, turning reflective. "Then you shan't."

Abruptly, she spins away, gown billowing behind her. She strides to a table with parchment and ink, grabs a feather, and starts scrawling.

"What are you doing?" I ask her, daring a glance over her shoulder.

"I am detailing what occurred here today, so that none shall blame you for my demise."

It's not a thought that had occurred to me until she mentions it. I glance over my shoulder back toward the door, wondering what would've happened if the guards had returned to find their queen dead and myself standing over her.

"Guards!" she yells.

They enter so quickly they almost tear the doors down. But the queen eases their fears with a simple beckon of her hand.

"You shall bear witness," she tells them. "To what is about to happen."

Meanwhile, my head is spinning. It feels like I've been hurled into the center of a cyclone and I'm being thrown about every which way. What did she mean I wouldn't lose her? What does she want them to bear witness to?

We all stand in silence as Queen Miva finishes her letter.

"There," she says, rolling the parchment up and sealing it with wax. She hands it to one of her guardsmen. "This document officially announces Sinisa as my blood, and therefore part of the royal family."

The guards exchange a quick look of confusion.

"Rest assured, upon my death, it will still be Sokkolf on the throne. I simply need to ensure that Sinisa will be taken care of, and that she will be welcomed into the family by her siblings."

"Your Majesty, you speak of your death like it is imminent. Do you fear your life is in danger?" The guard closest to her, the one with the scroll in hand, glares at me.

"I fear nothing. What I do now is of my own accord, in the name of Ghamaya and Tayaraan as a whole."

Turning her back on her guards, she reaches up to untie her pendant again. My breath catches as she pulls it away from her chest and walks toward me with it extended like a gift.

My voice cracks. "I won't take it."

"You must, Sinisa. If what you say is true, and I know it to be, then this is a moment in history that has been impending for a long while. Everything has led us both here to this moment. Every decision either of us has made, every loss we've ever endured, they only matter because of what happens now."

I think of Hayliel then. Of Dethoc, and Rory, and Avalanche. Of the man I killed and became a Reaper for, then the young girl I saved by renouncing my crow. I think of Acari and the path he is on, of my father and the journey he never returned from. All of them. Every way our lives entangled themselves into each other's and the moments our paths parted. I can never do any of it over again, but if I don't fulfill my fate, then it will all have been for nothing.

The pendant spins from its chain, suspended before me and dazzling in the light from the windows. I shake my head, but Queen Miva holds it out firm.

"You will not lose me," she says. "Because you will have your brothers. They are lovable boys, tender and smart. They are just and curious. They are strong. You will like them, and since you will see me in them, you will learn to love them. And in so doing, you shall never lose me. Not ever again."

With tears streaming down my cheeks, I reach out. My hand

hovers around the pendant for a second before I finally muster the courage to wrap my fingers around the gemstone. My mother releases the chain.

I tuck the pendant close as I watch her fade away. Her skin turning ashen before hollowing, the rich darkness of her hair turning as white as the mountains outside. She staggers forward, and I catch her in my arms before we collide to the floor. She shrinks inside my grasp, skin withering away like a rotting apple, until she is nothing but black flesh, and then bone, and then ash.

18

THOSE WHO ARE BRAVE

ACARI

"This is as far as I go," the sailor shouts back at us.

I peek out up ahead expecting to find the white beach resting just beneath us. Instead, it floats ahead in the distance, way farther away than I thought it would be.

"Are you suggesting we swim?" I ask the sailor, face contorted with fear.

"Apologies, my king. But please, do not make me go any closer. The Howling Isle is cursed. Not a boat that docks ever leaves. Not a soul who sets foot there ever finds their way off the island again."

Miengha comes up behind us and pats the trembling man on the back. "That's what they said about the neko cave and Pyrethi Tower, but Sinisa survived both."

"Who's Sinisa?" the man asks.

"Sinisa isn't here," I remind her, the ache in my chest at the mention of her name making my words sharper than I intend.

Miengha only shrugs. Then, with a sly smile, she hops up onto the wooden banister, swings her legs over the side, and leaps off the edge of the ship.

I race to the ledge to look over just as she splashes into the waters down below. The waves crash into the side of the boat, mist spraying the base and making it nearly impossible to see anything else but churning waters. The sailor, too, stares over with me, and when we see no sign of Miengha, we share a horrified look.

"Water's fine," she finally calls out, drawing my attention back to her just as she starts propelling her arms. "Let's go! The satyr awaits."

Hesitantly, I signal to my men to follow. A few of them are forced to stay aboard as they are not strong swimmers, but most jump without hesitation. Sungema takes to the sky, along with my father-crow. Borgravid and I are the last to leave.

"You do not need to sail any closer," Borgravid tells the man. "But we ask that you return every day to this very spot to retrieve us, should we need it."

"And what if you don't need it? What if they satyr gets you first?"

"A week," is Borgravid's response. "Give us one week before you give up."

As I stare down into the bottomless, churning waters, I grow wary myself. The ocean, the satyr, there seems to be many dangers lurking between us and freeing Lorik.

"Maybe we shouldn't—"

Borgravid's hand collides into my back before I can finish expressing my doubt, and I plummet.

The water is frigid, sucking the breath away from me on impact. I bob back to the surface, choking and gasping, but I have no other choice now but to swim. And swim I do. Anything to put distance between me and the ship that seems like it could be the death of me if I catch the wrong wave.

I wrack my sweeping arms through the blue waters, ignoring the sight of my father-crow flying high overhead, as dry as a desert. By the time I reach the sandy shore, my muscles are throbbing. My teeth chatter as the sun starts to make its descent.

We pull ourselves out of the ocean, sopping and heavy. To start our exploration of the island now would surely mean death. Nightfall will soon bring out every dangerous creature that dwells here, at least, that is the consensus. My men whisper among themselves about how death will find us regardless, while the rest of us set about fixing our camp.

Miengha returns from the jungle an hour later with a collection of twigs and branches just in time for the sun to blink out of view. Darkness surrounds the men like a horde of deadly scorpions. They twitch and jump at the slightest noise, exchanging horror stories in hushed whispers among themselves.

As Miengha arranges the wood, she stares over at them. "I've heard that the satyr only hunts those who truly fear it. I'm told fear turns the flesh into a delicatessen. The satyr can smell it on us all, and he will strike only those who smell juiciest."

The taunt lands its mark, and the men immediately clamp their mouths closed. But unlike me, they fail to see the smirk Miengha's wearing when she returns her attention to the logs.

"Do you need help?" I ask her.

She lays a bundle of moss on a thin strip of tree bark, not bothering to look up at me. "And do you know much about making a fire, King Acari?"

Wincing, I cast my gaze across the ocean instead, to the black sky that has become undistinguishable from the even darker waters.

"I didn't think so. Even if you did, it would be unwise to let you near this perfectly good lumber, lest you sap what little life remains inside it."

Coming from anyone else, I'd think her words were meant to be an insult. But the sly tilt of her lips says otherwise. My hands hang heavy at my sides. I flex and release my fingers, trying to feel the power that's in there, but finding nothing but grimy skin. Then I look to her hands, the ones covered in runes as bright as a clear blue sky, matching her eyes.

"Sinisa has those runes too," I mutter. "Hers are lavender though. Do they mean what I think they mean?"

She levels me a flat look. "They mean we are stronger than you."

Her answer leaves me perplexed and far less certain of my

previous deduction than I am now, but before I can question her again, a spark flies from the rocks she's banging together. The moss catches beneath the logs, a small flame igniting.

Belsante walks over to us then, crossing her arms as she watches Miengha. "Give the king a rest, will you?"

Miengha frowns, standing. "I don't like Reapers. What can I say?"

"You realize how hypocritical that makes you, right?" Belsante asks.

The Ghamayan shrugs, leaving us without another word.

"Why does that make her a hypocrite?" I ask, thinking again about the runes that she shares with Sinisa and hoping that if Miengha wouldn't tell me the truth, that Belsante will. Before today, Sinisa was the only person I'd ever seen with them. She's also the only person I know of who was once a Reaper but is now something else. "Those runes on her hands...they mean Miengha used to be a Reaper too, don't they?"

A knowing, enchanting smile blooms between Belsante's full cheeks. I want to ask her how it's possible. The only Reaper I've ever heard of escaping was Sinisa. Even Nerul seems to only have known of her. How is it possible that both of them have escaped, that they bare the same markings, possibly even the same powers?

"Sleep well, my king," Belsante says, spinning on her heels. Her hips sway as she walks, voice low as she adds over her shoulder, "Tomorrow we face the satyr and we will all need our rest."

The next morning, I arise to the bloodcurdling cries of someone off in the distance.

I clamber to my feet, the rest of the dozen or so people who had been sleeping doing the same, as we stare out into the jungle, to where the screams become choking gasps and sputters. Whoever it is, they're not far, close enough to rattle the bones of everyone at the camp and make them realize just how easily it could've been any one of them.

As the cries come to a guttural halt, echoes rustling throughout the tropical trees, the only comfort I find is in knowing that I could never suffer such a fate. If the satyr were to pluck me from the group in the middle of the night, *it* would be the one howling in agony as my dark magic coursed through it and sent it on its way to the underrealm.

There's little comfort to be found from that thought though. I can't let the satyr die, especially not at my own hands. It would ruin every chance I have at changing the way people view my sister, and others like her. I need the satyr—need Lorik—to help me change the Law of Mother's Love. If we are to defeat the creature, if we are to free the Divine Lorik from his prison inside it, then we'll have to do so without killing him, and preferably without losing any more lives.

Suddenly aware that I don't know who the satyr has killed, I scan the faces around me. I become frantic, searching for the only one I care for among them. When I find Borgravid up ahead, hands planted firmly on either hip, my chest collapses with relief. It's not that I want any of them to die, but I'd feel his loss more than any. Though I don't remember my upbringing with him and therefore should have no ties stronger to him than anyone else I've met or re-met over the past few days, there is an intrinsic bond of time between us, one that I've felt since the moment he found me in the bathing house with my father's corpse.

I go to him, catching my breath and finally wiping the sleep from my eyes. "What happened?"

He leans toward me but doesn't take his eyes off the jungle. "The Divine Sungema sent scouts out this morning. From the sound of it, one of them located the satyr. Whether it was unintentional or not, their dying cry just might—"

Shaking my head violently, I cut him off. "Sungema did what?"

Twisting back around toward the fire, I spot the Altúyur talking with another group of men—*my* men. I feel the injustice of it, the direct defiance and challenge of my authority, and though I'm not one to embrace confrontation, as king I cannot let this go unchecked. Her actions just got one of my men killed.

I stride across the camp to meet her, fists clenched as solid as rocks.

When I finally reach her, she either ignores me because she thinks so little of me, or she is so immersed in the conversation— what sounds like her next set of orders—that she really is oblivious to my presence. Something tells me that the Altúyur, even one as seemingly self-invested as her, have an acute sense of awareness, something akin to a predator lurking in the night.

"What do you think you're doing?" I snap, finally done being ignored.

Her sleek eyebrows raise. "Finding the satyr."

"No, I mean—you can't just command my guardsmen. They don't serve you; they serve me."

She cocks her head, flames sparking behind her golden irises. "They *serve* their Altúyur. But rest assured, I sent only those who volunteered to be of use. Come. It appears one has been successful. We should follow his cries immediately, before the satyr changes course."

I want to argue that we do the opposite, but the instinct is so mammalian and foolhardy that I bite my tongue. The only reason I want to contend with her is because I feel challenged, threatened, but we have already agreed to work together. Not to mention, what she says is true. We now know where the satyr is, and the sooner we find and free Lorik from him, the sooner we can part paths.

With a begrudging sigh, I call over my shoulder. "Captain Borgravid, ready the men! We set out for the satyr now."

"You heard the king!" Borgravid shouts. "Grab your shields! Make sure your armor is intact! We leave now!" As Borgravid directs the other guards, he crosses the camp, making his way to stand beside me. "And what is the plan?"

Miengha and Belsante join us as well, as Sungema reaches up

to tuck the blue and orange stripes of hair behind her dark ears. "The plan is to free the Divine Lorik."

Borgravid bows his head. "Forgive me, but that is no plan. It is a goal. We need an actual plan, a strategy for how we will find the beast, what we'll do when we spot him, and how we will make it out of this alive."

This time, it's Belsante that speaks. "Sinisa said all she had to do to free the Divine Iracara was perform an act of compassion in front of him. Sungema was restored when—"

"When the Divine Iracara ate the memory leaves and reclaimed a memory that had been forgotten. Yes, I know, I was there. We still need a—"

"Then it stands to reason," Belsante continues. "The Divine Lorik must witness an act of bravery. All we must do is confront him, show him we are fearless, and he will be freed."

"Fearless," Borgravid barks out a humorless laugh. "Have you seen the men I just readied? They're terrified. There isn't a brave bone among them."

Sungema straightens. "They have nothing to fear but fear itself. Fear will only get us all killed. I suggest you control yours and hope your men will do the same."

Without another word, her wings unfold. She takes to the sky in a blustering gust of sand. The four of us stand there, eyes shielded, utterly speechless as she ascends overhead. My guards see her take flight as well. With her trajectory headed toward the jungle, they jump to action, ready to follow the Divine Sungema to their deaths.

"This is madness," Borgravid growls, sputtering sand from his lips. "These men will die if they chase after her and the satyr right now. No mortal human knows fearless bravery. It's impossible."

"Then," Belsante mutters. "Divine Owlena, protect our fates."

She weaves into the group of guards, and although I agree with Borgravid, I know that my own options are limited. I am no mortal, so perhaps I'll be able to do what must be done, and perhaps I'll be able to do it before anyone else has to die.

I set after Belsante, Sungema, and the others, intent on joining the guards at the front of the group, but Borgravid's hand catches my shoulder.

"I won't see my king on the frontlines," he says quietly, firmly.

"I'll be fine. Just because I'm king, doesn't mean I can't—"

"If the satyr touches you, it dies. Not just the satyr, but the Divine Lorik himself. Tayaraan cannot afford to lose him. *You* cannot afford to lose him. The people would be trapped in fear forever and humanity might never let people like your sister exist in peace if that were to happen. You must keep your distance and let the men do what they are here to do."

Though my mouth opens to protest, I can't find a compelling enough reason to argue. Despite wanting to help, despite wanting to prove to my guard that I won't leave them to do the dirty work for me, it's too risky for me to lead them on this mission, even if I am immortal and possibly the only one who can see it through.

I hang my head instead, glaring at the dirt beneath my toes.

"You proved your loyalty when the whisper wasps attacked. Now let them prove theirs."

When my eyes drift back to his, I see the fierceness in them, the loyalty and devotion. Silently, I nod, agreeing that I will do my best to allow my men to serve me.

By the time we join the rest of our party, they're already entering the jungle. They comb between the bases of the tall, exotic trees and plants with leaves as wide as hay bales and flowers as bright as Sungema's eyes.

The overgrowth is so immense that I have to tuck my hands under my arms just to keep the foliage protected from me. Ahead of me, Borgravid does what he can to hold back the branches, but I still duck and dodge every limb and leaf that he misses. Any unwarranted deaths will summon the Wraiths, and I have no intention of alerting the underrealm of my presence here.

We quickly realize how futile our efforts are though. This jungle is far denser than the forests of Oakfall. Almost everywhere we step, branches are intertwined. Where they aren't, vines drape across them instead, like they're desperate to wrap the jungle in an everlasting embrace.

Eventually, Borgravid unclips his cape and tosses it over my head.

We keep trekking, through the ficus, anthurium, and philoden-dron—as Miengha points out—the jungle swallowing us in its expansive tapestry of foliage. For hours, we hike, even though the screams we heard while at camp seemed like they were so near.

Half the day has past by the time we finally reach a clearing. The grass lies flat here, trampled beneath the hooves of a large beast. At first glance, it appears like a bed of red flowers have bloomed here, their petals glistening in the light that shines through the trees. But at closer inspection, we realize with horror that we are not walking through a bed of flowers, but the carnal spray of viscera.

At the center of the clearing, lays a body, or at least what remains of one. The guardsmen fall silent as Borgravid examines what remains of the poor man's torso and head.

As quiet as a leaf falling from a tree, Sungema floats down from where she soared above the trees and lands softly beside him. "The satyr has not gone far. He heads west. We must continue before he reaches the mountain and gains an advantage that would only cost more lives."

With a dutiful nod, Borgravid rises. I'm surprised by his response. I would've thought he'd fight her about leaving one of his men behind like this. But I also forget the hold that the Divine Altúyur have over the people of Tayaraan, and the loyalty bred into his bones. He made his case back on the beach, but now, here, in the middle of the jungle, hot on the satyr's trail, he is a soldier. There is no time for second-guessing commands, and Sungema made that apparent.

She returns to her element above the treetops and Borgravid starts to lead the others west.

"We can't leave him here like this," one of the other men insists, apparently less a soldier than he is. "We should light a pyre at least—"

Borgravid curls his hands into fists. "The satyr is our priority. We leave him for now."

"But, the other animals, they'll come for him."

"I said we leave him. That's an order!" His roar echoes across the silent rainforest, scaring the birds and whatever other critters have managed to call this place their home.

But his isn't the only sound to disturb the jungle.

A bone-chilling roar rattles the very earth beneath our feet. I glance nervously to the other guardsmen, fear present in all of our faces now. Long after the roar fades, the earth continues to pound, a rhythmic beat that sounds like the drumming tune of our impending deaths.

"It comes," shouts Sungema from above. "The satyr comes! Be ready!"

Hooves beat against the earth, growing louder, faster, shaking the very knees beneath me. The guards do their best to stand ready, but the tremors tear through them as well, making them unsteady on their feet, as if they wouldn't have been already. The stringent stench of urine wafts through the air but none of us tear our eyes away from the satyr's impending approach to find out who among us have lost control of our bowels in the face of death.

A claw strikes through the trees, sharp and stained crimson. The guardsmen scream. Terror fills the air as the beast's horned head appears next. Its red eyes scan us, hungry and deranged, like it hasn't eaten in decades, like the man it plucked from us earlier wasn't anything but a mere snack to wet its palette.

The satyr's chest heaves as it takes in the scent of the soon-to-be-dead, the meal laid out before it.

It throws its head back again and bellows.

Chaos ensues. The men scatter, some diving deeper into the jungle while others head back toward the beach, the only landmark and beacon of hope that they have. I am the only one to remain where I am, utterly frozen by the menacing nature of this horrifying, divine creature.

In Sungema's presence, I felt my insignificance, sure, but nothing like how I feel it now. Much like Veltuur, the Divine Lorik —the satyr—exudes raw power. My neck cranes back to stare up at the creature towering over us, at the sharp teeth that jut from its jaw and the black claws readied at his fingers. His breath seeps through Borgravid's cloak, hot and putrid, and suddenly I can't even fathom what it would take for anyone to face this creature without an ounce of fear in their heart, immortal or not, Reaper or not. The way its lip curls back, the way its tongue flicks out at the sight of the men who dart for their lives, makes my knees feel like they're going to suddenly give out.

But I hold them in tight. I don't know what it will take to face this beast without fear, but I know giving in now won't do. I have to be strong, if not for myself or my men, then for the mission I set out upon, for Gem and all the others like her.

Though my guards have scattered, none of them get very far before the satyr takes his first strike. It's like seeing them dash about, aimless and frenzied, ignites the predator in his wild eyes. The creature cranks a lanky arm behind him, one as long as two carriages parked front to back, and I just barely have enough time to duck before he swipes it through the clearing. His talons, sharp as steel, cut through leather and iron and flesh like they are just as easy to slice through as water or air.

With a single swipe of his hand, he tears through three of the guards, and I understand why he's left the blade at his hip ignored. My men become limbs and ribbons, their agonizing cries churning the contents of my stomach and riling the rest of the jungle.

"Get the king to safety!" Borgravid shouts over his shoulder.

He raises his shield just in time for another of the satyr's mighty swings. The shield shatters. Borgravid cries out, one of the claws slicing clean through his belly as he's sent flying through the trees.

"No!" I shout, scrambling to my feet and bolting.

But in slow-motion, I watch his spine slam into a thick tree trunk sideways, see his limbs flail backward, practically wrapping around it, before he drops to the forest floor, utterly still. Even from this distance, the blood is bright and visible from where he lands in the foliage.

"No!" I cry again.

Only this time, when I thrash forward, my legs don't seem to be working. They slip and slide beneath me, vines and something else tangling themselves around my feet.

Miengha catches my arm before I fall into the viscera and pulls me in the opposite direction.

"This way," she says, pulling me deeper into the jungle, farther away from Borgravid.

My most trusted guardsmen.

My friend.

Gone.

I trip over fallen trees and vines, trying to fight against Miengha, trying to return to the man I'm told that I've known since my birth, to the man who believed me when I first returned to Oakfall as a new Reaper, the man who has helped me on every step of my path. He didn't deserve such a brutal death. He wouldn't have even died if I hadn't been the one to convince him I needed to come here.

But despite Miengha's leather gloves—or perhaps even because of them—our hands do not slip apart, and I cannot break away from her.

"We have to go back for them!" I shout.

"No, we don't. The dead are dead, and we can't do anything about it."

She pulls me harder, fingers gripping my wrist so tightly that I start to lose the feeling in my hand. I glance over my shoulder to the screams behind us just as the Reapers arrive. They pillage what's left of the souls, making sure to keep their distance from the satyr as best as they can. Even though my willingness to admit Miengha was right is buried beneath a mound of guilt and grief, I know that tearing me away from there was the only option she had, the only option I could've lived with. If I had been seen, if anyone knew that I was working with Sungema or people like Miengha, Veltuur would summon me back in an instant. He still might, for all I know. I don't know how closely he pays attention to all the deaths every Reaper is responsible for, but if he notices these, he might realize that a group of Oakfall's guards have just fallen on the Howling Isle, the same place I had my father-crow tell him I was heading.

Worry sets in. There's nothing I can do now but run.

When I turn back around and stop fighting Miengha to run alongside her, I notice Belsante and another guard have joined us.

"Where are we going?" I ask no one in particular, trying to swallow the bubbling abyss of grief welling inside my chest.

"Wherever *she* is taking us," calls Miengha as she nods to the sky.

My eyes flit upward, Sungema flying high above the trees and leading the way. It's a small comfort to know that she is still with us, and that she at least has an aerial view of this place, and therefore some idea of where we might find safety. From down here, we can't see anything through the thick underbrush.

Hours go by, but eventually, we reach the northern side of the Howling Isle. Sunset already approaches, but still the cries of the men we left behind carry across the land like curses cast out to condemn us all.

Having already landed, Sungema awaits us on the beach. We jog to her, limbs heavy, lungs heaving, and hearts broken. Our first attempt to face the satyr was a disaster. Worse than a disaster. Lives were lost in vain because those of us who survived weren't able to fulfill our quest for them. We just ran. Even knowing what we know about how to free the Divine Lorik, and we still ran.

"None of those men showed bravery," Sungema says snappishly. It's the most emotion I've ever seen from her, and even still, her chin is lifted, her brow undisturbed by any scowl I might've expected to find. "None of them have conquered fear."

She carries herself like the cold mountains of Ghamaya and for the first time since meeting Veltuur, I can finally understand why he had her trapped. We just lost friends, loyal men who could've lived long and prosperous lives, and it's all her fault.

And I'm not the only one her callous comments rile.

"Of course they were afraid!" Miengha snaps, arms flying. "They were ambushed. They faced the most frightening creature any of them have ever seen and they were completely unprepared."

Sungema stands taller. "They knew what they were walking into—"

"No, they didn't," I snap, a quiet fury rising inside me. "The one thing that mortals fear more than anything else is the unknown, and you walked my guardsmen straight into that fight blind."

"Acari's right," Belsante adds. "None of them had seen the satyr before, so they didn't know what to expect. None knew what he was capable of. But we do now."

"That still might not be enough," Miengha counters. "Can any of you honestly say you feel any braver than you did this morning?"

Belsante lowers her gaze. The guard beside her all but whimpers.

Sungema though, stares off into the dimming distance, an idea brewing somewhere behind those golden eyes. "The only guarantee we have is with the Fatebringer Pendant."

Belsante looks up from her folded hands, brow furrowed. "You want me to ask Aulow and the others to join us?"

"No," Sungema says flatly. "Do not alert them of anything. Do not ask them anything. Last update you received, Sinisa hadn't even retrieved the pendant yet."

"No, but she's gone to find it. By now, she might've—"

"We can't risk distracting her. Sinisa needs to focus on retrieving the Fatebringer Pendant. If she discovers you are in danger, she will abandon her task and come for you, but she will be ineffective with her aid if she does not bring the pendant."

This is the first time any of them have named Sinisa's task, and though I have questions about what such a pendant can do for us, and why it is so important, with the satyr still thrashing somewhere behind us, we have more pressing matters.

"What do we do then? My men were just slaughtered. If the satyr finds us—"

"He mustn't. If those among us here cannot face him with pure bravery in their hearts, then you must ensure that you remain hidden, at all costs. If he finds you, you all will die. Or worse," she says, looking to me. "He will die, and all will be lost. You must ensure that does not happen."

I swallow hard, lost in the idea of being stuck on this island, running from the satyr for...for I don't know how long.

But Miengha thinks more quickly. She's already figured out that there is something else Sungema isn't saying and asks, "And what will you do in the meantime?"

Sungema gives a nearly imperceptible incline of her head. "We will not attempt telepathic communication with the others through Belsante, but I will go to retrieve Sinisa and the others. Once I arrive, assuming she has the Fatebringer Pendant in her possession, I will return with her so that we may face the satyr again and free the Divine Lorik."

"How long will that take?" Belsante balks. "How long do we have to remain alive until your return?"

Sungema is silent for a moment, but even her hesitation comes across cold and unfeeling. "If they are still in northern Ghamaya, it should only take a few days—"

Collectively, we gasp.

"Three days?" Belsante guffaws.

"We'll be dead by then," Miengha assures her.

I would offer my own protests and complaints, but I feel like the stakes aren't as high for me. With one look to my father-crow, I get the feeling he'd take me anywhere the moment I needed him to. I'm not trapped on this island like the others, I'm here willingly, determined to see my mission through. Besides, I can see in Sunge-ma's eyes that she doesn't care about anyone's protests. Her mission is not to keep us alive, but to free her brethren. In fact, I think she believes that we should all feel similarly, like it would be an honor to die trying to ensure Lorik's safe return.

But we've already lost too much to give up now, and it's obvious that the mortals still standing are seconds away from mutiny against their beloved Sungema. I can't let them give up. Borgravid's death can't mean nothing. Me becoming a Reaper can't be for nothing. We are here to free the Divine Lorik, and if we are to succeed, then we need all the help we can get.

"There's no time to argue," I say firmly, drawing the silence out of everyone. I wait until all eyes turn to me, concerned but attentive, before speaking again. "We will do what we can to survive, and also what must be done to protect the Divine Lorik. Tayaraan needs him and has been without him for far too long. Belsante, it's Lorik's disappearance that put fear into the hearts of mortals and made them believe people like you deserved to die. His entrapment is why all those men back there just died, good men, loyal men, whose only faults were wanting to return help one of their Divine Altúyur.

"If we don't do this, who will? We've come all this way with purpose, and if this pendant is our only hope, then we shouldn't delay Sungema any longer than we already have."

I glance to the others around me, to the blood splattered on Belsante's face and the twigs caught in Miengha's hair, to the guard who managed to escape with us. Each of them nods, solemnly, but I can see the spark of determination reigniting in each of them. We will not give up. We've come too far and will push ourselves just a little farther.

I turn to Sungema to give her the order that I don't think she needed from me, but the one she waits for anyway.

"Fly hard," I tell her. "And return to us as quickly as possible."

"I will do what I can to ensure a swift journey there," she says. "But it's the return that will cost me. I do not travel well while carrying others."

"Do what you can," I tell her, settling my gaze back to the jungle.

The screams of my men have finally faded, leaving nothing but the exotic calls of birds and monkeys to sing through the trees. But somewhere deep in the jungle, I know the satyr still lurks, *my* men and eating his fill of *my* people.

I turn back to Sungema, eyes hardened as stones. "When you return, we'll be ready for you."

19

FATE BECKONS

SINISA

Hunched over my second mug of ale, the hoppy aroma wafts up around me, smelling far less stringent than whatever foul drink Brükmir had offered me back on his ship. It seems like such a long time ago when Hayliel and I mistakenly thought we were on a mission to free Acari.

If I had known then what I know now, I would've ripped Brükmir's tankard from his hand and chugged, all too eager to drown the pain that awaited my future.

Even though my head spins from my last drink, I welcome another with my mouth wide.

Once the last of the foam has fizzed away, I slosh the contents of my beer around, toss it back again, and take another swig before setting it down on the table. Every now and then I glance over to the pendant beside it, the electric blue that is as bright as a lake beneath an open sky.

I've been sitting here, alone and contemplative for a couple of hours now, and I still can't tell how much longer I'll stay. The bard in the corner keeps the room bright and lively enough. There's singing and dancing and games, friends locked shoulder to shoulder as they chant and sway, and let's not forget the drinking.

Despite the jubilation in the room though, none of it quite reaches my heart. Their laughter can't erase my mother's death, nor the years I was left thinking she was dead. Their songs that recount the great feats of the Divine Altúyur do not make me feel any less guilty for my part in all of this, any less angry at the path that fate has carved out for me. And, of course, the icing on the cake is knowing that very soon the smiles of every patron in this establishment will fade too. Once news of Queen Miva's death makes it across the city, everyone will be in mourning, not just me, the daughter that no one knew of.

The boisterous sounds of the tavern die down around me, replaced by hushed murmurs as two newcomers enter. I don't need to look behind me to know who they are. Even if Iracara's talons weren't tapping on the floorboards as he approached, only he could make an entrance that would silence a bar full of drunks.

"She's drinking," Iracara whispers to Aulow while they approach, but they're already close enough for me to hear them. "I didn't know she drank. Isn't she too young?"

"The Ghamayans make their own rules," Aulow replies to him quietly. She takes a seat beside me, reaching across the table to rub my bicep. "Are you all right? You look like...what happened?"

"Why don't you ask him?" I snarl. When I discover my voice is steadier than I expected after the ales I've chugged, I become emboldened and can't stop myself. "I'm sure he knows exactly what happened. I bet they all knew, but they like to keep their secrets."

Out of the corner of my eye, I catch the exchange between the two of them, her look of worry met by his blatant show of denying what I already know to be true.

I slam my mug atop the table and rise, albeit a bit wobbly. "Don't lie to me! You knew! Just admit that you knew."

"I-I'm not sure what you mean."

If we didn't have the full attention of the bar before, we certainly do now. Every eye watches us, the girl arguing with the man in feathers, the creature who can only be one of the Divine

Altúyur. They watch me with shame and fury, but I've spent years building armor to deflect the judgmental gazes of mortals.

However, despite wanting to scream at Iracara, I am sober enough to know that I have to be selective with my words here. Hearing that the queen has died cannot come from me, a nobody, especially if I have any plans of connecting with the family my mother left behind. If I mention the queen's death, I'll be labeled a threat and persecuted, though, admittedly, there's a part of me that thinks I might deserve such a fate.

My eyes float back to the table, trailing over the bright jewel resting there. It's the first time I realize how foolish I've already been. If my mother had never parted with her necklace until today, then her people have likely seen it dozens of times over the years and they could easily recognize it.

When I slam my hands back on the table, leaning over it to stare Iracara down, I'm just as strategic with my words as I am with the placement of my hands, and I conceal the pendant.

With lethal quiet, I speak only so he and Aulow can hear me. "You knew she would die once her fate had been fulfilled."

Iracara balks, swaying as he blinks at me with a truly convincing display of shock. "I—I didn't... I hadn't even considered..." He slumps into a chair before he can finish.

I stay where I am, poised above him like a viper ready to strike, but even through my rage, his surprise seems genuine.

After dragging the pendant across the table toward me, I tuck it into my lap and return to my seat.

"There's nothing to consider now," I say softly, taking the tankard into my other hand and letting the last of the amber ale rush down my throat to warm my stomach. "It is done. My mother is dead. All because I took her pendant away from her."

Aulow's hand finds mine still clutching my mug. "It isn't your fault."

"Oh, I know. I know exactly whose fault it is."

My glare finds Iracara again. I see all of the Altúyur in him, the lying, selfish, absent divinities who seem to only want what's best for themselves. But even though I want to hate them all, looking into Iracara's sorrowful eyes chips away at the stone encasing my heart. I believe him when he says he didn't know, and so I can't bring myself to blame him.

"It's Owlena's fault for wrapping my mother and I up in fate," I snarl. "And Sungema's for not bothering to warn me about what I was walking into."

"Try to understand," Iracara says softly. "Perhaps she didn't warn you because she feared you might not follow through. I'm not saying it was fair to you, but Sungema made a promise to Owlena to see the prophecy through. She bears the responsibility of—"

"She bears nothing!" I roar, my mug-less fist pounding the table again. "*I* am the one who lost my mother. *I* am the one who lost my friends. *I* am the one whose entire life has been predetermined. Sungema risks nothing."

Iracara stares at me with pleading eyes. His voice softens with even more compassion. "She, too, has lost much. Might I remind you that we all have. Years of our lives, we waited for you to emerge. Our Prophets were stolen and forced into the servitude of Veltuur. The Guardians we made and befriended have all long since died. The realm that we so cherished has fallen apart in our absence and we bear the burden of that. Humanity has barely held onto any of the gifts we once bestowed upon you all. Everywhere I look, I only see Veltuur's mark. The hatred, the deceit, the fear he gave the mortals—it's poisoned everything, and we weren't here to stop him.

"If it is anyone's fault that your mother is dead, that she forgot about you and built a new life, it is Veltuur's."

Chewing my lip, I hail the tavern maiden with my mug. I try holding onto my hate, but as she refills it, the truth of Iracara's words seep deeper into me. Perhaps he is right. Perhaps I'm taking my anger out on the wrong Altúyur. After all, was it not Veltuur who created the Deceptive Serpent who took my mother, father, and Hayliel away from me? Was it not Veltuur who forced my parents onto their separate paths of destruction? Was it not Veltuur who claimed me as a Reaper when I finally defended myself against the man who'd abused me for years?

My hand feels numb and limp when I raise my two fingers to the tavern maiden. "Bring two more."

Iracara grimaces. "I worry that drinking might not be the best decision right now—"

"I disagree," Aulow says over him. "A life has been lost. We can afford a moment of mourning, of meaning, of memory."

I offer her a grateful smile.

"Besides, it's late. We should rest here tonight before embarking on the next leg of our journey. There will be time enough tomorrow to secure a new horse, restock provisions, and to figure out how exactly we'll restore Pecolock to his Altúyur form."

"I think I've already figure it out," I say, slurring my words a little, and they both turn their attention to me.

The tavern maiden comes and delivers the steins. I hold up mine and await the clink from theirs, something I've seen other mortals do, but have never before done so myself. In fact, tonight is the first time I've ever even tasted ale. As a Reaper, there wasn't much opportunity for socializing in taverns.

We each take a drink, and as we set our mugs on the table, I tell them the simple solution.

"If Pecolock was the Altúyur of Inspiration, what could be more inspiring than seeing a fellow Altúyur freed from his prison?"

"You think all we need to do is show him that I'm myself again?"

I shrug. "Or maybe seeing me will do it. The *Prophesized* One."

Once we've settled into our drinks and stopped yelling, the patrons find the courage to approach us. We spend the rest of the evening telling them that Iracara has returned, as have some of the other Altúyur, as will the rest. Iracara basks in the attention, and with an occasional friendly wave of his feathers, he grants each individual request for his power.

When we finish our tankards, Aulow secures us a couple of

rooms at the inn next door. They have to aid me to mine, each of them on either side of me as they walk me to my bed. Sleep finds me quickly, and I'm glad that the ale keeps the dreams at bay.

My head pounds at the greeting of the rising sun through my window. I'm blurry eyes and uncoordinated feet as I stumble out of bed and toward the table with a glass of water waiting for me. It's the most succulent water I've ever drank, and I'm sorry that it goes so quickly.

The night comes back to me in hazy waves. The tavern, the ale, the mountain. My mother and Avalanche's deaths ache through me like a fissure breaking me in two. But just before I can slump back onto my bed, before the tears can take hold once more, there's a knock at my door.

"It's me," Aulow says. "When you're ready, there's breakfast downstairs."

The promise of food is too tantalizing to ignore. I haven't eaten since yesterday morning, while we were still hiking up the mountain, while Avalanche was still with us. With the Fatebringer Pendant tucked safely inside my pouch, I leave my room and find Iracara and Aulow waiting for me at a table.

The bread is stale, nothing like that of the breads my aunt Theffania would make me, but it fills my belly all the same. But it's the warm coffee I appreciate the most. Even with a fire going most of the night, my toes have still not quite fully warmed since our trek through the mountains. It feels like my bones have been replaced with ice, but each sip of the dark, bitter beverage takes me one step closer to warmth.

"The innkeeper has been so generous as to offer to send us off with some of the bread," Aulow says.

Taking a bite from his own loaf, Iracara adds, "And don't forget the nice fellas from last night who offered us one of their horses so that we can head south to the Magrok Mountains. Sinisa's plan is promising, though I'd feel better if we had other options as well. Just in case it isn't as simple as we hope."

"Well," Aulow says. "What did Pecolock find inspiring?"

Iracara chortles. "What *didn't* he find inspiring? Pecolock could find beauty and magnificence in every blade of grass, from every grain of salt. It was his nature."

With my lips pressed against my mug, I blow on the steaming coffee, the umber pool swirling before me. "Then I stand by my original idea. Veltuur would've ensured that the Divine Pecolock couldn't have been inspired by everyday simple things anymore. After all, he's been banished to a mountain that's known for its breathtakingly beautiful views and he remains trapped. It will need to be something truly magnificent to free him."

"Like seeing you or me."

My nodding is interrupted by the ruffle of wings as someone bursts through the entrance behind me. The three of us turn to find Sungema striding across the room, and though she's not one for much expression, the air of fear and danger about her is palpable.

"You are needed, Sinisa."

I swallow the unchewed bite of bread and it goes down like a rock. "Needed where?"

"The Corraeda Isles. I fear that only you can free Lorik."

"Is Belsante all right?" Aulow asks, pushing herself up from the table.

It doesn't go unnoticed by any of us that Sungema dodges the question. "Do you have the Fatebringer Pendant?"

I reach down to my waist and free the pouch from my belt. My tired fingers fumble on the knot, but once I finally manage to get it open, I pull the pendant out for her.

"Wear it always," she says. "You never know when you'll need its protection."

Without protest, I tie it around my neck, the weight of the blue stone heavier than it should be on my chest, but it brings with it a burden greater than fate.

With a toss of her vibrant hair, Sungema scans the others, her golden eyes roaming from Iracara, to Aulow, back to me.

"Pecolock is not with you yet."

"We were just about to head out," Iracara starts to snivel, like he's in trouble, like he's failed her.

It's enough to ignite the rage inside me.

"Excuse me for needing to take a break after my mother died before my eyes," I sneer, fire burning through my very core and melting any part of the ice left inside me. "I might've been able to continue, if you had bothered to warn me."

Sungema doesn't flinch; she just stares me down, ever unreadable and silent. I stare right back. Altúyur or not, she does not scare me. What's the worst she could do? Remove my memories? What good have they done me so far anyway?

When her green wings pop out behind her, I'm not the only one who jumps.

"You two will continue with the task of freeing Pecolock, while Sinisa will come with me to the Corraeda Isles."

"I'm not going anywhere with you! You...you lied to me! My mother..."

"Your mother would've died millennium ago if not for the destiny bestowed upon her. If you are feeling guilty because she lost her life upon giving you the pendant, then might I suggest you consider that you *gave* her lifetimes of vitality because of the fate connected to you. She lived more than most because you were destined to be her daughter."

The anger in me simmers, grief bubbling up inside me all over again. I don't know how to mourn her, I don't know who to mourn—the mother I lost years ago, or the one I only just met—but I feel myself sinking into the reality that Sungema is right. If it hadn't been for the Divine Owlena's prophecy, if she hadn't protected my mother with the Fatebringer Pendant so that she might live long enough to birth a daughter—to birth *me*—I would've never even met my mother. She would've died a long time ago, long before I could've been born.

"If you are ireful with me because I declined to tell you your mother would perish upon the exchange," Sungema says with a ruffle of her feathers. "So be it. But to decline to come with me now is to abandon your friends to their deaths."

I look to Aulow and see the fear already clawing its way through her.

"No more lives will be lost, not if I can help it." Standing from my chair, I spin and face Sungema. "Let's go."

20

TROUBLE IN PARADISE
ACARI

"**R**un!"

The satyr clambers through the trees, all muscled limbs and glistening teeth. Though it already knew we were on the island, seeing us here, out in the open, ignites the fire behind its already burning eyes and it throws its head back and roars.

We were supposed to remain hidden. The satyr was supposed to be on the opposite side of the island so that we might have time to find food before its return. It wasn't supposed to see us.

Now, we might've ruined everything Sungema had planned.

My legs are pumping before Miengha even commands it, but the soft sands of the beach fight against any quick progress I should be making.

"We should head inland," Belsante huffs with each bounding stride.

"No!" I shout back. "I can't go into the jungle. If I kill anything else by accident...Veltuur will come for me. He would come for Lorik."

I don't add that I'm surprised he hasn't already. After the Reapers came for my guardsmen, I half-expected Veltuur to arrive in a tarry, ominous cloud that filled the sky above, stretching as far as the eye could see. But Veltuur never came. Maybe he didn't think he needed to. After all, the Divine Lorik is still imprisoned as the satyr, and isn't that what Veltuur wanted all along: for the Altúyur to remain trapped?

Miengha growls behind us both. "Less talking, more running!"

We stick to our path along the shoreline and race for the rocks up ahead. My arms ache, my thighs burning from every hurdling leap as I dash for my life. For Lorik's life. Sure, I can heal if I return to Veltuur, but I don't think Lorik could survive slicing through a Reaper. My power would have no choice but to take his life, and his death would ruin everything...

My father-crow cries overhead before swooping down beside me to stare into me with that knowing look. I shake my head at him. There may be a time for me to disappear, but this doesn't feel like it. Not yet. If the satyr gets closer though, if he puts himself in danger...

"To the cave!" Miengha yells over the crashing of the waves and another bloodcurdling snarl from the satyr as it gains on us.

For two days, we've explored the island. It started as a search for the ship and the sailor who Borgravid had asked to return for us every day for a week. The one guardsmen who had made it out of the slaughter, had not done so unscathed. He was egregiously injured, a deep gash that not even Miengha could see to, not here in the middle of nowhere. We thought we might be able to send him back to the mainland with the sailor so that he could get some help, but there was no sign of him since our arrival, and my last remaining guard died on the beach the following morning.

From then on, we mostly kept to the beaches and explored for food and shelter. We found a few places where we just might hold the advantage over the satyr, if we ever had to face him again, the cave being one of them. The entrance seemed too small for the large creature to squeeze even an arm through, let alone the rest of his lumbering form, so we decided to stay nearby, just in case he ever returned. Just in case Sungema and Sinisa did.

But I think we all kind of hoped they'd get here before we ever needed to test our theory out.

Belsante veers farther up to beach to even drier sands. I follow after her, my feet sinking deeper with every uncoordinated and flailing step, making the chase even more challenging and tiring. But none of us slow. We have to reach the cave. It's the only way we're all making it out of this alive.

I glance back over my shoulder to find the satyr closer still. It's tongue sloshes around its mouth as it barrels after us, spittle flying freely like it can already taste the juicy, lean meats fleeing from it.

"Don't look back!" Miengha yells, and I promptly obey.

The rock wall looms closer, its shadow swallowing up the sands.

Belsante disappears inside the cave first, and I am relieved to see at least one of us find safety—*hopeful* safety. I follow just a moment after her, slamming face-first into the rock wall just on the inside. Miengha nearly collides into me next, but fortunately I roll away just before she, too, dives into the confines of the cave's mouth.

Outside, the satyr slams into the rock wall with such force that the entire enclosure quakes. Dirt and rocks sift down from the ceiling, and I'm not the only one to look up and wonder whether we'll be safe in here and for how long. Any more collisions like that, and this entire cavern might come crumbling down on top of us.

Though the entrance was too small for the satyr, the beast isn't senseless. It sees the opening, assesses it with eyes alit with frenzy, and then jabs a lanky arm inside. It reaches its clawed hand toward the three of us, and we all tense against the wall at our backs. Snarling and growling, it presses itself harder against the cliffside, but with its shoulder crammed against the opening, it can't fit through any farther, and therefore can't reach us.

I slouch back against the wall with a sigh.

Belsante smirks. "See? I told you he wouldn't fit."

"Yes, but now what?" Miengha asks, incredulous. "We're trapped in here with no way out."

She veers left, to a pocket just inside the cave where we had the foresight of storing some clean water and what little food we were able to forage from the beach.

"Now, we wait," I say, joining them in the alcove and putting some distance between myself and the thrashing satyr. "We wait and hope that Sungema will return with Sinisa soon and finish this."

21

BLADE OF IMMORTALITY

SINISA

We've flown over so many different patches of land floating in the ocean below by now that I've stopped getting my hopes up when yet another comes into view. The Corraeda Isles seem to have once been a solid chunk of land that at one point shattered like broken glass. The isles splinter throughout the sea, leaving thin drizzles of rivers and channels to separate the country into dozens upon dozens of small, private islands. Each is unique by shape, and color, and height, but all bring out the same question in me:

Is this the island where the Divine Lorik has been kept?

Is this the island where my friends are in danger?

But as I feel Sungema's trajectory shift, notice the horizon tilt as we descend toward the waters, relief overcomes me as I realize we've finally reached our destination.

Relief and fear, for I know that once we land, only danger will greet us there.

It's like the danger hears my thoughts, because it greets us with a resounding guttural bellow that shakes the very air we fly through. Even from this distance, I see the beast's black, hulking body charging across the beach. I see the three dots it's chasing, the ones that become more and more mortal-like the closer we get.

"That's them, isn't it?"

"I would assume," Sungema replies. "Though when I left them, there were four."

Something sinks into the pit of my stomach, but I try ignoring it. If I am to face the satyr—face Lorik—I will need to be focused, not distracted by who else might or might not have died.

Sungema lowers us onto the yellow sands from across the beach, far enough away that hopefully the satyr can't smell us—if it can even do such a thing—but close enough that I can just make-out Belsante diving into a cave, Acari right behind her.

My heart bounces back up from my stomach and into my throat, buoyant and warm. I realize with immense joy that Acari's here, he's with them. For all our efforts, he has finally left the underrealm behind and joined—

Before I can finish the thought, I see the black bird circling high over the rocky cliff, never veering too far from where it can see the entrance below.

Brow creasing, I look to Sungema. "Acari's with you?"

Her eyes don't exactly roll, but there's a bored quality to her flat stare all the same. "We found him in Oakfall on our way to Illistead Harbor. He is here to free Lorik as well."

"But...how? How is that even possible? Veltuur wouldn't—"

"No, he wouldn't," she says to me flatly. "But that's neither of our concerns now, is it? We have to free the Divine Lorik."

Miengha clambers inside the small opening seconds later, and I watch with my breath held as the satyr slams himself against the rock wall. He snarls and roars as he reaches a gangly arm inside, grasping and clawing for the prize that had only narrowly escaped that he likely believed was his.

"You're right. But how do we free him?" Realizing that it's the same answer as it was with all of the others, I mutter, "Show him bravery."

She holds up a thin finger. "Not just an act of bravery, but one of pure bravery. You can hold no fear in your heart otherwise it will not count."

"That's impossible," I balk.

"Not impossible for the Prophesized One. The Fatebringer Pendant should help you."

Still groaning at the unwanted title, before she can say anything else, I bound toward the beast and where it has my friends trapped. The creature slams itself again and again against the hollowed entrance, boulders tumbling down the sides and crashing all around it. *If it's not careful, it might be the cause of its own demise,* I think snidely. But then I remind myself who the satyr really is. It's not just some bloodthirsty creature, but the Altúyur of Bravery, the Divine Lorik, and he can't die here, like this, crushed by falling debris.

The only way we will save him is by facing him, by proving to him that there is still courage left in the realm.

But right now, I feel little courage. Three of my friends are trapped inside a rock dwelling that could crumble at any minute and I have no way of knowing if they are all right. From my vantage point behind the beast, I can't tell if he's able to reach inside deep enough to slice them all to pieces, or if they've managed to survive.

Despite my doubt and fear, I continue my charge, panting and heaving as the beach sand slips beneath my every stride. My fists pump at my sides, like they are grasping ropes tied to the cliff and helping to propel me farther.

As I gain on the satyr, the sun catches on something metal at his hip. A curved sort of blade, a weapon that would be so small in his colossal grasp that it would look more like a dagger wielded by him than anything. But in my mortal hands, it would become a mighty sword.

The blade hangs low and hapless, the belt that once kept it tucked tightly at his side now barely hanging on by the leather. As my feet work, legs pumping harder and faster, I realize that the blade is so low to the ground, that I might even be able to—

Once I'm right behind him, I leap into the air. My hands grasp the hilt, rough with leather and glistening black beneath. It's just like Sungema described: a blade crafted from the forest of the underrealm, forged in the black Pools of Prophecy.

I let my weight yank both me and the blade downward, unsheathing the weapon in one fluid movement. The satyr notices me the moment I hit the ground, but I don't give it time to react. Instead, I run for the cave's opening, dragging the blade through the sand behind me, never once stopping to look back over my shoulder to see the angry eyes of the beast I'll have to face.

Darkness greets me inside, so I'm unable to see the wall of rock I run face-first into, but at least I'm safe. For now. I spin around, press my back against the wall, and aim the blade out toward the satyr.

Realizing it's been confounded again, the creature bellows, shaking the enclosure that feels more like a tomb now that I'm inside. I look around into the darkness, but the space seems hollow, empty. There are no signs of Belsante, Miengha, or Acari. But as my eyes start to adjust, I notice the curve of the cave and push myself off the wall, minding the thrashing claw just behind me, and decide to venture a little farther into the enclosure.

"Sinisa?" comes a voice from the shadows, a voice I still hear in my dreams and think about daily. His is a voice that makes my heartbeat quicken, reminds me that I am no longer a creature of death, but am now alive.

"You came," Acari breathes into the darkness. "You're finally here."

The young king steps forward and into the dim light the entrance provides, a hopeful and goofy twist to his mouth, and my heart all but melts at the sight of him. Even if he is still stubbornly remaining a Reaper, and even if I don't yet understand why or how he's here, I know that all that matters is that he *is* here.

"So are you," I say, a soft smile meeting his own.

But our reunion and any chance I had at getting answers is cut short when Miengha and Belsante appear behind him. When the Ghamayan looks at me, pain seers through us both. I know she's thinking of Avalanche, and the final moments he spent alive with me and Aulow. I want to tell her that I'm sorry, that I wish I could've saved him, but before I can, Belsante points to the necklace around my neck.

"Is that it? Is that the Fatebringer Pendant?"

Nodding, I gaze down at it, cupping the blue jewel in my palm. "It is."

"Then why is the satyr still here?" Miengha asks. "Sungema said once you had the pendant, you could free Lorik."

Reminded of my mission, I shake my head and twist away from my friends to face the beast in the entryway. "I can. But first, I have to face him. I have to show him what pure bravery looks like."

22

BRAVERY AND BEAUTY

ACARI

S inisa fidgets with the pendant around her neck before raising a blade that I'm just now noticing is clutched in her hand. It seems far too ancient and foreboding to be in her possession, like a weapon raised from the underrealm itself. Power exudes from it. Even in the dim light that the cave provides, the hilt glimmers like it's been dipped in black blood, like some ancient force of magic dwells deep within it. The steel of the blade is just as dark and lethal.

But it's not until I notice the bird skull crested in the hilt, the feathers etched alongside it, that I know for certain who this weapon belonged to: definitely an Altúyur, and who else but the one who has us cornered in here, the very one I saw with a blade sheathed at his hip during our first encounter.

"Are you ready to face me!" Sinisa yells, tightening her grip and standing firm.

The three of us watch in awe as the satyr slams his body once again into the cliffside, and though the creature's claws are just a hair away from nicking Sinisa in the face, and though the cave ceiling continues to crumble with dust and small rocks shaken loose from the cracks, Sinisa doesn't flinch once.

She is iron.

She is steel.

And I know I should be terrified. I should be worried beyond comprehension. But instead something else stirs inside me, a desire I haven't before realized was there. Perhaps it's because I just lost a friend; perhaps it's because we just ran for our lives and narrowly escaped; perhaps it's because my goal is so close that I can almost taste it; or perhaps it's just the sight of the powerful, striking young woman standing between me and danger yet again that has me so awestruck, so inspired, so impressed.

Sinisa is so breathtakingly courageous and selfless, and I don't even think she realizes it. I think she still paints herself the villain, despite having broken free from her bonds.

When this is all said and done, I vow right here and right now that my next mission will be helping her see her true nature. Her bravery. Her resiliency. Her compassion.

In slow strides, Sinisa walks toward the cave's entrance, calm and determined. She dodges each wild swipe of the creature's claws. She shields herself with the blade when she has to, uses it to slam the satyr's arm to the wall when it gets too close. And though it *is* close, on more than one occasion, never do her footsteps waver. When she's knocked down, she stands back up. When she's thrown to the wall, she pushes back until she's freed. When she's knocked back a step, she takes two more forward.

It's like fear has no place inside her heart, and suddenly it's so obvious to me why Sungema left to retrieve her.

Call it fate, call it destiny, call it the pendant dangling from her neck—whatever it is, Sinisa was made for this moment.

On the next blow, the satyr's arm stretches right past her. Sinisa seizes the opportunity. She slams the blade into the creature's hairy forearm and wrenches the weapon upward. I flinch, remembering who is trapped inside the beast, but I know she had little choice. Eventually, he was going to land a blow, and the only way out is if his arm isn't blocking most of the entrance.

The satyr screeches, an ear-piercing shriek that echoes in the cave like the torturous wails that reside with the Wraiths. He yanks his arm back, but the blade has him pinned in the wall. With another cry, this one more enraged than the first, he tugs his arm again, once and then twice, and finally snatches his arm back, the creature's hand falling clean off and dropping to the floor with a thud. The satyr recoils back in agony and Sinisa lunges toward her escape, leaving the rest of us inside, slack jawed.

She is dangerous.

She is lethal.

And she is about to save us all.

23

AN ACT OF COURAGE

SINISA

"Don't make me remove the other one," I growl up at the creature.

Though my voice is steady, as I exit the cave's mouth, embraced by the sea breeze, my hands tremble at the sight of the magnificent beast towering above me. I am a cyclone of rawness. My grief over the death of my mother is entirely entangled with my fierce desire to protect my friends and the ones I love.

I have never wielded a weapon like this before, or any weapon, for that matter. I know nothing about how to fight other than where to point the sharp end of the blade. But none of that matters because I have fate on my side, and as long as I'm wearing the Fate-bringer Pendant, I will be protected.

At least, that's what Sungema says, and I am inclined to believe her, considering how well this is going for me so far. I let it embolden me.

Staring up at the satyr still writhing in pain and coddling the nub where its hand once was, I spit. "Haven't I proven myself yet? Return to your true form, Divine Lorik. I do not fear you."

I say his true name, hoping that it will serve as a reminder, but instead the mere mention of it only seems to enrage him.

The satyr tilts his head to the sky and roars. He swipes his long arms—even the one now without a hand—and I swing the blade I stole from him. But he's too fast. Out here in the open, without the cave walls to confine his reach, he knocks the weapon from my hand. I'm still stunned, gaping at the blade flying through the air when he slashes me again. The blows lands across my chest, sending me spinning and tumbling to the ground.

I shove myself up, spit the sand from my mouth, and on hands and knees, my eyes flit down, expecting to find my chest ripped open and bloodied.

But my garments are undisturbed. Despite what should've been a deadly blow, the satyr's claws didn't tear through me at all, and I know this time I truly do have the Fatebringer Pendant to thank for—

Terror ripples through me. Staring at my chest, I find no pendant dangling there. It's gone. Suddenly electric with dread, I search the sand beside me, frantically scooping and digging, but I find nothing. Even if I did, the steady rumbling of the satyr's steps behind me confirm that I have run out of time.

Slowly, I raise my head. The satyr is just a few paces away, taking his time as he, too, surely knows what it looks like to see defeated prey. Hunger twist his mangled lips into something that could resemble a smile. Every step he takes sends a new jolt of fear rippling through me. I don't want to die. I've only just reclaimed my life. I have a Prophet to protect now, a life to figure out how to live, new powers to discover, and a friend who still needs to be saved.

All of my bravado is gone. I recognize my end and realize there's only one thing I want now.

I twist back around to the cave to find my friends huddled in the entrance, watching, helpless and desperate.

But I only have eyes for one of them. Acari stares across the way, mouth torn open in an agonizing wail that is muted by the distance and the waves. From all this way though, I know what he's feeling: fear, desperation. And I suppose, at first, I felt those things too. For so long I've fought to survive. The night I killed my abuser, the night I let go of my past, the hours I spent in Pyrethi Tower, and every moment before and after then. I wanted to live; I wanted a chance at living a normal life, and I realize now that in a way, I had one. Maybe not normal, but mortal. I escaped Veltuur's clutches. I made friends with Guardians and Prophets, and even a king. If I am to die here, now, at least I know I lived. At least I know that I died trying to protect the people I care about.

Peace surrounds me. The peace of a quiet morning in the woods; of dipping my body into a warm bath after a long day; of standing in the sun in an open meadow.

I wish that Acari and I had more time together, but I'm grateful for the time we had. I'm grateful for him, for all the ways in which he helped me, and made me a better person.

Bowing my head, I prepare for the searing pain that will whip across my back, for the claws that will rip me to shreds, and the fangs that will devour me. I tell myself it will be okay, that I did everything I could and I have nothing to regret.

But when the strike doesn't come, I start to wonder. Maybe I've done it after all. Maybe all that I needed to do to face Lorik without fear was to accept whatever death he could bring me.

I look up, finding the creature snarling, malicious intent returned to his eyes, only, they're no longer resting on me.

In the distance, the sound of a battle cry draws nearer. I look up.

Acari charges toward us, hands clutched to his abdomen. As he races, drawing closer with each bounding—albeit stumbling—stride, I realize he's folded his tunic up and there's something heavy and jagged weighing it down.

He reaches inside as he nears. The satyr belts out another malicious roar but its cut short by a rock Acari throws at the beast's face. He chucks another one, hitting the satyr in the eye, sending him staggering a step, long enough for Acari to reach me.

He extends his free hand. I'm so touched by the gesture, so relieved to see him, that I almost take it, but thankfully Acari jerks it away before our skin can touch. I should've remembered the significance of his runeless face, but all I could think about was how good it is to see him, to know that he was fighting on our side.

Acari stares at the bare skin of his palm, but as I stand, the two of us face the ferocious beast together, stronger and more determined than ever. With Acari at my side, I'm emboldened once more. We don't need fate. We don't need bravery, or intellect, or any of the other gifts. If I've learned anything since we met it's that we only need each other.

The satyr leans in close, drool dripping down from its sneering lips as it roars in our faces. But just as it starts to pull back, to give itself enough room to strike us both dead, I see the light emanating from its chest. It blooms and blooms, shining as bright as the sun above, as bright as Sungema's golden eyes.

Before the light becomes too bright, I see the creature changing. His horns shrink back into his skull. The hair on his arms, legs, and torso shift and grow into feathers, bright and orange.

I turn to Acari, breathless. "It's working. You did it."

"We did it," he says, looking down at me with so much warmth that I can't tell if I'm burning because of his proximity, or because of the light that bursts in one final, blinding blow from Lorik's chest.

The light consumes us but Acari and I shield each other from it. We step closer to one another, our noses barely apart, surrounded by nothing but white and the sounds of the ocean somewhere behind us. Just a Reaper boy and a Guardian girl, our roles all but reversed since the first day we met, and I am suddenly so overwhelmed by all we have endured, all we have done for ourselves and each other, that I can't control the fire blooming inside me. It rises like smoke and steam, coursing through my every molecule like it is screaming for Acari, for his closeness, for his touch, for him.

With one hand still shielding my eyes, I thrust out the other. A strange power surges through me, hot and white, unlike the cold, dark touch of a Reaper's magic that I had once been used to. It rushes from my hand, invisible but palpable, and encloses us in a Guardian's shield.

Cut-off from Veltuur's reach, Acari's runes appear instantly, the mint green brightening his eyes.

"You saved me," I whisper, grabbing his belt and pulling him closer. I need him closer.

My lips crash against his, clumsy and hungry. He's dehydrated from the days he's spent stranded and running for his life, and so I try giving him the moisture from mine. Our mouths open, and I become fire and air. I am drifting out of my burning body into eternal bliss and I don't ever want to leave. I never want him to leave.

I have spent so many years associating touch with death that I had no idea how much life it could bring. My body pulses with it, loud and bright. As I taste him, I become drunk with all that is possible, everything that lays before us.

But his hands find my arms, his grip hard and alarming. He shoves me away, the two of us staggering backward. By now, the blinding light has all but diminished, so when I open my eyes, I'm able to see him clearly as he wipes the taste of me off of his mouth and fixes his shadowed eyes to the ground.

I lose hold of the shield I placed around us. His runes disappear, and with them, every hope I had that the two of us might actually have had any kind of future together.

24

THE UNREST OF PEACE
ACARI

What was I thinking? How could I let her put herself at risk like that? I could've killed her! My touch—I-I *should've* killed her. Why didn't I kill her? How is it that I can smack a whisper wasp out of thin air and it dies the moment its body touches my skin, but Sinisa will survive a kiss?

"Welcome back," Sungema says to Lorik as she lands on the beach.

I avoid Sinisa's hurt gaze as I, too, bring my attention to the new Altúyur among us. He is as colorful as the tropical forest behind him. Feathers as green and as large as leaves cover the back of his head. They trail down his neck and shoulders, becoming as slender as blades of grass by the time they reach his forearms. He has the blue face of a bird, a lorikeet, presumably, but unlike Sungema and Iracara, I find no wings.

"Where am I?" Lorik asks, and Sungema begins the task of catching him up on everything that has transpired over the last millennium since he's been imprisoned.

As Belsante and Miengha jog out from the cave to join us, Sinisa turns away, retreating toward the jungle.

"My turn!" Belsante says in her singsong tone. She reaches for Sinisa's face, lips puckered, and pulls her forward.

Sinisa swats her away. "What are you doing?"

"I told you I'd kiss you the next time I saw you." When Sinisa only blinks, Belsante adds, "For saving Aulow."

That seems to jog her memory. "Oh, right. Well, there's no need for that."

Our eyes lock, if just for a moment, before Sinisa turns her back to all of us.

"Where are you going?" Belsante calls after her.

Her question goes unanswered, and instead we all watch in silence as Sinisa kicks about the sand. It's not until she finally bends over that I realize she's not just moping. She pulls something silver and blue up and dusts it with her fingers before placing the Fatebringer Pendant back around her neck.

She continues meandering the shore, kicking sand as she goes. I want to go to her. I want to explain that I didn't push her away because I wanted to, but because I had to. We can't do things like that. It's too dangerous. If I had accidentally killed her—I can't even bring myself to think about that. She's done so much for me. She vowed to protect my sister, she helped restore some of my memories, she came all the way to the underrealm to try to save me—I can't be responsible for her death.

Part of me wants to run to her, but it's obvious from the distance she's putting between us that she would rather be left alone right now. And so I do. I leave her to her solitude and instead bring my attention back to the Divine Lorik.

It's only then that the full weight of his presence finally hits me: my quest, it's done. According to the Wraiths, Sinisa freed the Altúyur of Compassion days ago. All I needed was to restore the Altúyur of Bravery, and I did. Now the people of Tayaraan will finally leave people like my sister alone.

I did it. I have proven to my father that I am worthy of being a king. I have given my sister the greatest gift I could ever hope to give. And most of all, I've proven to myself that I know where I belong. I am King of Oakfall. I am sworn to serve and protect my people, and serve them I will.

My father-crow lands on my shoulder. It's the first time I've seen him in what feels like forever; I'd almost forgotten he was still here, still lingering.

He leans his head against me, and I stroke his oily feathers. Only, he's not as solid as I remember. My hand glides over him almost like he's made of water, then vapor.

"Oh," I say to him, the sad realization settling in. "I guess this means you're leaving. That's all it takes, for peace to be made with our pasts, and now that compassion and bravery have been restored to the realm. I... I guess I did it."

And as I speak, the weight of him continues to lighten. His press against my cheek melts away. The place in my shoulder where his talons keep him balanced dissipates as my father-crow finally coalesces into smoke.

"Goodbye, Father," I say to him as the final sliver of gray fades into the ether.

Tears sting my eyes and assault my throat. I've been looking forward to this moment for days now, and yet, somehow, I didn't feel ready.

But I hardly have time to mourn him. With his departure, a whole lifetime flashes before me. I'm five years old, holding my mother's hand while we stand before the royal court in the throne room, listening to my father deliver his wishes. I'm ten, riding horseback with Rikeet and dreading every minute of it. I'm fifteen, meeting my new handmaiden from Ngal and blushing at the beauty of her sun-kissed skin and meadow-green eyes.

Years pass again, and I'm wandering the halls of the palace alone, the bodies of my mother and brother only recently retrieved from the road. I'm crying in my bedroom as my handmaiden comforts me, telling me that she knows it's hard, but things will get better.

Weeks pass, and I'm learning of the Reaper that my father sent after Gem. I see Sinisa for the first time in the Hall of Altúyur, feel the chill of death in the air at her presence, even as I'm simultaneously struck by her beauty. As our paths intertwine, I learn of the fire inside her, I help her uncover who she really is, the person she buried long ago and the one she's prevented from rising from within herself.

It took a lifetime to amass all of those moments and more, but only seconds to relive each one of them.

But by the time they fade back into the depths of my mind, my face is slick with tears. Tears of joy, tears of heartache, tears of triumph, tears of guilt.

I've lost so much in this short time—my father, Borgravid—but perhaps the death I feel the most is Hayliel's. She died at my hand, a woman that I once thought I loved, someone who I think loved me as well.

I lift my hands to my face to bury myself and my shame, but stop mid-track. Mint-green designs swirl on the backs of my hands. They line my fingers with twisting, floral patterns that I've only ever seen on—

"I'm not a Reaper anymore," I say, breathless and unblinking.

Miengha gives me a hard pat on the back. "Welcome to the club, Guardian."

My eyes bulge at her. "What does that mean? What are these runes? Why have I never heard about Guardians before, nor ever met one until I saw Sinisa?"

Sinisa returns just in time to catch the end of my rant, blade in hand having retrieved it from where it had been discarded.

Examining his hand to find it somehow still intact—although, covered in blood—Lorik answers, "The runes are gifts, bestowed upon you by your beloved Altúyur."

"What?" Miengha balks.

"You've got to be kidding me..." Belsante utters.

Sinisa looks to her hand, the blade rising as she holds it in front of her. "No one has ever said that the runes came from the Altúyur."

"That's because no one ever knew that!" Miengha cries, incredulous. "We were always told they were earned during key mile-stones in a person's life: the four-pointed star for birth—"

"Oh! The armband that parents develop," Belsante adds.

"If that's not true though, then why do we earn them?" I ask the Divine Lorik.

He looks down his beak at me. "It's not that difficult to deduce. Surely, you're aware of the other gifts we share with the mortals, aren't you?"

Nods go all around.

"Well, when a mortal first encounters our gift, they earn the rune that corresponds. You call it the four-pointed star of birth, but that rune is granted by Sungema, and earned for the first memory a child ever creates. Pecolock bestows the armband of inspiration. And so on."

"No, not *and so on*," Miengha says, crossing her arms. "If they're gifts, I want to understand them all. Each and every one of them."

I'm grateful she's the one saying so, because I'm not sure I could've brought myself to demand anything from the Divine Altúyur, especially not one that I just saw shift from a malevolent satyr with talons that could've speared me.

"What about the runes people get when they become too sick to recover?" Miengha continues. "You're telling me those are gifts?"

"A marking of fate, from Owlena," Lorik answers.

"And the three dots we have on our foreheads?" Belsante asks, pointing emphatically. "We were told they are for language?"

Lorik tilts his feathered head, the green and blue just as bright as his orange body. "In a sense. Those are given by Macawna to mark one's intellectual progress."

Between the two of them, they force Lorik down the entire list. He tells them that the runes we've always believed were for experiencing our first moments of fear are actually to show the first moment we experienced bravery—his gift. The lines we earn above our eyebrows, the ones many assumed marked a person for heartbreak are actually symbols for learning compassion—a gift from my namesake. Dovenia's rune of peace is earned upon death, and

Veltuur's gift of balance, the gloves of runes, are earned once a person has walked with death and returned back to the land of the mortals.

Confusion crinkles Sinisa's brow. She looks down at her hands, then over to me, but she quickly averts her gaze to Belsante beside me instead, and examines the runes on her face.

"What about Quetzi?" Sinisa asks. "She's the only one you haven't mentioned yet. What's her rune?"

Sungema responds. "Quetzi grants no rune. She believes mortals should be intrinsically motivated to find integrity, not motivated by whether a rune would appear or not, and so she did not grant one."

"If we're done with all that, I have a more pressing question," Lorik interjects. He reaches across the group to snatch the blade from Sinisa. Turning to glare at Sungema, he adds, "What is a mortal girl doing with the Blade of Immortality?"

"She is no mere mortal girl," Sungema says. "She is the Prophesized One."

With a raise of his feathered eyebrow, Lorik twists to take Sinisa in. His hawk-like eyes rove over her, up and down, and when he finally does speak again, his voice is as hard and sharp as his beak. "Well that's great news. Where is he then? Where is Veltuur?"

Sungema sighs. "He awaits us in the underrealm."

Lorik snorts. "He's still claiming the realm of prophecy as his own?"

"He is. But not for long. Sinisa has set out to free the Altúyur. She has restored the Divine Iracara, Dovenia, myself, and now you to our true forms. We have allies who seek to release Pecolock, and others who search for Quetzi, whom we believe she already inadvertently saved."

He nods, once and resolute. "We go to the realm of prophecy then, free Macawna, and then face Veltuur. Once I get my hands on him—"

"Not yet," Sungema says at the same time I yell, "No!"

All eyes turn to me. I look down to my hands, see the runes of a

Guardian there again. It startles me again. It doesn't seem real, to know that I am truly no longer a Reaper, that I have finally escaped that dark and damp place for good. But then I remember what Aulow told us about those who become Guardians, how they become connected with the souls they save, and I remember that my last contract was for Sinisa's life.

Wide-eyed, I bring my gaze up to hers. Once more, we are bound by forces greater than ourselves, our paths intertwined in ways that feel...fated.

"You have something to say?" Lorik asks me, jarring me from my thoughts.

"I just meant...first, will you restore bravery to the people? They have been without it for years—for ages. They could use some now. Help them see the err in their ways. Help them undo the damage that's been done by the Law of Mother's Love."

The Divine Lorik snorts. "No matter my absence, the mortals have always been granted the courage they need for the events they must endure."

"They haven't been given enough," I growl.

He holds my gaze, eyes narrowing. "What would you have me do? Pump them so full of fearlessness that they lose sight of caution? Fire is beautiful, but they do not walk into it for fear that it will kill them. They sleep at night in the comfort of their homes instead of roaming the forests aimlessly because they know what dangers lurk about in the dark. If you're asking for me to ensure that mortals only ever feel bravery, then I refuse. It is part of the balance. For all the wrong Veltuur has caused, he was wise to bestow fear upon them."

Sinisa watches him curiously. "The way you talk, about balance and the importance of fear...I'm surprised you—"

"What?" Lorik asks. "You're surprised Veltuur and I aren't better friends?"

I don't see her nodding, I'm too fixated on the energy pulsing through me, the failure, the untruths. Lorik begins to explain himself and his complicated relationship with the underrealm ruler, but I cut him off.

"Stop..." I say. My head won't quit shaking. My hands, they tremble like rapids surge through them. "No... Th-this can't be. The Wraiths, they said—"

"The Wraiths?" Sinisa sneers. "The Wraiths are nothing more than Veltuur's pets. Why would you believe anything the Wraiths said?"

"No, you don't understand—"

"Enough," Sungema calls out over us. "What I don't understand is why we're still here. The Fatebringer Pendant is in our possession. Lorik is freed. Now is the time to return to the camp and await the others. Dovenia will likely be returning with Quetzi any day now, and Iracara will be back with Pecolock soon as well."

No one seems to argue, and as she leads the others away, back to the southern tip of the island where she and Sinisa apparently asked a boat to come for us, I fume at Lorik's words. What good is balance when good people are being harmed by it? What good is balance when fear rules the actions of everyone in the kingdoms?

Balance is overrated. The people—*my* people—could thrive without fear.

And so, it appears I have a new investment in Sinisa's destiny.

I, too, want to see Veltuur destroyed and the balance he brings ripped from the realms.

25

WELCOME HOME

SINISA

T he journey to camp is fraught with tension. Miengha mourns the loss of Avalanche, Acari the loss of Borgravid and the rest of his guard. Sungema spends her time answering Lorik's questions about what has come to pass since he was last himself, and Belsante mostly keeps to her thoughts, to the conversation she has with the woman she loves across Tayaraan.

So my woes seem pitiful by comparison. I do not mourn the fallen, nor the danger my loved ones may be facing. Instead, I grieve over the pathetic shattering of my ego.

It was ridiculous of me to think Acari could feel for me the same way I have grown to feel for him. Not only is he a king, and I a mere orphan girl without a place to call home, but our diverse upbringings are only the beginning of what separates us. I was sent to kill Gem. I am the person responsible for why he became a Reaper. His father is dead because I did not act quickly enough and I can never expect to receive his forgiveness.

Not to mention, Acari loves another. Though she no longer walks the living realm, I know his heart is still with her. By the way Hayliel talked about him, they would've married if they'd had the chance.

And I don't know what's worse, feeling heartbroken or embarrassed by his rejection.

Mostly though, I just feel foolish. Never had he given me any indication that he felt the same. Never had I caught him gazing at me the way Aulow does Belsante. I didn't think, I just acted, and now I will spend the rest of my life regretting ever having kissed him.

Acari doesn't say a word the entire boat ride between the isles, nor during the trek back through the forest. He keeps to himself near the back of the group and I let him. There's nothing more for me to do or say anyway. He is free from the underrealm. Isn't that all I wanted for him?

By the time we arrive back to the Guardian camp, Rhet and Dovenia have already returned. They wait in the main hut with Quetzi, a woman of aquamarine and cerulean. Her feathers drape behind her, long and flowing, like she drifts deep in the ocean even though we stand on dry land. Her dress, too, flows down her body, sleek and as smooth as rose petals.

"We found her in a tree at the swamp, not too far from the gate," Rhet reports, making sure to step out of Quetzi's earshot. "She was too frightened to leave for fear of becoming the serpent once more."

Sungema nods, turning to Belsante. "And what news of Iracara and Aulow?"

"They located and have freed the Divine Pecolock. They make their return trip now and expect to be back within a day."

"That is good news," Lorik says. "Then we have one day to prepare for our infiltration of Veltuur's nest. Have you a plan already in mind?"

"In fact, we do," Sungema answers. She comes to the center of the room and waits for the attention of us all. "Now that Sinisa has the Fatebringer Pendant, she will face Veltuur with the Blade of Immortality and put an end to the suffering he causes, once and for all. The prophecy will be fulfilled, and all will be right in the realms once more."

With a grunt of approval, Lorik grabs the hilt of his blade. It rings as he pulls it free, holding it out for one final gaze of approval before crossing the room to stand before me

"Then it appears this belongs to you."

I glance up at the blade, note the blood dried along the edge from where I removed the satyr's hand. Death has never bothered me, but I can't say I have much experience with blood. To kill as a Reaper is a clean affair. It's quick, some might even claim painless. But to thrust a blade through a heart—assuming the Altúyur even have hearts—it's not something that I think I will enjoy.

But my mother died for this prophecy to be brought to fruition. So did Avalanche, and Dethoc, and Hayliel, and so many countless others.

I grab the blade from Lorik, the black hilt warm and rough against my palm, take the sheath he offers next, and nod a silent promise that I will do what I must so that all of the lives lost won't be for nothing.

"Very well. For now, then, we rest and wait for the others to return. Tell me, is there food here?" Sungema asks, turning to Rhet.

With his arms crossed, Rhet nods for her to follow. Lorik goes too, as does Miengha. But before Belsante leaves as well, with a silent flick of her eyes, she encourages me to talk to Acari.

I shake my head, but she insists.

"Take him to see his sister," she whispers. "He's worked so hard to give her a better life. As have you."

She pats my cheek, a little harder than I expect, and her smile widens before she turns and leaves us.

Rolling my eyes, I turn around and clear my throat. "Would you like to see Gem?"

It's the first time he's looked at me since our kiss. My heart swells beneath his gaze and thoughts of the taste of him boil me alive again.

His eyes fill with hope and surprise, but he reins it all in and says softly, "Yes, I would like that very much."

We make the short trip to Gem's hut, my feet groaning the entire walk, no matter how brief. I feel like someone's shaved off the soles of my feet they're so raw. When this is all said and done, if I never trek across the Tayaraan realms again, I'll be thoroughly pleased.

Before we reach her quarters, the same hut where Hayliel and I rested the night we stayed here, a gaggle of children run out from behind it, their giddy giggles and energetic squeals enough to stop us in our tracks.

Acari's voice quivers. "Gem?"

The young girl stops as if her feet have just been captured by vines. She blinks over to us, finding me first before spotting her brother, a ghost she likely thought she'd never see again.

"Acari!" she squeals, racing for him with her arms wide.

He takes a knee, envelops her in his arms, and lifts her into the air.

"Y-you said my name," he says into her hair, squeezing tighter. "Ah, I've missed you."

Gem squirms from his arms, and though he's reluctant to release her, he does. She points to me. "Sinsa save."

"I tried, little one," I tell her. "But your brother didn't need my help. It was you that brought him back. He fought to make sure you would never have to be afraid again."

Gem tilts her head, looking back to her brother.

He reaches up to his neck and buries his face. "It's not like it worked. The Law of Mother's Love still exists. The Divine Lorik and Divine Iracara won't do anything to change it."

I shrug and offer what I hope is a reassuring smile. "It just means you still have more work to do as king. It doesn't mean you failed her."

He sighs. Gem barrels into him again, hooking her arms around his legs until he can't help but smile down at her. "In the meantime, I guess it's a good thing she has a Guardian to look after her."

With a snort, I look away. I don't bother reminding him of the task I'm meant to complete, of how in two days' time I'll be entering the underrealm again to face Veltuur and I'm not sure I'll make it back. Prophecy or not, who says he won't just kill me when I arrive? Who says I'll be able to find him and get close enough to shove the blade through his heart?

"Thank you," Acari says softly. "For looking out for her, for keeping your promise and protecting her."

I almost snort again. I didn't do much for the poor girl. I abandoned her to the other Guardians and went on a wild goose chase for her brother, only to return unsuccessful. Then again, I suppose out of everyone I started this journey with, Gem is one of the few who remain alive. It's a low bar, but it does make me feel a little better.

"I should leave you two alone," I say to them. "Let you catch up."

I turn my back to them and walk away without another word, ignoring the urge to look back. I'm not sure what's scarier, the thought that I'll find them both so quickly returned to themselves, or seeing that they care enough to watch me as I go.

The excitement of the camp grows loud and boisterous. Many gather, Prophets and Guardians alike, to greet the Altúyur and give their thanks. I'm dizzied by the crowd that floods the path, by the shouting and hollering as the mortals sing their victory songs and hymns.

Never has the silence of the forest beckoned me more, and so I let my feet take me there. Out here, I can breathe. I can think. I can move without fear of accidentally touching anyone, even though I know my skin won't kill them anymore.

There's a log, one freshly fallen on the forest floor and I take my seat upon it and gaze up to the sky. I doubt I will have another moment of peace before I depart tomorrow, and so I savor every breath of fresh air, every chirp of a bird singing overhead, and try not to think about whether facing Veltuur will go as planned. I have a whole day's journey ahead of me before I make it to the Kallinei Swamp; I can fret about it then.

A twig snaps, silence ringing through the air.

I stand from the log, legs damp from where they rested on a patch of moss, and examine the dense trees around me. Everything is still. It's like even the wind is too frightened to move, the leaves too frightened to even rustle.

The shadows feel no fear though. They slither along the forest floor, black eels of torment and torture. They close in on me like they are ready to feast, like I am a meal just seconds away from being devoured.

"Well," purrs a voice from behind me. "How fortuitous to meet here once again."

I feel his breath on my neck, smell the sickly stench of death that follows everyone who dwells in the underrealm, especially the Shades.

Nerul leans closer, his pale lips almost pressed against my ear. "I must admit, I've looked forward to this moment for far too long."

I remember the blade a moment too late. My hand closes around the hilt just as his closes around my neck. He pulls me back, throwing me to the cold, forest floor, and stands over me. When he sees me grabbing for my blade again, he kneels on top of me, pinning my arms in place and weighing my chest down with the weight of a boulder for someone so thin.

He cocks his head. "You didn't die."

And for a moment I think maybe I can talk my way out of this. Maybe I can convince him I'm now invincible and that he should leave me alone before he finds out just how dangerous I am. But instead, Nerul shrugs, calls for his crow, and thick, heavy smoke rises all around us.

Not just smoke, I realize. But Nerul has brought with him the Wraiths.

My chest pounds a their claws tighten around my ankles and calves. It's all too familiar. I'm a young girl again who's just made a terrible mistake.

I'm not ready to return to the underrealm yet. I haven't thought anything through. The other Altúyur aren't even ready to join me.

But as the smoke clears, all of my worries fade with it when I see the mammoth, winged creature waiting for me.

"Hello, Sinisa," Veltuur says, his voice like a low rumble of thunder. "Welcome home."

26

GEM

ACARI

"They're treating you well here?" I ask, dipping a piece of naan into the steaming bowl of curry.

Gem nods and takes a bite entirely too big for her mouth.

A laugh escapes me. "I see they've taught you to eat like an animal."

Gem scowls, a frightening but playful thing.

My hands go up in mock defense. I return to my meal, savoring every rich flavor and spice, grateful to once again be able to eat tomatoes and lentils.

With a mouth full of food, I ask her, "Do you think you're ready to return to the palace soon?"

Her eyes flit to mine long enough for me to see her tears forming there. "No go...friends." She hangs her head.

"We can still visit. Your friends, they'll still be here. Or, once I change the Law of Mother's Love, perhaps they can even join us in Azarrac City. They'd be welcome there and placed under the king's protection."

Her eyes snap up to mine again, sorrow edging the only words she can muster. "King gone."

I wince under the weight of her eyes, feel the guilt I should've felt days ago but haven't been able to. I killed our father. He didn't die an honorable death. Instead, his traitorous son snuck into the Forbidden Garden, retrieved one of the aacsi that was possibly responsible for the queen's and prince's deaths, and released the bug on him while he was naked in a bath.

I avert my gaze back to my bowl and take another bite.

And I jump when Gem's little hand finds my arm and her gentle smile peeks beneath my hanging chin. "Bad choices, not bad people."

A crooked smile of my own meets hers. "You're too gracious."

She frowns again as she returns to her seat. But before she can lift her bowl back to her lap, she goes rigid. Her eyes roll to the back of her skull and she collapses to the floor as stiff as a brick wall.

I crash to my knees beside her, take her head into my lap. "Help! Somebody—"

Gem's hand claps onto my wrist, forcing my gaze back to hers.

"Wings give me strength, you're all right."

Her eyes are wide and feral as she pushes herself up out of my reach.

"Are you all right?" I ask when she begins pacing. "We should get a healer. You fell—"

"Sinsa," Gem whimpers. "Sinsa."

"What? What about her? I'm sure she's..." But I can't bring myself to finish that thought because this moment is all too familiar. The panic and desperation. The camp. Sinisa disappearing without a trace. "Where is she?"

Gem shakes her head, her bottom lip quivering. "Gone."

Rhet comes up behind me, flanked by the Divine Sungema. "What is it? Gem had another prophecy?"

"She says Sinisa is gone."

"What do you mean *gone*?" Sungema asks. "She was with you, wasn't she?"

"Sh-she was, but she left. She said she wanted to give us some time alone to catch up."

"Which way did she go?" Rhet asks.

I simply point toward the main entrance.

They exchange a look, one that stirs Rhet into action. He calls over the nearby Guardians, sends them out into the woods to search for her. He summons Dovenia and Lorik as well and asks them to take to the skies to see if they can spot anything.

But neither of them move. Despite the stimulation from the rest of the camp, the three Divine Altúyur remain in place.

"What are you waiting for?" Rhet growls. "Sinisa is gone. With any luck, we'll find her before—"

"Before what?" Sungema asks. "Before destiny takes her under her wing?"

Rhet falls silent. Enraged understanding burns through his eyes as he looks from the Divine Altúyur to me. "Gem said she's in danger?"

I grimace, shaking my head.

"Danger or not," Sungema says, staring Rhet down as if they were eye to eye as opposed to him being large enough to trample over her. "Sinisa is both guided and protected by fate. Whatever has occurred, it has done so because it must. We do not intervene."

Still shaking my head, still unable to believe what I'm hearing, I ask, "What if fate wants us to go after her? What if that's why Gem saw what she did?"

The Altúyur glance between themselves.

A gust a wind blows over them as two winged beings land beside the firepit. One of them releases Aulow and she jogs to Rhet's side.

"What's going on here? Why is everyone in such a panic?"

"Sinisa has gone missing." He snarls at Sungema. "She says it's fate and that they won't help us look for her."

Aulow's eyes find mine, but before she can speak, Sungema does.

"Fate does not compel us to seek her, but perhaps King Acari is right. It is clear that he feels such a compulsion. If fate wanted him to find Sinisa, it would allow." She steps forward and looks me in the eyes. "If you feel you must go after her, then you should, for perhaps that is your destiny."

All eyes bore into me. I'm not sure if I'd call it fate or destiny, but I know I am compelled to search for her. I can't let things end where they left off with us. I can't let her face Veltuur alone. She forgave her abuser just to protect me and my sister. She trekked across Tayaraan and returned to the underrealm just to free me from being a Reaper.

Whether or not it's fate, I will find her, and I will be at her side for the worst of it.

I ignore the Altúyur and Guardians staring at me, and turn only to Iracara.

"Sinisa said you were the key that allowed her entry into the underrealm."

"I—I suppose I was," Iracara says, puffing out his scrawny chest and beaming.

"Then I cannot fulfill my destiny unless you accompany me."

The Divine Iracara fluffs his black wings. "It would be an honor. Anything for the Prophesized One."

"What happens if she isn't gone?" Aulow asks. "What if she's found taking a stroll through the woods?"

A level a look at her, and she shrinks away as I square my shoulders and prepare for Iracara to take me in his talons.

27

A PLACE TO BELONG

SINISA

"**I** did it, Master. I brought Sinisa to you," Nerul says, his nails digging into my throat. "What do you want me to do with her?"

"You can start by removing her weapon."

Nerul flinches. His attention drops to the blade still sheathed at my hip, but his hold does not loosen from my neck. He grips me tighter, a warning for me not to try anything rash. Standing before Veltuur, somewhere deep within the underrealm, with Wraiths swirling all around me ready to pounce if need be, I have no choice but to let him slide the blade out of its sheath and toss it to Veltuur.

"Ah, the Blade of Immortality. And what were your plans with such a weapon?"

Realizing he already knows the answer to that, I decide there's no reason to lie. "To shove it through your heart," I growl.

It earns me another yank back, Nerul's claws almost certainly drawing blood now.

Out of the corner of my eye, I see the grotesque creature that is Veltuur smiling through his mangled beak. He examines the blade, once again it appears much more like a dagger in the hands of an immortal. He runs a feathered finger from hilt to point before returning his attention to Nerul.

"There's too much bite in her. Send her to the Wraiths. I will retrieve her when she's feeling more...cordial."

My eyes pop wide. "No. No, no, no. Don't send me to the Wraiths!"

I claw and kick. I scream and squirm, but for all my efforts, it's utterly useless. No one can outrun the Wraiths.

Nerul releases my neck, shoving me into the center of the unfamiliar stone room, and darkness rushes toward me. I feel their chilling, damp claws all over my body as they drag me below. Screams fill the atmosphere, some distant, and others so close I could swear they were right behind me.

I land somewhere dark and black. Nothing to be seen as far as the eye can see, nor as close. I bring my hand to my face, straining to see something, anything to help me get my bearings, but it is void of all light. I see nothing.

I feel them, though, the Wraiths as they descend. They scuttle through the ether like whispers carrying on a winter night's wind. I reach for the blade, only to remember that it is no longer there. Instead, I clutch the pendant around my neck.

"It is protected?" the Wraiths hiss, their voices as one. "Fate guards it closely."

"It does," I say, and then even more emboldened, "I am. You cannot harm me. I am here with a purpose, and nothing can stop me from fulfilling it—"

"It freed the remaining Altúyur. It is ready to fulfill its destiny."

Lowering my fists, I straighten. "You know about the prophecy?"

"Of course they know, dear Sinisa," purrs a voice from the darkness. "I kept them well-informed, should the day come that you found yourself unfortunate enough to meet them."

Collectively, they hiss.

"Leumas?" I say. My hands reach out through the heavy black until I brush against the silken robe. He steps closer, and I can feel the hobble in his walk just as it has always been. "Leumas! It's really you!"

I surprise myself when I throw my arms around him. He pats the top of my head with one slender hand until I finally step back from clutching a rib cage that felt like it could crumble to dust any day now. If he was alive during the War of Divinity, it's no wonder he and the other Councilspirits have always seemed so decrepit. I do, however, wonder how they managed to survive. My mother required the Fatebringer Pendant to ensure she lived this long, a necklace that Owlena herself created as a way to ensure the prophecy was fulfilled, so I don't imagine all of the Councilspirits have one too.

But instead of veering off track, I ask, "What are you doing here?"

"I already told you Veltuur was going to find me. For now, this is where he keeps me."

I glance around the room, to the Wraiths I know still linger but I cannot see. "Yes, but, why are you *here*, with me? Why are they letting us speak?"

"Because I asked them to."

"It behooves us," the Wraiths sigh.

"But why?" I ask. "What's the point? I've already failed. Nerul kidnapped me, Veltuur stole the Blade of Immortality, and I'm trapped down here with the Wraiths, until who knows how long. Veltuur could leave me down here forever, if he likes, bringing about the death of the prophecy once and for all."

I can hear Leumas' smile as he speaks. "No, he will not. He is too intrigued by you and too invested in holding on to the power he's built for himself over the years to let you live down here forever. When he retrieves you, he will try to kill you. But first, he will have questions."

"Like what?"

"He will want to know who you've freed, where they lay in wait, their plans for him."

I bite my lip. "Then I'll have to stall him long enough to get the blade back."

"I am sure you will think of something."

"Why?" I breathe. "Why have you guided me all this time? Why have you believed in me? And don't just say *it is your fate* because I know that's not all."

Leumas takes in the quiet. I hear him breathe it in like it is oxygen to his lungs. "In part, it is because you are fated. But you are right, there is more. I would've assumed the Divine Sungema would've told you by now—"

I snort. "She doesn't tell me anything."

"Yes, well, when you are the holder of all memory, I imagine that sometimes certain things don't seem as important to share." He pauses, letting me ruminate on that thought while he returns to the question at hand. "Allow me to have the honor in shedding some light on my loyalties. I was Prophet to the Divine Owlena, and in fact, I was more."

My cheeks blush, remembering the sight of them before the battle in the desert, the gentle way he kissed her hand.

"I...saw," I say awkwardly.

Leumas considers this for a moment before continuing. "Before the War of Divinity, we bore a child. It was an unexpected miracle, as no other Altúyur had borne children before. As you can imagine, Owlena claimed it was fate that brought us a daughter, though it was many years before we truly understood why.

"Like her mortal father, the girl bore the mark of prophecy. However, hers was a hidden malformity, one that society never wrote into the Law of Mother's Love, for it was not one that could be easily identified."

Confused by where this is going, but curious nonetheless, I ask, "What was that?"

"Tetrachromacy," he says. "It's a term that philosophers use to describe when someone has greater access to color distinctions than the average person."

My scowl deepens when no revelation comes to me. It's obvious from the way he speaks that he thinks I'll be able to piece together whatever puzzle he's laid out for me, but it's like I'm still missing pieces. Even without them though, I can tell from the sinking pit in my stomach that whatever understanding is approaching, it will be a shattering one.

"Our daughter could see hues and vibrancy like no one else I'd ever met," Leumas continues. "Where I saw the green of a blade of grass, she could point out the dark seaweed color of the vein, the way the darkness bled into the bright emerald until it was practically as bright as a lime along the edges. Where we saw red, she'd find scarlet and rose and blush.

"But I think what I envied about her most of all was the way in which she saw gray. It was like to her, it was—"

"Blue..." I utter. "She always called my eyes blue." The words are like an anchor that I hoist from my lips, and just as I expected, the weight of them sends me plummeting. Disorientation makes my stomach churn. "You're...you're talking about my mother."

I'm grateful when his hand rests upon my shoulder, for it's the only thing that steadies me.

"You are so tightly bound to fate, dear Sinisa, because your mother, Khastyl, was Owlena's and my daughter. You are not only a descendant of the Altúyur of Fate herself, but you are my kin. I could never have doubted you."

Blinking, I stagger still. "So, you're...you're my—"

"Grandfather."

"And Owlena was my...grandmother."

"Indeed she was. It is why she fought so hard to ensure your fate was fulfilled. So many things could've interfered with or disrupted your destiny. She had to ensure you had the opportunity to exist. All of Tayaraan depended on it, but also, you were family, a rare gem that no other Altúyur was granted."

If there was a chair behind me, I would fall back into it and rest. Most of my life I believed I was alone. I never knew what happened to my father. I never knew my mother was still alive. But Leumas had been there for me. He was the first to greet me when I arrived in the underrealm for my initiation. He aided me in more ways than I can even keep track of anymore. Even still, from the darkest depths of the most horrific corners of the underrealm, he is here for me now.

"What will happen to you once I fulfill the prophecy?"

I hear his cloak rustle as he shakes his head. "Never mind what happens to me. I've lived a long enough life for one person."

"You would die then?" My chest cracks when I say the word. "You would die just as my mother has."

"It is a price I've been eager to pay since the moment I heard of the prophecy. Sinisa, do not grieve over me. We have been fortunate enough to be reunited, you and I. It's not something I ever anticipated, but I cherished every moment of it."

"You can't die." My voice chokes. The tears welling in my eyes seem to clog my throat instead of washing my face. "I can't lose you too. What's the worst that could happen if I just let Veltuur live?"

"Sinisa!" Leumas scolds. "That can't even be a consideration. Need I remind you what he's done to you?"

"He made me stronger! He brought us together!"

My words echo throughout the chasm of nothing. Leumas quiets, and I know him well enough to know that he's devising a wise monologue that will make me doubt everything.

But as his lips part, the Wraiths stir around us. "They come."

"Sinisa, you must promise me," Leumas says, grabbing my shoulder. "No matter what you do, you must—"

The Wraiths hiss louder. "They come and only one must be here when they arrive!"

Leumas exhales, a begrudging noise. "Do what you've been brought here to do," he advises, before the two of us are ripped apart from each other.

I fall backward, darkness buzzing below me, behind me, and all around me, until the underrealm—the habitable levels—reappear, gray and desolate. I find myself standing in a small room that smells like moss and wet stone. My eyes drift to a black pool at my feet, and I wonder if that's where the Wraiths dwell. The water certainly seems dark enough. Not even a glint of light reflects off its inky, still surface.

Nerul breathes hungrily in my left ear as he once again wrenches the back of my neck so that I am staring at Veltuur.

"Tell me, Prophesized One," Veltuur says. "Are you ready to talk?"

Thoughts of Leumas return to the forefront of my mind. I know what he wants from me, but what about what *I* want? Family. A place where I belong. A purpose. The only place I've ever had those things was here, with Veltuur.

"Tell me, what brings you here?" Veltuur asks. He stalks around the room, dark wings wrapped over his hunched shoulders. "Obviously, I'm aware that my Shade retrieved you, but you were on a path that would lead you to the underrealm regardless. But why? It can't *just* be to fulfill a prophecy. That is too cliché for someone like you."

All I can do is shake my head. "Truthfully, I no longer know."

He perks up. "Very interesting. It seems your time with the Wraiths was more impactful than I'd realized. Then I'll change my question. Tell me what it is you want, what you *truly* desire and have always desired."

My eyes water again.

"Go on. Say it."

Once again, I become that little girl left at the orphanage, the one who felt all alone and lost. "I want a family. To be loved. I want a place where I belong and can call home."

Veltuur nods his long beak. "And what better place than in the underrealm? Have you not always been accepted here? Have we not always loved you like one of our own? Up there, the mortals are cold and cruel. They only care for themselves and their blood, but you no longer have blood living. You are all alone. But you wouldn't be here."

Metal clangs on the stone floor and I startle. When I drop my gaze to my feet, I'm surprised to find the Blade of Immortality resting before me.

"Has anyone told you what this blade is capable of?"

My eyes flit to his, but my mouth is sewn shut. I look back down at the blade, my heart drumming inside me yet again. Nerul's nails are still too tightly wrapped around my neck for me to bend over for it, but then why throw it at my feet? Why tempt me?

"It can kill any of the Altúyur. I'm sure they've told you this. But did they mention that the blade's powers can go both ways?" A wicked smile curves Veltuur's beak when he sees the understanding flash across my face. "They didn't? Need I remind you who I am?"

And suddenly it hits me. I close my eyes, the realization so painfully obvious that I can't believe I didn't think of it before. "You're the Altúyur of Balance. It is your job to ensure that everything has equilibrium."

"Precisely. This weapon is not named the Blade That Can Kill An Altúyur. Where it can remove immortality, it can create it as well."

With a nod to Nerul, his grip around my neck releases.

"Pick it up."

I hesitate, glancing from the blade back to Veltuur.

"Pick it up," he says more encouragingly.

Slowly, I do as he instructs. Once it's in my hands, there's something about it that feels different. No longer does it just represent the life it can take, but also that which it can give. I run my thumb along the black leather, notice the feathers that swirl around the bird skull on the hilt.

"You have two options," Veltuur tells me. "Kill me and disrupt the balance of the realms, but do so feeling emboldened that you have fulfilled a primeval, forgotten prophecy. Or, plunge the blade into your own heart, embrace immortality, and rule with me here in the underrealm."

Though I try stopping my eyes, they bulge again. It is the dichotomy of decisions, a choice between life and death, of fate and choice, of past sacrifices and future ones. I cannot be the only person to make such a choice. To let Veltuur live means to let him continue binding Reapers to the souls of those they killed first. It means condemning every Reaper—past, present, and future—to never knowing who they were, who their crows were, who their families were.

"You would have family here, and love and acceptance."

He doesn't know how right he is. I already have those things here. Leumas has been more family to me than anyone living has ever been. When my parents disappeared, my aunt Theffania let me rot away in an orphanage in Oakfall. My own mother, even once I told her who I was, still chose to die without the memories of my childhood, of our family, rather than accept me into her life.

But Leumas has always been there.

And I've never felt more at home anywhere than I do beneath the blackened branches of the underrealm's forest.

Would it truly be so terrible to choose this place? To make my own destiny and find happiness?

With the blade in one hand, I reach up with the other. I wrap my fingers around the blue stone, the silver encasing embedding itself into my fingers, and yank the Fatebringer Pendant from my neck. Before I can change my mind, I chuck it to the ground. I ignore the *tink-tink-tink* as it pings across the stones somewhere far behind me, and instead I lace my fingers around the hilt of the Blade of Immortality and aim it at my heart.

"Strike true, and you will never feel alone or without love again."

28

THE HERO
ACARI

"**A**re you sure you know where you're going?" I yell up to Iracara, unsure if he'll even be able to hear me over the flapping of his powerful wings.

"Have faith. Not many would learn the location of a gate to the underrealm and dare forget where it lay."

He glides lower, the swampy treetops nearly smack against my feet as we soar. I pull my legs up, trying to avoid any unnecessary injuries, but Iracara continues his descent and weaves us through the trees, down to the swampy marsh.

When my feet finally meet the earth again, it's with a hollow thump.

"See? I told you I knew where we were going."

For a whole day we traveled. From sunset to sunrise, through a rainstorm that I thought was most certainly following us just to spite us, through mealtimes and bedtimes, until we arrived here. I'm exhausted. My arms feel like they're made of dough, but Sinisa stands on the other side of this doorway, and I cannot make her wait a moment longer.

I bend over, grab the rusted handle, and lean back. The door doesn't budge.

"Oh right!" Iracara says, sticking a feathered finger into the air. "*I'm* the key. Sinisa could not open the door either. Here, step aside."

I do so, keenly, and watch as Iracara yanks the door ajar from under the swampy water with a heaving splash. We both glance down into the entrance, through the ominous fog that fills the inside.

"The underrealm is underneath Tayaraan," I say flatly. "I don't know why I never realized that before."

Iracara shrugs. "Don't beat yourself up about it. I'm not sure any mortal ever questions it."

Nodding, I peel my gaze away from his and look back into the dark hole. "Do we jump?"

"We've come all this way," he says, and without another word, he jumps through the doorway.

Immediately following him, I step through as well, and the familiar sounds and scents of the underrealm greet me. We fall until we can fall no more, until our feet meet the moist earth, and everything rights itself.

"We should separate."

I guffaw. "Why in the realm would we do that?"

"Because if we do, I can search for Macawna. She's down here somewhere, and her best chance at returning to her true form will be to witness whatever crafty plan the two of you are about to complete. Who knows the next time a mortal will be down here?" With his arms outstretched, feathers splayed, he shoos me away. "Go. Find Sinisa. Aid her as best as you can. I will find you both once I have Macawna. And then we can all get the feather out of here."

A smile cracks through me. "Do you know what you're looking for?"

"Sungema says Macawna became an abyss fly."

My eyebrow twitches at the sudden memory of the glowing orb that lured me through the underrealm's forest and into Veltuur's den. Could it be her? Could she have been trying to help us just as Leumas had?

"Try looking in the Pit of Judgment. It's like a deep dungeon where the Councilspirits held trials for the Reapers."

"I am familiar with the place. Once upon a time, all the Altúyur convened there to conduct our own trials, of a kind."

"The place was flooded with abyss flies. Maybe the Divine Macawna is there."

Iracara bows briefly, thanks me for the clue, before leaving me where I stand. If only I had the foresight to ask Iracara where I might find Sinisa, where Veltuur might've taken her, perhaps I wouldn't be stuck standing here looking like a clueless idiot.

Shadows pool at my feet.

"Not this again," I mutter, just as the claws reach out and drag me below.

"It returns and it is mortal once more," the Wraiths groan, their collective voices like the howl of wind. "It has come to fulfill its promise."

Realizing they're not entirely wrong, I shake my head. "I believe Veltuur brought Sinisa here. I think he's trying to stop her from completing the prophecy and I need to help her. It's the only way to defeat him, the only way to ensure your release. Do you know where they are?"

"I'm afraid you may have your work cut out for you," rasps a voice from the darkness. It's distinct from the Wraiths though, clearly the voice of a single man as opposed to thousands.

"Leumas? Is that you?"

"It is, boy."

"Do you know where Sinisa is?"

"I do, and the Wraiths will take you to her. But we fear Sinisa may not be up for the task."

I frown, only aware after that he can't see me just like I can't see him. "Why not?"

Guilt plummets in my stomach. I fear I already know the reason. I fear I'm the one that has caused her to doubt herself. She had been so sure on the beach, hadn't hesitated at all when she kissed me, and foolishly, I couldn't give her the same.

"There is no time," Leumas says. "Do you still have the feather?"

My hand floats to my chest, a gesture that goes unnoticed, so I say, "Yes."

"Then you must go. You must finish what Sinisa cannot. The realms depend on it."

Again I'm tossed through darkness. I'm pulled through the ether like I'm falling upside down and sideways and every which way possible. It's not until I land that I'm able to tell down from up again; it's not until I land that I realize where I am.

The slate corridor towers around me. Up ahead, I hear the hushed voices of a man and a woman, but I can't make out any of their words. My instincts reassure me it can only be Sinisa and Veltuur, and so I make my quiet journey down the hallway.

As I reach the end, I hug the flat wall.

"You would have family here," Veltuur's voice rumbles. "And love and acceptance."

Panic tells me to jump out from where I hide, it tells me to confess that I should've kissed her back. But panic also tells me to stay put. My hands rise to the feather stuffed between my shirt and my chest. If what Leumas says is true, if Sinisa can no longer make this choice, then I am her only hope, and the only way to save her and the rest of the realms is by getting close enough to Veltuur.

Something clinks across the floor, like that of a small vial. It rolls to the hallway, and my eyes widen when I see the Fatebringer Pendant at my feet. Another wave of fear spikes through me. What could cause her to remove the only necklace that's protecting her? What will Veltuur do to her while she's vulnerable?

Muttering a curse, I bend over and retrieve the pendant before storming into the room. "Sinisa!" I roar, but my voice breaks when I see her aiming the Blade of Immortality at her own heart. "Sinisa."

She jolts, her hold on the blade weakening. "What are you doing here?"

"Me?" I gesture to her weapon. "What are *you* doing here? What is he making you do?"

"Nothing. He's not making me do anything. I was... He made me an offer."

With a snort, I dare a step closer, eyeing Nerul beside her, and noting Veltuur lurking in the dark corner. If I can just get closer, if I could get around the pool, I might be able to blow on his feather and my breath might reach him.

"And what offer was that? To die and abandon all of Tayaraan?"

"I'm not abandoning anyone. I can stay here and rule at his side. I can make the underrealm a better place and maybe even—"

"That's absurd. After everything, you really think you have no better place to be than down here, surrounded by death? I'm sorry about earlier. I didn't mean to—I was just afraid what my touch would do to you. I didn't mean to hurt your feelings. I like you—"

Her eyebrows shoot to her hairline, her jaw practically coming unhinged. "You think this is about you? That I'm some petulant, heartbroken girl who is going to lock herself away just because some boy rejected me?"

Abashed, my hand floats to the back of my neck. When she puts it like that, I sound like the biggest egotist in all the kingdoms. Wincing, I meet her eyes. "I'm...sorry. Is that not it?"

"I don't belong up there, Acari! I never have. My father abandoned me to search for my mother rather than taking care of me. My aunt gave up looking for me. And my mother completely forgot I even existed until I confronted her, and even then, she didn't want me. She chose death and supposed fate over being with me."

"That's not true—it's not fair."

"All that Tayaraan has ever given me is grief and pain. Why wouldn't I stay down here? It's the only place I've ever truly belonged, the only place I have family."

Lowering my gaze, I become solemn. I don't want to hold this over her, but it's the only card I have left to play. "Because you made a promise," I grit out. "You told me you'd protect Gem."

Sinisa scoffs. "She has her brother to protect her now."

I shake my head. "She needs more than just a brother. She's grown attached to you. I can see it. She, too, has known only pain from her short life in Tayaraan. Her own father locked her away in a tower for three years. Her mother and brother died. Her only living brother killed their own father and abandoned her when he became a Reaper. If you left too, she'd be heartbroken. So would Aulow and the others. So would..." The words catch on my throat, jagged and heavy, but if this is my last chance to tell her everything, then I know I can hold nothing back. "So would I. I would miss you."

The blade in her shaking hands lowers a little more, and so I continue.

"You talk of wanting family and a place where you belong—well, you've found it. The Guardians are your family. Gem is your family. And whether you decide to stay at the camp or come to Halaud Palace with us, you have a home regardless."

Sinisa's brow twitches, a cyclone of emotions raging just beneath her surface. She looks down to the blade, blinks furiously, and then, to my great relief, lowers it all the way down, until the tip is nearly touching the stone floor.

I offer her a grateful smile, one that she returns in kind.

But in a flash of smoke, Nerul disappears from beside her. He blinks into existence before me and roars, reaching his hands for my neck.

29

MOMENT OF DEFEAT

SINISA

I lunge for them.

The Fatebringer Pendant has already proven itself, and yet, I still lunge. Dethoc's death flashes before my eyes, how all it had taken was a single touch from Nerul and he was gone.

Nerul's hand closes around Acari's neck and I scream.

But Acari does not collapse. His skin does not turn sickly white.

Instead, they vanish.

Smoke fills the space where they were standing, thick and roiling. I fall through the cloud, arms pinwheeling, searching for the two bodies who had just been there, but all I grasp is the stone floor where I crash.

Out of sight, Nerul says through gritted teeth, "What's wrong, Sinisa? Afraid you'll lose someone else?"

I spin around, finding the two of them standing alongside Veltuur, Nerul's hand still clutching Acari's neck.

I raise the blade. "Put. Him. Down."

"Fool!" Veltuur roars. The stones beneath my feet quake, the walls surrounding us trembling as if his very words travel through them. "I did not command you to grab the boy."

Nerul looks wounded. "But...Master. She was about to turn on you—"

"I promised her a family, somewhere she will know nothing but acceptance, and you make me out to be a liar!"

This time, the force that rolls through the underrealm is no mere tremor. The black waters splash against the ridge of the pool. Rocks tumble from somewhere high overhead. The floor cracks, steam rising like it's boiling from the underrealm itself.

Hesitantly, Nerul releases Acari. He gasps for a breath of air, falling to the ground, and I race to his side.

"Are you all right?" I whisper, trying to keep a third eye on what's happening beside us between Nerul and Veltuur.

Massaging his neck, Acari nods through a fit of coughs.

At least he's breathing, I reassure myself, leaving him on his knees as I rise. From this distance, when I raise my blade, it catches the ball of Nerul's throat. The blade bobs when he swallows.

"Forgive him," Veltuur says to me, voice cloyingly sweet as he reaches up to gently shove the blade aside. "He only acts because he fears what you may do to *his* family. I'm sure you can understand."

I narrow my eyes. I try fighting the logic of it, but despite my best efforts, Veltuur's words reach me. If the underrealm is all I've ever thought I had, surely it feels the same for Nerul, and right now, I threaten it all.

I lower the blade from Nerul's neck, but keep it readied, just in case. After all, it's not the neck I need to aim for if I decide to end him or Veltuur. But if I'm being honest, I'm still not sure I want to do either. I've had enough killing for one lifetime. I've killed innocents and those who are guilty, pigeons and coyotes, snails and stigrees. I don't want to add Shades and Altúyur to that list. I just want to start over, build a new life for myself, maybe even return to the newfound family Acari reminded me I have.

"What are you waiting for?" Acari rasps. "Kill him. End this. You don't have to be stuck down here for the rest of your life. It can all be over—"

Once more, Acari is consumed by black clouds, only this time, when he reappears, it's in Veltuur's massive grasp. With one single hand, though it has only three talons, he grips Acari by the chest and holds him up. Every sense in my body, every alarm, bell, and whistle, goes off.

"If it isn't the Reaper King," Veltuur says, examining him with his black, beady eyes. "Ah, he isn't a Reaper anymore though. Which can only mean—" He glances over his shoulder at me before turning his back and shielding Acari almost entirely from sight. "Of course *she* would be the one you decided to give up your Reaper life for. I should have known. Fate is wound so tightly around the two of you, you couldn't resist the pull of it. Maybe you're right, Nerul. Maybe this is a lost cause."

My eyes widen with understanding and fear. We are about to die, and I hadn't even once wondered who Acari had become a Guardian for when he regained his runes on the Howling Isle. I had been too consumed by self-pity to even think about it. But I know he had been sent to kill me in the Forbidden Garden, and since Veltuur banished him back to Oakfall shortly after, I doubt he was given any new contracts.

And even though it all seems so obvious now, not once had it even occurred to me that Acari was my Guardian. He is sworn to protect me until the end of his days, bound to me like I am bound to Gem, like Aulow is bound to Belsante. No wonder he's here for me. Veltuur was right. Fate really has ensnared us—

At the same moment understanding rushes over me, Nerul's elbow cracks into my nose. I stumble backward, falling to the ground with a heavy thud, as white-hot pain sears across my face.

He leans low over me. "Just because I can't kill you, doesn't mean I can't make you feel pain."

This time it's his knee, and when it slams into my face, I hear the bones crack. I fall all the way back. My world spins, gray and blurry. My fingers lose their grip on the blade, though I can still faintly feel it beneath my hand.

But it's Veltuur's voice that brings me back.

"What's that in your hand, Reaper King?"

There is no response, but it catches Nerul's attention too. Instead of swinging his raised leg into my ribs, he freezes, turning to watch Veltuur.

"Go on. Show me."

My eyes flutter as I scrape around for the blade. When I finally find the rough leather wrapped around the hilt, the feathers embossed in inky black wood, my fingers know what to do, and they do not disappoint.

"It looks like some kind of necklace. Is that—"

I grip the Blade of Immortality as tight as I can, and I heave the blade up and over my body. It slices through Nerul's shins with a sickening squelch. The Shade collapses, an agonizing howl filling the small room and arousing me back to reality.

I scramble to my feet, turn to face Veltuur and Acari. "Release him," I say with force, but the wobbling blade in my hand betrays me.

Veltuur looks over his humped, feathered shoulder. "Or what? You'll kill me? I fear you plan to do this anyway."

"Release him," I demand again.

"Do not move or I end him now. Only I control the balance of life and death, so surely, you know I am able."

Seething, I steady my hand.

"What do you think will happen if you kill me? Might you become a Reaper again? Or does that thought not frighten you? No, of course it doesn't, not when you'd be killing me to protect those you love. But what might happen should the Reaper King die? If I deem his life useless, finished, would your *family* in the mortal realm be able to forgive you? Accept you? Would his sister? You'd be lost and alone once again."

Fear consumes me. It's like lightning, coursing through me, turning me into a bundle of nerves. I can't lose him. I can't lose Gem or Aulow or any of them.

"Put down the Blade of Immortality, or I stop the Reaper King's heart from beating and you have to live out the rest of your days knowing that his death was your doing."

"No," I breathe, the blade growing heavy.

I don't want this; I don't want any of this. Acari must survive. And me? I can't live here any longer. For all Veltuur's talk of family and acceptance, the kind of love I'd find here is only toxic and decaying. Leumas said himself, we've been fortunate to have the time together that we've had, but that time is over.

I steady my hand, aiming the blade at its mark.

"You can have it," I growl, and thrust the Blade of Immortality through Veltuur's back.

30

WRONG

ACARI

"Put down the Blade of Immortality, or I stop the Reaper King's heart from beating and you have to live out the rest of your days knowing that his death was your doing."

The threat reminds me just how fragile and mortal I am again, and whose company I'm in. Divine beings. Creatures of the under-realm. Sinisa and I, we are mere blips in time compared to the long life Veltuur has lived, compared to the years yet to come for him.

But it's that thought, the sudden realization that he isn't going to die, that reminds me that the Blade of Immortality isn't the only weapon at our disposal. I too, possess one, but from where Veltuur grips my chest, the feather is almost entirely rendered useless. I'd have to loosen my belt, find a way to reach into my tunic without drawing too much attention, or fumbling the feather completely.

However, it's not the only feather in this room.

"No," Sinisa mutters, a sound that breaks my heart.

I won't let her do this. I won't let her sacrifice herself for my sake. We have one other option, and she doesn't even know it, but my heart swells with pride at knowing that this time, I'll be the one doing the saving. This time, I get to repay a debt to her.

I grab the wrist that Veltuur is using to suspend me in the air. His beady eyes assess me, a flicker of concern passing over them before he deems the action unthreatening. Why wouldn't he? From every angle of the room, he appears to have the upper hand, in this case, quite literally. He's a divinity, an immortal, and I am nothing in his eyes but a pest.

But he doesn't know what the Wraiths have told me; he doesn't know that, I, alone know his and every other Altúyur's weakness; doesn't know that I know how he trapped them all.

My head feels like it might burst from where he's squeezing my neck so tightly. I can't breathe. I know I only have seconds before the darkness creeping up through my vision finishes taking its hold, and so I act fast.

Sliding my hand up the wrinkles of Veltuur's arm, I reach farther back, up to his chest, until I can just grasp his black feathers. My vision fades until all I can see is his face, the realm blackening around me. My eyes grow heavy, but not before I pluck one of his feathers free and watch his own eyes widen with recognition.

"You can have it," Sinisa growls.

There's a heartbeat of a second where I wonder what she's saying, but not long enough to distract myself from what must be done. There is no time. I act now, or I die.

I bring the feather to my lips. There's no air left in my lungs but I mimic the motion of blowing anyway, scraping and scrounging the hollow of my mouth for any remnants of air left. The bristles of the feather sway, if almost entirely imperceptible, and I'm not even convinced it's true—I might just be imagining it in my delirium— but I have no choice but to hope it is and that it's enough. I can barely breathe, but I move my lips, forcing them to form the words, even if I have no air to carry them out.

"Conundrum...Become..."

It has to be enough. It just has to.

"No," Veltuur growls. "No!"

And the moment my lips stop moving, the very second blackness overcomes me and my head sways, the pressure around my neck is relived. With a deep, gasping breath, I suck in the damp air of the underrealm, taste the death around us and drink in my life once more.

And as my eyes burst wide, I see it. Veltuur begins to coalesce. His dense body turns opaque, just as my father-crow's had. His talons disappear from where they still rest against my neck. As I plummet, I watch him shrink and shift until he's nothing more than a large, black egg rolling on the stones, and I swear I can hear the soft moans of the souls trapped below, the Wraiths sigh as they make their exit.

But before I land beside what Veltuur has become, before I can see the shadows fade from the dark corners of the room, something metal punctures the air I've swallowed and skewers me.

Hot waves burst from my torso. I blink down at the Blade of Immortality embedded in my chest to the black hilt, blood seeping around it. It looks so strange, the way it juts from my chest like a broken rib, like it's somehow a part of me.

I look up, eyes wide, to find Sinisa at the other end.

She releases her hand with a gasp, lip already trembling. "Acari...no..." she breathes. "You can't... I didn't mean..."

I stagger a step back, then another. My hands find the leather hilt, warm and slick with my blood already, and I crash to the ground, sending a new bolt of pain through my abdomen. Blood spills down my sides; it bubbles in the back of my throat. I sputter, trying to breathe through the thickness of it, trying to stay alive—I wanted to stay alive.

"Wings give me strength," breathes someone in the doorway. "What happened?"

"I didn't mean to!" Sinisa cries. She falls to her knees beside me, fretting over my wound. "I was trying to kill Veltuur, but he disappeared and...the blade just...I didn't mean to...I don't know what happened."

She finally meets my gaze and I realize, I'm afraid she's going to look away, afraid she's going to leave me to finish what we started, not realizing it's already done. I reach up and clutch her hand before she can leave; I hold her in my gaze.

"If I am to die," I say, my words escaping my lips in an anguished whisper. "I want you to be the last...person I see. I want to remember...everything you've done for me...how much you mean to me."

She shakes her head but leans in closer, until all I can see is her beautiful face. Her smoky eyes, her red lips, the runes on her face that are as bright as lavender.

Her soft and warm hand brushes my dark locks away from my eyes while someone enters the room behind her, though I still can't see them—I don't want to see them. All I care about right now is *her*.

"You are not dying here, Acari Halaud," Sinisa vows. Tears stream from her eyes, unrestrained and wild. "You have a realm to right, a kingdom to rule, and a law to reform. If I've learned anything, it's that you, of all people, have a greater purpose than dying here in this gloomy place..."

She pauses, tears her eyes away from mine and I swear it's like having my heart ripped from my chest. I know I have but a few precious moments, and all I want from them is to be with her. But the flare of hope that burns through her is as contagious as wildfire. It spreads to me the moment she starts scanning the room and I don't pull her back in. If anyone can make this right again, she can.

"That's it," she exclaims, voice echoing in the small slate chamber. "Your fate. You can be protected by fate!"

An Altúyur leans into view above her and I recognize Iracara at last. He looks down upon us, and there's a hint of calculation about him. "You might be right, Sinisa. Where is the Fatebringer Pendant?"

She shakes her head, pointing to the entrance behind her. "I took it off. I threw it over there somewhere."

As she jumps to her feet, I choke on another pool of blood. It was meant to be a small laugh, a sound of relief and disbelief, but it stops her in her steps. She sinks back into the stone floor at my side, worry consuming her.

"It's too late," she says. "By the time we find it, it'll be too late."

I shake my head, ignoring the pain that throbs through my abdomen, and before she can lose all hope, before Iracara can race to the entrance in a futile search for an ancient piece of magic that is no longer there, I hold up my hand, the one still clutching the Fatebringer Pendant.

A smile finds its way out on Sinisa's next sob. Its radiance is met only by the halo of light bursting behind her, the one I assume is emanating from Macawna who only needed to witness a mortal's intellect. Sinisa doesn't seem to notice that she's freed yet another of the Divine Altúyur. Her eyes never leave mine, and I swear, even though her lips don't move, I can hear her promising that she will never leave me again.

Iracara notices the light, but he only allows himself a small moment to acknowledge it before he looks down at me sympathetically. "Then Owlena watch over you because this is going to hurt."

I only have a second to register what he means before he steps a foot on either side of me, wraps his hand over the hilt still sunk deep into my chest and says, "Don't let go of that pendant."

And then he pulls.

Agony explodes inside me, white and searing. I cry out, my voice echoing up the never-ending walls like an aimless soul loosed from death. Despite the blade being out, despite the pendant my knuckles have turned white just to hold on to, I'm still choking on blood. I feel the warmth of it pumping out of the hole in my chest and spreading, falling down my sides like a waterfall of carnage.

Panicked, Sinisa cries, "It's not working."

"Give him time?" Iracara suggests.

"It's not working!" Sinisa growls louder.

"Perhaps he needs a healer," a woman says from the other side of the room.

As she draws Sinisa's and Iracara's attention, I rock my head to get a better look just in time to see her vibrancy. Her feathers are the brightest shade of red. Not like blood or rust, but like the petals of a flower. She has green and blue feathers as well, equally as bright and radiant. Like many of the Altúyur, she also has a beak, one that's white and curved and sharpened to a point. I don't have to have met Macawna before to recognize her presence now. Iracara did it, then. He found her and brought her to Sinisa.

"You are a Guardian, are you not?" the Divine Macawna asks. "Shouldn't you heal him?"

Sinisa nods, wiping at her tears.

Straining to regain her focus, she turns back to me. She looks incredibly, debilitatingly worried, like she's not sure she can do what is being asked of her. *I'm* not even sure she can. The powers of the Guardians are still an enigma to me, even though I am one now.

Regardless of fear though, Sinisa scoots closer to me. She holds her hands over my heaving chest and closes her eyes. I feel the warmth radiating off her, and it helps distract me, if only a little, from the burning inside me.

But the longer she sits, the longer she hovers her hands over me, the more soothing her warmth becomes. It battles with the searing pain inside me like a cool breeze trying to temper the summer sun. Where my entire torso felt scalded, the heat begins to rescind like a toxin being leeched from my body until there is only rawness, then tingling, then nothing.

With a heaving breath, Sinisa falls over me. I flinch, expecting a new flash of pain when she lands, but instead I just feel warmth, comfort, ease. Our bodies contour to each other's like she was always meant to be there. I bring one hand to my chest, to the blood still soaked in my tunic, and feel the absence of a hole. The other hand, I place gently on her shoulder and close my eyes.

But it doesn't last long.

"Are you immortal now?" Iracara asks, peeking over us again.

The thought sends a bolt of fear through me. To be immortal means to watch everyone I love die while I'm left living out my days without them.

Sinisa and I both jolt upright. We stare at each other, our eyes wide. Our lives flash before me, what could've been and should be. The friendship that continues to grow, the romance that would follow and stand the test of time. We would be beloved by the people, by all the kingdoms for what we restored to them.

And yet, if I am immortal, where does that leave her?

31

TO UPHOLD BALANCE

SINISA

"Judging from the wound," Macawna says, her beak pointed in the air. "I'd say the blade just barely missed his heart. I doubt he is immortal. Though, I suppose in a decade or two he will know for sure."

"A decade?" I choke out a gasp.

"She's joking," Iracara says. "She thinks because she's so smart, she gets to laugh at everyone else's...ineptness." He glares at Macawna. "But, excuse us for not seeing what you find so blatantly obvious. How are we supposed to know whether a blade reaches someone's heart or not?"

"Know you not the anatomy of a mortal body, Iracara? Or at the very least, the placement of the heart. That's your domain, isn't it? You should know, the heart is rarely as low as the sternum—"

"I know, I know," Iracara grumbles.

Acari and I smile at each other, a look that's says something between *I'm so grateful we're both still alive* and *I can't believe that things are continually so crazy*. But truthfully, I feel more of the first. This moment feels as if it has been in the making from the first time we entered each other's lives—for lifetimes, even. Even though defeating Veltuur was only a goal I've had for a handful of weeks, I fought harder than I've ever fought to be here, to earn this victory. Now, having won it, it almost feels unreal. Impossible.

And that feeling, that sense that things are not yet finished, brings my wary gaze to the place where Veltuur last stood. Before my blade could reach him, he disappeared, and in the frantic, desperate moments that followed, I hadn't had a chance to consider where he'd gone.

But now I see the egg, as black as charcoal, resting on the stone-cold floor.

"What happened to him?" I ask, twisting back to face Acari. "You did something, didn't you?"

Propped on his elbow, he nods, then points to a single black feather that has fallen beside the egg.

"Before Veltuur sent me back to the palace, I wandered in here by accident," he begins, pointing to the dark room around us.

"It was no accident," Macawna reminds him.

"Right. Sorry, I forgot. Fate apparently exists. Anyway, once I was here, I found a feather, and I don't know why, maybe it's all part of this fate thing, but it seemed important, too important to leave here. I hid it away before Veltuur found me, before he knew it was in my possession. He sent me to the Wraiths shortly after, who told me that it was with the feathers of the Altúyur that Veltuur was able to imprison them all."

I whip around, searching Iracara's expression for confirmation. It's not that I don't believe Acari—I do, I really do, him above all others even—but if what he's saying is true, then this is just one more of the lies the Altúyur have told me. They led me to believe the only way to defeat Veltuur was with the Blade of Immortality.

"Is that true?" I ask Iracara.

His mouth tightens into a thin line. "It is. Our feathers possess the magic to—"

Before he can finish, I spring to my feet, my hands clenched at my sides. "You knew we could imprison him? You knew there was another way to defeat Veltuur than by killing him with the Blade of Immortality, and you didn't tell me?"

"I—well, yes, I suppose. I hadn't really thought about it. The prophecy said that you were to defeat him. The feathers are but a temporary solution."

I balk, fury welling inside me.

But Macawna spreads her winged arms, indicating to the dim room. "Whether dead or trapped, look around you. It is done."

"I almost killed him," I say through gritted teeth. "I was almost responsible for ending all balance!"

The Altúyur fall silent. Iracara won't even meet my eyes, too cowardly in his withholding. Macawna, too, doesn't look at me, though her eyes wander more with purpose than guilt. She takes in the room like she's seeing it for the first time, like there is beauty buried somewhere here beneath all the slate and shadow.

"This was once a place of vision, of sanctity," she says at last. "And Veltuur poisoned it until it was nothing more than a nightmare. This realm was meant to bring about a peaceful, joyous future, guided by the prophecies foretold from these very Pools."

She gestures to the black water in the middle of the room, and this time, when I gaze into it, I see a glint of light in its reflection. I can't tell where she's going with this yet, but I'm curious enough to listen. There is still so much I don't understand about any of this, and since I am somehow intrinsically connected to it, I want to know all I can.

Macawna nods at me. "Whether by death or feather, you've done the realms a service. Fate must've intervened when she needed to, to prevent you from being the undoing of balance. But everything worked out. By trapping Veltuur, you rid this place of the pollution he unleashed upon it. For too many years, he has flooded this realm with nothing but visions of death until all the Prophets could see were the dying, until the very Pools were black, until the trees were charred and decayed. With time, now the realm can return to its former state of glory."

A knot twists inside me, one that I don't understand. If what she is saying is true, then why do I still feel guilty about it? She's right; either it was fate that intervened or just luck, but either way Veltuur is not dead, merely trapped. But even that doesn't feel like justice. He imprisoned the rest of the Altúyur in the very same manner that Acari has bound him. He's become an impossible puzzle, an egg that must find balance before ever being restored to his true state.

Staring at the black egg, a muscle feathers in my jaw. "He wasn't always like this. He just wanted to bring balance and thought the rest of you were abusing your powers. He thought he was doing the right thing."

Macawna scoffs, but Iracara placates her.

"He was not always so misguided, that is true, Sinisa," he says gently. "I believe living millennium without Sungema's memories though, nor without the gifts of any of us, forced him into a place of darkness. What he created here and above...he lost sight of the balance he once held so dearly."

"But maybe now that all of the Altúyur have returned, maybe he can change," I say, heart cracking. "If given the chance, he could return to the way he was before, right?"

I can't tell if I'm pleading for him, or for myself, but I know in my heart that I have to be right. If none of us can change, if none of us can be better, then there is no hope.

Macawna rolls her eyes.

With a sympathetic wince, Iracara says, "Perhaps."

Around us, the room continues to brighten, the shadows seeping away like clouds blown through the wind. The inky black pools become clear. The dark stones turn from charcoal, to iron, to smoke gray. It's hard to deny that Veltuur's reign here was anything but toxic. He created the Reapers. He let people who had done nothing more than defend themselves be kidnapped by the Wraiths and forced into servitude alongside the very people they'd slain. He only met death with more death.

And yet...

How many souls did I claim before I earned my redemption? How many did Aulow or Rhet, or any of the other Guardians up in Tayaraan?

Without a word, I make my way toward the large egg. It takes two hands to pick it up, but only one heart to realize that no living creature deserves to live out their days trapped inside an inanimate object. Iracara should understand that more than anyone else, but I too remember what it was like to be imprisoned, to be bound to a crow that I had tried so desperately to escape in my mortal life.

My voice cuts through the silence like a knife. "What happens to the balance now then?"

"What do you mean?" Macawna asks.

"I think you know what I mean. You are the Altúyur of Intellect. Aren't you smart enough to understand the implications of what his disappearance will do? When he trapped Sungema, she took the history of Tayaraan with her. Without Iracara's and Lorik's presence, the people lost touch with their compassion and bravery."

"Not entirely," Iracara reminds us.

"Still!" I continue. "What happens when the realm loses balance, of all things?"

Patiently, I watch Macawna and await her *brilliance*, but I can tell I've already struck a nerve, already asked too many questions for being a mortal.

"I *am* smart enough to understand the implications, and they *are* minimal. Iracara has already explained as much, but I will elaborate. Even once the rest of us had been imprisoned, tendrils of our gifts remained. Just because Iracara was locked away did not mean that no one experienced a moment of compassion in the years that followed."

I know she's right. After all, what was it that drove Acari to protect his sister if not compassion and love? What, if not bravery and courage, emboldened him to try to outrun a Reaper? What, if not cunning and intellect, allowed him to best me outside the palace long enough to escape?

"The Tayaraan realm will not be in chaos," Iracara assures me. "The only thing that has changed is that now we have the opportunity to set things right again."

"If you're so worried about Veltuur though"—Macawna sneers —"rest assured that once you restore balance back to the realms, once your fate has been fulfilled, he will be released." Upon seeing my look of confusion, she explains. "As with all of us, we had to bear witness to our gift. Quetzi needed to be shown truth, Sungema memory, and so forth. Veltuur only needs to witness the return of balance here, and from the looks of it, it has already begun. But there is still far to go before true balance is achieved."

"Wait," Acari says, pushing himself upright. He still clutches his chest, a phantom wound where the blood is still damp. The look of worry in his eyes brings concern to me as well. "What do you mean once her fate is fulfilled? She defeated Veltuur. He's gone. She's done here."

Sinking. I am sinking. The realm moves slowly, like it's been swallowed in a pool of misery, and I turn to face Macawna with dread in my eyes, hoping that Acari has only misunderstood her.

"Foolish mortals," she sighs. "Prophecies are rarely as they seem. Though the words were that Sinisa defeat Veltuur, there is more to defeat than his body. His impacts are lasting. It will take time to truly defeat the tyranny he wreaked on the realms and those who live within them."

"What are you saying?" Acari's voice catches.

Though he is expecting an answer from Macawna, it's me who answers, finally putting all of the pieces together.

"They need me to stay here," I say hoarsely. "I am the descendant of Owlena. These Pools, this realm, it belonged to her before Veltuur claimed it as his own, didn't it? It was a realm of prophecy."

Macawna gives a deep incline of her head. "And as such, it needs a ruler, someone to oversee and guide the visions."

"It's why Veltuur could never leave," I continue, everything coming together like a fog clearing. Only, this fog isn't making way for a peaceful field or blue skies. It's only revealing more darkness, more doom, and the agonizing realization that after all this, my life is still not my own.

"It's why even after Veltuur thought everything he stood for was being threatened, he had to send his minions out to do his bidding," Iracara explains. "Otherwise, he would've come after you himself, Sinisa."

"And now," Macawna adds. "Someone needs to remain here to ensure things return to their natural order."

"Then let it be someone else," Acari growls. It takes him time, but with great effort, he pushes himself to his feet and staggers, taking my hand into his own. "Y-you can't...you can't stay here. You've already done so much—given up so much." He twists to the Altúyur, venom laced in his words. "Hasn't she done enough?"

Neither Macawna nor Iracara answer him. There's nothing left to say, really. Now that the truth has been spoken, I feel the reality of it, the purpose of my path, of my fate.

Acari reaches up, cupping my cheek with the bloodied side of his palm. I lean into his hand, into the embrace I've wanted longer than I've even realized. I don't want to say goodbye to him any more than I want to live without air. This is what I've been fighting for, for him, for whatever hope I might have at exploring whatever's been building between us and drawing us together.

I step closer to him, Veltuur's egg resting in my arms between us as his other hand finds my chin. But the memory of his rejection is still too fresh and stinging. I can't bring myself to take the leap like I did last time, no matter how much my heart aches to pull him closer.

Instead, I gaze into his dark green eyes and try steadying my shallow breaths.

Just when I think I've slowed them though, he leans into me. His lips brush against mine, soft and warm. I breathe the scent of him in, pine needles and clear lakes, cedar and cloves. I grow dizzy with the anticipation of being able to taste him one more time before everything is taken away again.

A longing sinks into me. As I stare down my nose at his mouth, I know there's nothing I've wanted more than wanting him.

And just when I think I can't stand it any longer, just before I give in and risk everything for the possibility of rejection again, my heart flutters when he closes the distance between us. Our lips press against each other, and I am spinning, I am floating, I am sinking into the sweetness of him, the gentleness he's always brought.

He is family.

He is acceptance.

He is love.

My tongue flicks against his lips, begging for entrance and he gives it. I welcome him in like the night welcomes the moon. Never before has anyone meant more to me than Acari. In more ways than he knows he has saved me, and I, him. If fate is such a thing, then I have no doubt of its involvement in bringing the two of us together.

He wraps his arms around my waist and pulls me in tighter. I gasp into his mouth, a soft moan, a breath of pent up longing.

I get so carried away in tasting every inch of his mouth, in closing the space between us, that I almost forget about the egg pressed in my arms.

Saddened by the memory of it and what it represents, I take one last taste of Acari before, slowly, pulling away from him.

He feels the sadness instantly, like it too is clawing through his chest.

"Don't do this," he says, his eyes still closed, his mouth still suspended where I left him.

"I don't have a choice," I tell him, cleaving my own heart in two. "If I abandon this place now, everything my family fought for was for nothing. Everything we fought for was for nothing."

"It's for nothing already if you are forced to stay here."

A sad smile comes to my lips. "That's not true. You still have a purpose. Besides, no one deserves to be imprisoned. Not Veltuur, not the crows, not the Reapers."

"And what do you call this?" he asks, incredulous. "Fate is imprisoning you."

"It's not. This is my choice. If I've learned anything through all this, it's that no one is safe until balance is restored. Not you, not Gem, not Aulow or Belsante, or any of the Altúyur. I am Owlena's descendant. I may be the only one who can change things and return the realms to normal, and it's a chance I have to take."

Acari presses his forehead to mine. His brow is furrowed when he tilts his lips to meet mine again. I never want our mouths to part, but the kiss is short, leaving me cold in his absence.

He slips something into my hand, a metal chain followed by something light and shimmering. I look up and meet his eyes.

He shrugs, a sad smile tugging at one corner of his lips. "If I'm immortal, I don't need a pendant to protect me through time. But you might." He closes my fingers around the necklace. "Hold onto it. Finish what you set out to finish here, and return to me."

He kisses me again, one last time before we say our goodbyes.

While Iracara and Macawna leave to return Acari to Tayaraan, I wander through the everchanging underrealm. Without the Wraiths to fill every crack and crevice, the corridor is brighter, the forest a little less gloomy. By no accident, I'm sure, I find my way to the Pit of Judgment, and for the first time ever, I notice a set of stone stairs that lead up to the Councilspirits' thrones. I look into each one to find a red robe resting in all but Leumas' and the throne that was always empty.

Making sure not to burn myself on the dozens of candles along the base, I step around Leumas' throne and take my seat. There was a time in my life when I wanted nothing more than to sit up here among the Councilspirits and be revered by all the Reapers and Shades.

Never once did I realize how lonely it would be up here in the darkness.

32

A FICKLE FATE

SINISA

A few months later

"Thank you all for coming." My voice carries throughout the chamber, much like Councilspirits' voices would when they oversaw the underrealm.

The candles flicker from my echo, an ominous rumble in the sky overhead that had once been black but is now light gray. It's still a far cry from the crystal white that Iracara has told me about, but we're getting there. In time, I have no doubt that I'll be able to restore the underrealm—the realm of prophecy—to its pure, true form.

The Altúyur are restless from where they stand in the pit below me. Some of them—mainly Macawna who doesn't appear to be too eager to be back here again—glares up at me from behind her colorful feathers. I could've invited them up to the thrones, treated them as my equals, but I'm still far too irritated by the way they've acted. If they would've just been able to respect the role Veltuur played in everything, if they wouldn't have become frivolous with the use of their powers, perhaps none of this would've occurred.

Not to mention, I may never forgive Sungema for not telling me that the Blade of Immortality wasn't my only option in defeating Veltuur.

"As you all are aware, some changes are coming to the under-realm," I begin.

It doesn't take long for Sungema to hold up a finger. "The realm of prophecy is what it was once called."

With a roll of my eyes, I groan. "Call it what you will, but things will be different here. It is my duty to restore the realms to the way they were, or at least to make them better, and I believe we do that by examining Veltuur's creation of the Reapers."

"We've wanted to do away with them forever," Dovenia says.

"Yes, but you had no plan on how to correct the mistake Veltuur made," I remind her. "Sungema showed me what happened. Your demand was only to have them destroyed. No matter their crimes though, or Veltuur's, they are still people. They deserve a chance at redemption."

"And I take it," Macawna says. "That you've finally decided what we shall do about them, oh *wise* Sinisa?"

I glare at her, but then remember where I sit. I reign over the realm of prophecy now, not them. I hold the power, and I alone have figured out a solution.

"Sungema will restore the memories of the Reapers," I say. "She should've never taken them away to begin with. Your fight was with Veltuur, not the lives he claimed along the way."

There are murmurs between a few of them, but Sungema bows. "Very well. Gather them together and it shall be done."

"I mean no offense," Iracara adds, stepping forward. He offers me a private smile before continuing. "You know I am all for showing compassion to the misguided, but what will restoring their memories do? Did King Acari not receive his and decide to remain a Reaper? Have others not done the same?"

"He did not receive all of his memories," I remind him. "Once the Reapers have every last one of their memories returned to them, those who are able to make amends and overcome the guilt they harbor for the actions of their past, they will be free to go. The transition from Reaper to Guardian is instant.

"Those who do not, or cannot, will remain a Reaper, but they will only aid in the essential deaths. There will be no more assassinations, no more requests for murdering the innocent and the prophecy-marked. And, I will claim no more murderers to serve the dead. The mortals will return to the way things were before there were Reapers: they will have to butcher their own meat, catch their own fish, and if they want someone dead, they will have to kill them themselves and reap the consequences that their monarchs enforce upon them.

"In addition, since the mortals will no longer be permitted to commune with the scripture worms, their efforts will instead be diverted to another task. The Guardians and the Prophets who reside in Tayaraan will help aid in ensuring the natural lifelines of the mortals are upheld. All of this is assuming what I've been told is true though, about the purpose of Reapers and the souls they collect."

"It depends on what you were told," Dovenia says.

"That a Reaper's crow needs to feast on something living in order to remain between the realms, and that the souls they collected became the Wraiths, trapped in torment for eternity, or until their release."

"I believe that is true, yes."

"And what used to happen to souls? Before the Reapers were told they needed to collect them?"

Dovenia intwines her pearl-white arms. She looks up to me from behind frosted lashes. "They were bestowed peace and released from the flesh that bound them."

"And my question to you is"—I ask her—"Would it put the Reapers at risk if their crows are unable to feed as often? If we limit the types of deaths they attend?"

She looks to the others before turning her innocent eyes on me.

"I wouldn't know, but I imagine not. There is death all around Tayaraan. And once you free some of your Reapers, there will be even fewer crows to fight over the souls of the dead."

"Good."

"All of this is very well," Sungema says. "But why have we been summoned here to hear all of it?"

Slowly, I rise from my place on the throne. "Because I want to make it clear that each of you shares blame in this mess. I am here to clean it up because you were unable to set aside your egos and desires to reach an agreement with Veltuur. I want you to know what I'm doing because it will impact your lives in Tayaraan. Some day, Veltuur will be returned to his true form, and when that happens, it will be up to you all to work together to ensure the realms do not spiral into chaos again.

"Which reminds me, from this day forward, no more Guardians shall be created by the Altúyur."

This, more than anything, unleashes their discontent. All but Iracara and Sungema seem to turn into writhing waves, vicious and enraged. The Altúyur yell at me that I cannot command them, that they only made the Guardians to help maintain the balance of the realms.

As they rage, it's easy to remember that I am just a mere mortal, descendant or not, prophesized or not. They are the Altúyur. Who am I to command them?

But fortunately, I am not alone. Iracara steps forward again, commanding them all. "I want to hear what she has to say."

I give him a small, appreciative nod and wait for them to quiet. "Veltuur was right. If the Guardians continue to heal people, then no one will ever die."

"And that's a problem now?" Macawna spits. "You sound just like him."

This time, it's Lorik who steps in on my behalf. "Sinisa is nothing like Veltuur. Might I remind you that she freed almost every one of us from his toxic chains. And she is not wrong. If we had listened to Veltuur from the beginning, if we had appreciated the balance he brought to the realms, things might've played out differently." When no one else protests, he nods to me. "Continue, Sinisa."

"If no one dies, the balance is upset. The realm would become overpopulated. The mortals would eventually grow hateful and bored and vile. If their lives were infinite, they would hold no meaning. We have to maintain the balance of everything, including life and death. As more Reapers make peace with their past, more Guardians will appear, but they are not immortal. Their lives will fade, and in time, when the final Reapers have returned to Tayaraan, the final Guardians shall come to pass. It will take time, but if things are ever to return to the way they once were—to the way they are meant to be—then we must begin now, and it starts with you all."

Before their grumbling can grate on me, I wave a hand. "Now, everyone may go, except Sungema. We have work to do."

She cocks her head, assessing my meaning. "The Reapers are here already?"

"Oh yes. I have no intention of taking my time with this. They've suffered for too long already."

Once the others have gone, Sungema follows me out into the forest. As we stroll between the trees, her golden eyes catch on the flowers that have already begun to bud. "I see you were not lying. You are making quick work on turning things around here."

"Unlike the rest of you, I believe Veltuur could oversee prophecy with integrity. It's not a throne I wish to fill forever, only until he can return to it."

When we reach an archway of tangled branches, I jerk my head. "This way."

We step into a clearing, one with a few rays of sunshine streaking through. One by one, Reapers begin to walk out from the forest toward us. They stare up at me with eager, uncertain eyes. I spy Nerul among them. The underrealm made quick work of healing his wounds, though the rage has yet to leave his eyes.

"You will each be given a choice here, in a moment, to decide whether or not this is the life you'd like to live." I gesture beside me. "This is the Divine Sungema. Many of you are aware that the mortals worship her for the gift of memory, but down here in the underrealm, we've often believed the Altúyur were false, or that they had abandoned us. Today I'm here to prove you wrong.

"Something was stolen from each of you, something that only she can restore. Once she has returned to you the memories of your life before you were a Reaper, you will decide whether or not to stay here."

Unlike Iracara, Sungema's wings drape down her back, entirely detached from her arms. Instead of waving an arm over the crowd, Sungema twirls. Her wings open wide, two fans casting a breeze over the hundreds of Reapers congregated. They each endure their own remembering, the lives they took, the ones they themselves lost. Some collapse with hitches and sobs for the children they abandoned. Others rage with pain and anger at the realization that they've been working alongside the very person they killed for years, decades, some even for centuries.

There are those who burrow into their life as a Reaper, the ones who claim no remorse for their actions, and no interest in leaving, but they are the few. In a matter of minutes, dozens of Reapers disappear all around us, their crows dissipating like a forgotten memory of the past.

With each Reaper who leaves, a little more light returns to the realm of prophecy. The flower that had only just started to bud reaches its petals out into a wide bloom. The blackened bark along the trees chips away to reveal white branches beneath. All around us, leaves grow through the branches, and a freshness returns to the air.

And once the forest is more alive and radiant than any I've ever seen in the mortal realm, the Fatebringer Pendant around my neck begins to shine as well.

I blink over at Sungema, afraid my eyes are deceiving me, but she's impossible to read. The only indication she gives me that I'm not mistaken is that her eyes are trained at my neck.

The glow brightens and brightens, until a blinding burst of white encompasses the whole forest.

With my arm raised, blinded but hopeful, I walk forward. I don't want to even risk thinking what I'm thinking, lest the hope be shattered when I realize I'm wrong, but I can't help it. The blinding light is too familiar, and it can only mean one thing.

On my next step, my arm presses into soft, cream feathers, and I have to catch my breath.

"They said you died," I manage to say. "Sungema said you sacrificed yourself to create the pendant."

The light returns to a more gentle glow and I look up to greet Owlena's wide, circular face. She ruffles her feathers and twists her head, every inch the vision of an owl.

"And so I did," she tells me. "I trapped myself inside a necklace that would protect my family until the prophecy had been fulfilled. I was as good as dead, if anything were to go awry."

Tears sting my eyes and she holds her wings out for me. I bury myself against her breast, her feathers fluffy against my cheeks.

"I am so proud of you." She folds her wings over me like a blanket and I embrace the warmth that surrounds me. "You have defeated Veltuur, the darkness that had invaded the underrealm is fleeing, and you are finally righting the imbalance brought upon by the whimsical wills of the Altúyur."

"I...I'm done?"

Gently, she holds me at arm's length. She gazes down upon me, her irises honeyed and kind. "It appears so. Your fate has been fulfilled. If it is what you wish, you are done here."

The last time I was asked such a question, I had too many doubts. This time, I know where my heart stands though. My life is not here, not the life I want, anyway. And if Owlena has returned and can resume her duties of overseeing the Pools of Prophecy, then I can leave knowing the underrealm has been left in competent, benevolent hands.

But I do have one matter of unfinished business left.

"What about Veltuur?" I ask her. "You can't just leave him trapped like that forever."

"Look around you," she says with a warm smile. "You have restored the balance. By now, I'm sure he's already returned to himself. But have no fear, I have no intention of banishing him. The changes you have begun, he will help me oversee them."

I snort. "What makes you think he's interested in working with any of you? He hasn't shown himself to be very interested in collaboration."

Another warm smile, one as radiant as a summer day. "He will. Veltuur is many things, but he is not one to be so willing to return to his prison. I'm sure I'll be able to persuade him to work with us if he would like to remain as he is." At my worried look, she adds, "And he will. He will see what you have restored here. He will realize how much he'd lost himself, and how only your plan will, in time, restore the realms to *true* balance. That's all he ever wanted.

"So, now I ask you, will you stay here and aid us in the progression of the realms, or do you have another path you'd like to follow?"

33

DESTINY UNCHARTED

ACARI

A few days later

Rhet leans over the throne toward me. The sight of him and the others who came with him, clad in the palace guard garb instead of his tattered leathers is still taking me some time to get used to, but I'm so grateful I was able to convince him and the others to join me at the palace. It is the best way I know to keep the Prophets and Guardians safe during this time of transition.

"You don't have to be the one to wield the ax," he says into my ear. "Let me, or any of the other Guardians take your place."

I hold up my hand, and he returns to stand at my side.

The peasant who has come before me waits patiently for my response to his call for help. Without meat, not only his family, but many will starve.

"The people are still frightened about taking a life," I say to the room. "They fear the underrealm is still ready to claim new Reapers, despite the word that we've received stating otherwise.

Until they are comfortable, it is important that I set the example. I was not a Reaper long, and admittedly my contracts rarely required me to kill anything that wasn't already on a path toward death, but I will help my people to my utmost ability. I will kill their chickens and hogs if it is food they need. I will show them that this is the new way of life and that they have nothing to fear from it."

The peasant bows. "Thank you, King Acari. We are eternally grateful. I will tell the others that you will be by the farmlands tomorrow."

With a nod, I dismiss him from the throne room. I wave to a guard standing post at the door for her to bring the next person in.

At the sight of the lavender runes that swirl like leaves through the breeze along her wrists, my heart nearly stops. Gripping the edges of my throne, I push myself up to my feet and have to focus heavily on not falling forward.

"S-Sinisa. We—I wasn't expecting you. I thought you couldn't leave the underrealm—is everything all right? W-why have you come? I mean—it's good to see you. I—"

Rhet places a hand on my shoulder. "Why not let her speak, my King?"

With a crooked smile, I sigh up at him. "Wise advice."

I look out over my court again, and with a wide wave of my hand, I address them all. "The rest of you may leave us. I will summon you when we're ready to resume court."

As the room clears, Sinisa continues the long walk up the carpet-lined path. She keeps her head lowered, but I see her gray eyes flit to mine every chance they get.

I am pulled to her by something I cannot see and will never understand, but I descend the steps to meet her on the carpet. Even this close isn't close enough. I want to reach out, take her hands into mine, and hold onto her as long as I can—as long as we have.

"I went to the camp," she says, her voice hoarse. "I feared the worst when I found it empty, but I'm relieved to see you here, Rhet."

He inclines his head, arms crossed. "We didn't know anyone would return to look for us. The king ordered us here—"

"I didn't *order* it," I say over my shoulder. "You were invented—*invited*."

She laughs, a soft, warm sound that spills into me like cider.

"We are all safe, Sinisa," Rhet tells her. "The king has ensured it."

"That is good to hear. Things are going well then with your plans to reintegrate the Guardians and the Prophets? Have you reformed the Law of Mother's Love then?"

Wincing, I rub the back of my neck. "Yes and no. The law has been reformed but, there are...good and bad days. The people are hesitant to accept it. They still fear difference, as I'm sure you remember. Many fear the Prophets, especially now that they know there is more to them than small scars and variances. More, still, don't understand the Guardians they never even knew existed, nor how to accept the loved ones who have returned from their lives as Reapers. Some days, there is a line outside the palace of people demanding we slay the...*deformed* newborns—their words, not mine—who fill the orphanages. Other days, people come requesting news of any new Reapers who might've returned from the underrealm, to see if their sisters and fathers and children have returned."

"I'd say that's about as good as one could expect," she says. "Change takes time."

"So I'm told, and yet, here you are." I swallow the lump in my throat, hope bubbling through me at what the presence of her here might mean—*must* mean. "Why have you come—I mean, how are you—is everything...is it done?"

A smile flickers at the edges of her lips, but I see it for only a second before she reaches up for me and pulls me into her. It is a kiss I've waited for months now, and feared I'd be left waiting years for. Decades. Centuries. I've dreamed about this moment, about what I'd do if I ever saw her again.

I reach my hand to the back of her head, tangle my fingers in her hair, and melt into her. Our lips slide against each other's, hungry and demanding. A soft moan escapes me when she presses closer still, her bodice so tight against my robes that I can feel the curves of her against my chest. This can't be real. I've had this dream too many times to count. She returns to the palace, I feel happier than I've felt my entire life, and then I wake up to a cold and empty bed.

But as her hands rove over my chest, up my neck and thread through my hair, one thing happens that never has in any of my dreams before.

Behind us, Rhet clears his throat.

She pulls away, pink brightening her cheeks. The scowl I throw back at Rhet is mostly harmless and he shrugs, turning his back to us and leaving out one of the back doors.

When I return my gaze to hers, her smile makes my heart dance out of my chest.

"Are you really here?" I ask her, combing my hand into her hair. I pull her closer, our lips just a breath away from each other's. "Tell me, can we finally live a normal life?"

With lips as red as cherries, and a smile as stunning as the moon, she brushes her lips against mine and says, "Normal? I doubt that. But everything is as it should be. Our destinies are finally our own now."

Thank you for reading *Fate of the Vulture*!

Leave a Review

Help other readers find this epic, dark saga, by leaving a review on Amazon, Goodreads, Bookbub, or any other reading website. Even simple ones like "I loved it" really help with a book's success!

Join My Newsletter

Stay updated on all of my upcoming releases, as well as gain exclusive access to early cover reveals, fan pricing, excerpts, and more! https://www.jessacawillis.com

Immortals of Shadowthorn

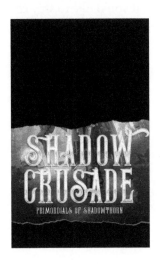

If you're looking for your next adventure, one with a badass demon huntress and a shadow realm that needs to be dealt with, be sure to check out my upcoming *Primordials of Shadowthorn* series! Read more below:

Halira grew up knowing to never wander into the Shadowthorn.

Demons prowl there, waiting to kidnap anyone they can and feast upon their hearts.

So when Halira's family is slaughtered by the very demons she grew up hating, she doesn't hesitate to join the Shadow Crusade alongside her best friend Dimitri. Together, they plan to eradicate the demons and reclaim their territory, once and for all.

But what happens when Halira discovers something far worse lurking on the other side of the realm...

Preorder your copy of *Shadow Crusade* now!

Social Media
And last but not least, if you'd like to stay connected, you can find my social media links here: https://linktr.ee/jessaca_with_an_a

ACKNOWLEDGMENTS

It's so crazy to me that the acknowledgments always come at the end of the book, the place where they are least likely to be seen, because in many ways, this is the most important section of the entire story. This is the place where the hard work of others is recognized and honored, and some people might not realize this, but without said hard work from others, the very book might not have ever been finished—at least, not in the state that you've just read.

Did you all know that if it weren't for my brother, **Michael**, *Fate of the Vulture*—actually, come to think of it, this entire series—would've been drastically different. He helped me decide where Sinisa's journey was going to take her. He also helped craft the idea of the Blade of Immortality—the first draft of this story didn't even have one! Can you even imagine that? If memory served, he was also instrumental in helping me decide what the purpose of the crows was—another decision that was fundamental to this story.

Someone else who plays a huge role in helping me write these book sis my partner **James**. If he wasn't always so willing to step in with the kids so that I can get some writing done on the weekends, it would've taken me decades longer to finish this series.

I'm eternally grateful to my editors, **Sandra Ogle** and **Kate Anderson**. They catch so many of my dyslexic errors, it astounds me! I don't know what I'd do without these two lovely people, but I'm sure that my books would've suffered without them.

She did a phenomenal job on all of the covers, but when I saw the cover **Luminescence Covers** created for book three, I was speechless! So grateful for being able to work with her to create some tantalizing covers for this series—and hopeful to keep working with her in the near future.

Lastly, here is a shoutout to **my readers** who have cheered Sinisa and Acari on from the start! I've loved reading your reviews along the way and I hope that you'll find this ending satisfying. It was a difficult one for me to write. I didn't want their story to end yet because I'm going to miss them both so much! But hopefully we can all rest easy knowing that they have each other at least.

Until next time friends, to Sinisa and Acari, may they face any future demons together, hand-in-hand and with love in their hearts.

~Jessaca

ABOUT THE AUTHOR

Jessaca is a fantasy writer with an inclination toward the dark, epic, and adventure sub-genres. She draws inspiration from books like the Nevernight Chronicles & ACOTAR, videogames like Dark Souls III, and television shows like Game of Thrones and The Chilling Adventures of Sabrina. She is a self-proclaimed nerd who loves cosplay, video games, and comics, and if you live in the PNW, you just might see her at one of the local comic conventions in one of her favorite RWBY cosplays!

CPSIA information can be obtained
at www.ICGtesting.com
Printed in the USA
BVHW040248221221
624681BV00013B/625

9 781733 992596